THE LAW PARTNERS

JOHN ELLSWORTH

COPYRIGHT

THE LAW PARTNERS

JOHN ELLSWORTH

1

Johnny Washington hit the pipe and the crack bugs went crazy. He caught a glimpse of ragged fingernails flying to the skin on his arms. The nails flailed at the imaginary devils. He then shook like a wet dog. But the crack bugs were persistent. He set to raking his arms harder from his perch on the upturned milk crate. The day was bright and sunny on the streets of South Chicago, but here, in the alley behind the Quik Stop, time stood still and heavy shadows came tumbling from the clouds that seemed to hang everywhere. He didn't know it was all a crack dream--the bugs, the clouds, the feelings of pure heaven. He just took another hit.

50 Cent's syllables pounded up over the Quik Stop, floating in the air over Johnny's head, begging to be injected into the veins of the empty black teenager whose inner life was composed solely of feelings, rhyme without meaning.

He moaned as the euphoria trailed off. Then his anger at the world returned and he looked around for something or someone to attack. The glass tube fell from his fingers into the dirt behind the Quik Stop. The pipe didn't shatter, and that would be a win for the crime scene techs who would be sweeping the area in about an hour.

Johnny climbed to his feet from the milk crate. He stumbled into the Quik Stop and immediately seized a quart of Budweiser from the cooler and unscrewed the cap. In one long slug he drained off half the bottle and belched. Joseph Arnold, the proprietor, watched Johnny saunter through his store up to the linoleum countertop where he placed his elbows, the beer bottle trapped between his hands like a squirming bird. Johnny saw it with a twist: everything he touched just wanted away from him.

Arnold looked at him with a look of intense hatred. Johnny wore his pants so low the belt loops underhung his white T-shirt, and the do-rag identified him as a Crip, a gangbanger, rhyme-sprung flesh on bones that sought nothing and gave the same in kind. He held out the beer bottle to Arnold and said, "See this?"

Arnold nodded. He didn't want any trouble with Johnny Washington. No one in his right mind did. The young man had a laundry list of criminal convictions attached to his name on his CPD juvie record. When he turned eighteen two weeks ago, he was released from juvie with one hundred dollars and told to go home. Except Johnny couldn't go home because there was no home to go to. His mother was dead and his father was long gone. He had two siblings, a brother and sister, but they were both in state lockup. There were some aunts but they had their own problems. With no place to turn, Johnny took the only job available to him in South Chicago: he joined the Crips. A famous gang of black youth with nothing to live for and everything to gain by a life of crime.

So when Johnny asked Quik Stop owner Joseph Arnold, "See this?" Arnold knew better than to respond. He only smiled at Johnny and the youth muttered an obscenity and banged through the screen door and out onto the sidewalk along Ballantine Street.

Traffic was light. It was mid-morning and everyone was at work. The only vehicles were delivery trucks, taxis, and the occasional white person driving a nice car who had blundered into this part of Chicago purely by mistake. They always fled once they realized where they were.

But Johnny wasn't thinking about all that as he stepped from the sidewalk into the street. He was thinking only about finding a certain girl. Crack always did that to him, made him crazy for female flesh. He began crossing the street. An eighteen-wheeler approached and laid on its air horn. Johnny returned from his somnambulant stroll. Jamming his fists into his hips he whirled around and dared the trucker to run him over. The trucker stopped and Johnny stepped out of the lane onto the centerline. He then proceeded to walk along the middle of Ballantine Street for half a block, causing traffic to swerve and honk in frustration. *Rage begat rage*, Johnny heard a voice say, and he looked around. "Who said dat?" he asked.

Which was when Officer Tory Stormont approached the minor traffic snarl. He pulled his squad car to the center of the road, facing Johnny head-on. He activated his emergency lights. He exited his vehicle and walked around front, where he shouted to Johnny, still fifty feet away but approaching, "Son, you need to get out of my street."

Johnny ignored the man. The truth of the matter was that Johnny couldn't tell head voices from real voices. Words floated by like handles; he grabbed at them when he could. When the officer called out to him again, Johnny heard yet another voice; it was about the street. So he proceeded toward the police car to investigate.

"Halt!" cried Officer Stormont. "Stop right there!"

Johnny ignored the command. He continued to close the distance between them.

"Freeze!" cried the officer.

Johnny became angry at the officer's tone. Nobody ever talked to him like that, especially when he was flying the Crips' colors. His arm drew back the beer bottle and flung it at the officer. The bottle hit the hood of the car, fell, and shattered on the asphalt. It had narrowly missed Officer Stormont's head. Officer Stormont's right hand went to his holster and he unsnapped the safety strap.

Johnny recognized none of the officer's movements as a threat. He kept coming, quickening his pace, breaking into a run directly at the officer.

Whipping the gun from its holster, Officer Stormont pointed it at Johnny's chest and again ordered the youngster to halt. But Johnny was having none of it and kept coming. Officer Stormont considered his universe in a split second: white cop surrounded by fifty thousand blacks, backup five minutes away: an eternity on this mean turf; several dozen citizens along the sidewalk, some of whom would be videoing him as they always did anymore at the first sign of a white-on-black confrontation.

His eyes darted around; anything to stop what was about to happen.

Still Johnny came on; the cop felt threatened with great bodily harm--which was the necessary legal standard to justify a shooting. A squirt of urine escaped his bladder but his navy pants covered it up. Frantic and losing control, he squeezed off a wild shot. The bullet struck the Crips soldier in the sternum and traveled off to the right side, away from the heart. Wounded but not mortally, Johnny kept closing the distance. He was half-running at this point, slowed somewhat, but he *was* running, according to the police officer's dash camera.

Rattled by the young man's staying power, Officer Stormont fired again and again, striking Johnny in the shoulder and the abdomen. Now Johnny was staggering and 50 Cent no longer inspired him, but still he approached. At the last possible second, the officer raised the muzzle of his gun, aiming it right between Johnny's eyes. He squeezed off one shot and then another. Witnesses would say the last two shots actually sounded like one long one. Johnny, reaching for the officer, crumpled to the asphalt. The officer stepped back from the dead teen, stunned. Witnesses along the sidewalks began pouring into the street.

"I seen it," said one woman wearing a pink dress. "The boy wasn't doin' nothin' wrong."

Two men wearing hardhats approached. "He was trying to stop when the officer cut him down. Cold-blooded murder, I'd say."

Officer Stormont stepped around the door of his patrol car. Shaken and his face drained of color, he keyed his mike and called Dispatch.

"Backup and an ambulance now!" he cried into the mike. "I've shot someone and I'm pretty sure he's dead but send an ambulance."

"Shot someone?" said the voice at the other end. "Where?"

"In the body and in the head."

"No, officer, where are you?"

"Fifteen-fifty Ballantine. Just down from the Quik Stop."

"I'm sending backup and an ambulance--now."

After an eternity, Officer Stormont heard distant sirens coming closer. But so was the crowd. He was sitting in the driver's seat of his squad car, his feet outside on the ground. Someone pushed forward and closed the door on his legs. He winced in pain and tried to stand up. But he was trapped in the seat and the crowd was pushing ever nearer.

"Get back," he cried in his best command voice. "Don't come any closer!"

"You murdered that child," said a woman in a cheap dress. She was maybe mid-sixties and quite large and the crowd seemed to make way for her. "That's my grandson and I seen the whole thing. You shot him down when he wasn't doing nothin'," she screamed. "You gonna get yours, officer nobody."

"Get back!" Stormont shouted again.

But it wasn't necessary. Two patrol cars pulled into the center of the road and approached at a high rate of speed. Then they slowed and four cops jumped out and moved in on foot, hands on nightsticks, nervously eyeing the angry crowd.

The new arrivals dispersed the crowd, sending them scattering back onto the sidewalks. Then they surrounded the dead body. One cop went for orange traffic cones while a second felt Johnny's throat. Clearly he was dead, but the determination of death was necessary, for it controlled the officers' next steps. The first man returned with ten orange cones and the men positioned them in a great circle around the body and Stormont's police car. An MSNBC wag would refer to the scene as the new American Stonehenge emerged from the fog of gunpowder and racial hatred.

Stormont was still sitting in his car, shaking, his head lowered and his mouth mumbling indistinct sounds. The others left him alone after checking to be sure he wasn't injured. No one wanted to be called as a witness to anything he might say, so they kept their distance and waited for the shooting team and CSI's to arrive from the CPD.

At last the shooting team arrived and took over. CSI's scattered throughout the scene and the crack pipe was found discarded behind the Quik Stop. The tech dropped it into a plastic bag and checked it into evidence. A crack pipe bearing the deceased's DNA could be huge.

A shocky Tory Stormont was helped into a black SUV which then activated its emergency lights and sped away.

Riots followed that night. The crowds grew and by the next afternoon several buildings were burning. A Walgreen's was looted, and the major news outlets were broadcasting from curbside. This went on for a full week.

Reverend Jesse Jackson came and had his say. Then came Reverend Al Sharpton. Black lawyers soothed the dead boy's mother's sisters, and plans were laid for a major lawsuit against the City of Chicago and Tory Stormont. CNN news anchors stalked the streets. Shots were fired but the news teams were fearless and trekked on in search of the next news-fathered story. The whole thing became surreal, with the Illinois National Guard having the final say when it moved Armored Personnel Carriers into position and passed out real bullets to the guardsmen.

The protests, lootings, fires, and random gunshots continued for ten days. In the end, the National Guard won an uneasy forfeit just because the weather had turned unbearably hot and the Guard was the only group left standing.

Officer Stormont was placed on paid leave. His name and file photo were on TV every few minutes day and night. He believed the crowds were hunting for him. He stopped leaving his apartment. He refused to answer his phone. Overnight he found he was a changed man, a man who had become willing to do anything to stay above ground.

2

Two weeks later, the Chicago Police Department's shooting team and the District Attorney were wasting no time, trading witness statements and reports and investigatory leads. Teams returned to the scene and more measurements were taken. Cameras clicked and whirred. Bullet trajectories were laid out in white strings and more pictures taken.

Meetings were held in which witnesses, deputy DA's, and police searched for insights and answers.

The entire community was watching. Without an indictment of the white cop there would be blood in the streets. It was promised.

In the end it all came down to the officer's dash cam. The video was clear and the view unobstructed. It was all presented to the DA's second-in-command, Darrell Harrow. Harrow took the case before the grand jury and laid it out. The grand jury came back with a true bill—

Officer Tory Stormont was indicted on a charge of first degree murder.

Harrow explained to the press that Stormont's final two shots were fired off as the young man was falling to the ground. It was an execution, he made the mistake of telling the *Tribune*. The Police Union responded with a threat of a recall election of the District Attorney. Cops called in sick by the hundreds. Black Lives Count filled the streets with peaceful marchers while opportunists from all sides set stores ablaze and looted a Target and a Costco. The nation was polarized.

CNN, Fox, and MSNBC had never left. They pointed their cameras at the new players in the case—the lawyers.

Assistant DA Darrell Harrow was a no-nonsense veteran of the homicide wars in Chicago. He went before the cameras, where he predicted a verdict that would satisfy the victim's family and neighbors and community.

Officer Tory Stormont took the news of the indictment hard. He hid inside his apartment while the cameras roamed the courtyard outside. According to the police union rep, Stormont was extremely emotional, spewing hatred at the authorities for abandoning him.

But Stormont had the support of his fellow officers and the police union. They swore that he wasn't going to go down just because he had followed departmental lethal force policy. Which was true, they said, and now look.

Indicted and enraged, he nonetheless pulled himself together and assessed his predicament. He morphed from outraged to calculating. Then he found himself calling in favors as he put together a dossier on the DA who had indicted him. On the day of his arraignment in court, Stormont followed Harrow out of the courthouse and tailed him home.

It was the beginning of his fixation on the man who represented everything Stormont saw wrong with the criminal justice system, the man who had indicted him, the man who had to be stopped.

The media went away. Stormont returned to the streets. He watched Harrow's house day and night. He had nothing else going on, being on paid leave. At night he pawed through Harrow's garbage and became satisfied that Harrow had a serious drinking problem covered up by hiding Jim Beam bottles at the bottom of his garbage bin.

Then, on July Fourth, Harrow attended a fundraiser put on by the Cook County Democratic Party. Stormont stood not five feet from Harrow as the lawyer argued with a woman who later made a speech. Clearly Harrow was intoxicated and the woman rebuffed him repeatedly. Harrow persisted. He warned the woman he was coming to her home that night to settle things. She tossed her head and laughed him off. He was demeaned and Stormont saw the man's rage take hold. His next move was easily predicted by Stormont so he tore away from the scene. He had been to the woman's home before and he was headed there now. It was important that he arrive first.

Stormont raced to the woman's home, a condo in downtown Chicago. He went inside the lobby and got clearance at the security desk. He was wearing jeans and a T-shirt and a hat pulled low on his forehead. But he was clean-cut and well-mannered. They wouldn't remember a nondescript nobody in jeans and a T-shirt. They didn't even ask to check his shoulder bag.

He avoided making eye contact with the CCTV cameras as he headed to the elevators.

He was cleared to visit unit number 2566. The woman lived in 2564. He didn't plan on leaving a record connecting him to her number.

Stormont stepped off the elevator and disappeared from camera range as he headed down the hall. There was no closed circuit TV allowed in the hallways; the owners had voted it down, preferring their privacy.

He stopped outside of 2564 and sprung the door with his picks. He stepped inside.

Into her bedroom he crept and removed his street clothes. Then, from the shoulder bag, he withdrew the Chicago Police Department uniform and put it on. It was the uniform with the stripe-less sleeve of a patrolman, a job he had once held in high regard. Now he just saw it as his downfall.

He slipped the police utility belt around his waist and adjusted the pepper spray, handcuffs, magazines, and semi auto. He settled the hat low across his eyes. His uniform made him feel powerful. When all hell broke loose and the duty cops arrived and he mixed in with them, the security staff and the district attorneys and the defense attorneys would have no record of him arriving there before the others.

He folded and carefully placed his jeans and T-shirt and porkpie hat inside his bag.

Thirty minutes later, he heard her key in the door.

3

Stormont stationed himself behind the front door. Once she was inside and the door was closing behind her, he clutched her in a choke hold. It was simple to do as he simply overpowered her. Her legs fell out from beneath her as if she had been head shot.

He caught her as she lost consciousness and crumpled. He carried her gently to the sofa. He stretched her out on her back and straightened her dress. Neat and unmarked--exactly like he wanted her.

He returned to the door and retrieved her gold lamé purse from the carpet. As he knew it would be, her pistol was inside. He knew that his hands, inside latex gloves, would leave no prints on the gun so he withdrew it from the purse and placed the purse on the coffee table beside the unconscious woman.

It was but minutes until lobby security called on the intercom. He keyed the unit and replied in his best impression of a female voice that yes, security should send Darrell Harrow right up to her condo, she was expecting him. Lights were clicked off. He took a seat in the chair beside the unconscious woman.

In less than five minutes there was a rapping on the door. It sounded almost like scratching and maybe it was, he couldn't be sure.

Whatever, he called to the visitor to come on in, the door was unlocked.

The visitor stepped inside a room that was as dark as night. Suddenly a light flared on and he froze; the police officer had turned the switch on the table between his chair and the sofa. In one continuous move Stormont fixed Harrow in his gunsights and pulled the trigger. Those hundreds of hours at the police shooting range hadn't been wasted. The single round struck the startled man squarely between the eyes. They remained open while the rear of his head spattered against the wall in the pattern of a large red flower. He fell to the floor, twisting, coming to rest partially on his back, one leg crumpled beneath him, both arms at his sides. He stared at the ceiling with the unblinking concentration of the dead.

Plucking a small nugget of burnt wood from the fireplace, the police officer drew on the wall above the victim's head. He rubbed the charcoal on the unconscious woman's hands. Pulling a wooden cross from his pack, he placed it on the carpet just above the victim's head. He cast a look around the living room. It was coming together just as he'd planned.

He then placed the gun inside the prosecutor's purse and placed that in her bedroom. Tucking his shoulder bag up under his arm, he pulled his cop hat low across his eyes and exited the condo.

The elevator lowered him to the basement of the condominium tower, down to the visitors' level, where the man stepped back into the shadows.

An hour later, he saw the black Mercedes arrive and take the only remaining visitor's slot. He watched as the lawyer exited the Mercedes and hurried for the elevators. Making him was easy: his license plate said SET U FREE.

Twenty minutes later, Stormont heard the sound of far-off sirens coming closer. When he heard the sirens shut down just outside the building's entrance, he rode the elevator back up to the woman's condo. His plan was to mix in with the arriving cops and enter the condo as one of them.

The uniform stationed at the entrance to the condo didn't give him a second look when Stormont walked inside like he owned the place. The on-call detective told him, "I need you to search the premises. We're looking for a gun." He was made a part of the crime scene team.

Officer Stormont started at the far end of the condo, the woman's bedroom. The rest was simple. He searched the woman's purse and there was the gun. A moment of inspiration caught him up and he jammed the revolver into his rear pocket. It was a tight fit but he didn't have time to worry about that. Just then, the lawyer came into the room and snapped his picture with his smartphone. Stormont turned and abruptly left. He then made his way downstairs to the parking garage. He exited the parking garage elevator and pressed his back to the wall and began making his way north.

He sidled along in the shadows until he was positioned directly beneath the CCTV camera. He reached above his head and turned the camera.

Alone at the rear of the black Mercedes, he jimmied the trunk with his picks and up it popped. He withdrew the gun from his back pocket. Behind the spare tire he placed the weapon. He was still wearing the same blue gloves he had worn while searching the woman's condo. Now he slammed the trunk, took a step back, and snapped the gloves from his hands. They went into the pocket of his navy pants.

Stormont rode the elevator up to the lobby, walked through and came out onto Jefferson Street. He hurried off into the Chicago night.

MICHAEL GRESHAM

4

"You have no idea how this happened?"

We are sitting in the living room of Cook County prosecutor Miranda—Mira—Morales. She was voted Top Female Lawyer in Chicago just last year and she is nobody's fool. But tonight a dead body is obtrusively stretched out on the shag with a bullet hole between the eyes, and she has no explanation for me, Michael Gresham, the lawyer she has called. Skull and soft tissue are spattered against the wall beside the front door. The eyes of the dead man are crossed, staring inward, as if gazing at the incoming round a split-second before the lights went out.

Assistant District Attorney Mira Morales is a woman of thirty-three years. She has invested the past ten years of her life achieving a trial record of 70-1. It's a world-class record and she is counting on it to win her the job of District Attorney in the November election. Her boss has announced his retirement and his return to private practice from whence he came some twenty-five years ago. The vacancy has attracted a crowded field of District Attorney wannabes in the Democrat primary election. Her competition is unaccomplished and mostly unelectable, as Mira Morales is the only career prosecutor among them. On the Republican side there is but one candidate, Lamont R. Johnstone. Until three months ago, Johnstone was the District Attorney's First Assistant. He jumped ship in order to run against his boss. But then his boss announced he was retiring.

She raises a hand to say something to me when an involuntary shudder wracks her body. It is only then that I realize I've been staring at her. Her skin tones are dark browns and deep ferrous hues. Her long, thin nose and violet eyes are stunning and I cannot stop staring. Everywhere in Cook County you will spot pictures of this beauty staring out from her campaign posters while shaking the hand of the Chief Justice of the Illinois Supreme Court. But even those posed shots understate her elegance. She is beautiful beyond any woman I've seen in years. But right now she is jangled and her hands shake and her voice falters as I try to question her.

"Mira, what happened here?"

She only looks at me. Her mouth opens and shuts but there are no words.

I am very tempted to call the police and give notice of the murder this minute, but Marcel, my investigator, is smartly holding me back. He's doing this to give us time to properly prepare the scene and the District Attorney candidate. Once the police are notified and the press intercepts the call, Mira's life will come crashing down around her. The election will likely be lost when the newspapers hit the streets. But right now it appears she'll be the last to know, as she sits on the couch wrapped in a fuzzy blanket, her face a blank, shut off from the world.

Her eyes close and remain that way. Marcel looks at me and shrugs. We both look at our newest client. She is still wearing the little black dress and string of pearls that carried her night at the annual Cook County Democratic Party Dinner kicking off the campaign season. It is July and elections are just four months off.

Her eyes open and swim back to reality. She focuses on me, the attorney she called when she realized there was a dead body in her living room. I say "realized," because Mira is claiming she was in a blackout when the shooting occurred. Of this she is certain: the dead body wasn't on her floor when she returned home from the dinner. She knows this to be a fact because she remembers coming inside her condo and locking the door behind her. The next thing she knew she was coming awake on her sofa. She sat up, dizzy and faint, and that's when she saw the body. She instantly recognized the man.

She lives alone, a single woman without children, a woman known in Chicago legal circles as a willing sleep-over partner and Chicago's very own Escoffier of intimate, morning-after brunch.

"Are you sure you hadn't invited him home with you?"

"I did not invite him. We argued at the fundraiser and I came home alone."

"Did anybody see you arguing?"

"Only everyone, I imagine. He was loud and under the influence."

Under the influence, I am thinking. Only a prosecutor would say *under the influence.* The rest of the unwashed--which includes me--would say he was drunk. Or maybe knee-walking. Or toasted. *Under the influence?* Only if we'd watched too much TV. No, Mira was a hands-on prosecutor, the kind who had learned the ropes by trial and error, and her words, while sparse, were always informed, always precise. That was the Mira Morales I knew from having defended three jury trials against her. We had each won one then split the third on a hung jury that went away on a plea after the smoke cleared. The score was tied, so she felt she was neither stooping nor reaching when she called me. I am known for being nuts-and-bolts in my trial practice. I am also known for smoke-and-mirrors. Mira evidently felt like she needed a helping of each. But for right now, the nuts-and-bolts lawyer will help her prepare for the arrival of the police once I put in the call to advise of a dead body in my client's living room. My goal is to shield her from all questions and to guide the inquiry away from her.

If I can do that, it's a first-round win.

5

Not ten minutes after my arrival we are joined by my investigator, Marcel Rainford. Marcel has been with me seven years, a one-time employee of Interpol and Scotland Yard. We crossed paths during that time. He was transplanted to America after a contract was issued on his life by a group of Sicilian Mafiosi upset with the inroads he had made on their European heroin kingdom. The U.S. State Department was instrumental in changing Marcel's surname and hiding his real identity in its cloistered terabytes of bureaucracy. He signed on with Chicago Police Department when he arrived stateside; two years later, he received medical retirement after being shot in the face on a routine robbery call. The wound left him disfigured even after six surgeries. But it didn't affect his investigator's bent for justice and truth-- two character defects in my world of criminal defense. But he works hard to overcome his better self. The fact of the matter is Marcel has crossed the line separating fact from fiction, as did I long ago when I became counsel for my first criminal client. We both are able to lie with ease. Criminal defense practice demands no less. Just now he is taking pictures of the scene with his Nikon.

He finishes up and turns to Mira and asks her to hold out her hands, palms up. She obliges, and he racks off maybe ten snaps on the camera. Then she's instructed to turn them over and he makes a recording of the top side. While the hand baseline is being set in this manner, I make a mental note. Her hands are blackened, sooty. I look back at the entrance wall. There is a large Satanic pentagram drawn there. It is done in what appears to be charcoal. Such as we have just recorded on her hands.

"Marce," I tell him softly. "Flip back through. Get rid of all the pictures of her hands."

He looks at me with a silent question. I roll my eyes to the wall drawing. He follows. The light goes on in his eyes. He immediately begins flipping back through his snaps. His fingers punch and the camera clicks and snapshots disappear. We know we must be very selective in what is preserved and what is disappeared.

Mira pulls an ashtray across the coffee table and manages, with shaking hands, to insert a Salem between her full, red lips and bring a flame to the business end of the tobacco. She inhales and the cigarette glows.

I ask again, "You have no idea how this happened?"

"Michael," she manages at last, "one moment I was out and the next moment I was conscious and aware. How he got there, I have no idea, I swear to you."

"It's Darrell Harrow?" I ask.

She nods and says heavily, "It is Darrell Harrow."

"Who hated him?" I ask.

She shrugs. "He's well-known around town and very well-liked."

My mind switches gears.

"So we need to figure out why Darrell, a married man, was in your condo tonight. Can you help me with that?" I cannot fend off my own sarcasm: of course she can help me—she had been bedding the guy.

Marcel looks up. "Let's try this. What *do* you remember?"

"I remember unlocking my door."

"What happened next?"

"That's the sixty-four-dollar question. I don't know."

"You regularly carry a gun?" Marcel asks.

"Yes. Our homicide prosecutors are armed. It goes with the job."

"Sure. So do you remember going for your gun tonight?"

"No. It's still in my purse."

"Where's your purse?"

She looks around the immediate area then shakes her head.

"I don't know. But I'm sure I had it when I came inside."

"Marcel?" I say.

"I'll have a look. Be right back."

Marcel begins an ever-widening search of the condo. After several minutes he returns. "It's in the bedroom. Gun's in the purse."

"What's it doing in there?" I ask her.

"I might have shot him and I might not have shot him. I honestly don't know," Mira suddenly offers. She semi-reclines, legs crossed, inhaling cigarette smoke and discharging it through her nostrils. In her black dress and silver-white pearls, slouching on the sofa, a swirl of smoke across her face, I am reminded of a noir scene from some long-ago movie. I can't name it, but the moral ambiguity of that ancient scene shades our work tonight: we are about to start hiding things from the cops who will arrive once I call them.

"Nobody came to see?" Marcel says to me. "Nobody heard the shot?"

I shake my head.

"Our units are guaranteed one-hundred percent sound-proof," she dreamily allows. "I can turn my stereo full on and nobody says a word."

Marcel and I trade a look. Then it's my turn to ask a few questions.

"Did Darrell come home with you?"

"Honestly, I don't know. He must have."

"Why do you say that?"

"How else would he get here?"

"Maybe he was already here when you came in," I say.

Marcel says, "Maybe you walked in, found him here, and shot him. Maybe he was stalking you. Maybe he was here to rape you--or kill you. There's a million and one possible theories. We just need to settle on the one that works best for you."

"Meaning, we've got to get my story pulled together?"

"Meaning exactly that," Marcel replies.

I don't disagree with him.

Marcel toes the dead man's shoulders with his ostrich-skin boot. Same with his arms and hands—toe of the boot, lift, drop. He's looking for a weapon of some kind.

"A weapon would be nice," he says absently. He fixes Mira with his hard gray eyes, waiting for the get-out-of-jail response, such as, "He had a gun," or "He came at me with a knife."

But there is nothing. The cigarette ember flares and her eyes drift off again.

Marcel turns to me and gives a slight shrug as if to say, "Your turn."

I try again.

"We need you to think with us, Mira. We're going to have to call the cops in the next few minutes and report this."

Marcel circuits the room, looking above and below. Then he disappears down the hallway, into the prosecutor's bedroom. I have been there and I know its layout. He is examining the mahogany escritoire right about now and looking beneath the ruffled skirt on Miranda's queen-sized bed, searching for anything the police might use against her.

Some minutes later he returns.

"Nothing out of place. Bed still made. Top covers undisturbed, smooth, no one's rolled around on them. I'm going downstairs to talk to the security desk. Be right back." He disappears out the front door.

Mira looks away again, obviously preparing to return to her mental la-la-land. But I head her off. I stare right at her, holding her attention. This is a question any woman can answer whether recently passed out or not.

"Have you had sex tonight? Any indication?"

"No indication."

"So you came to--for want of a better term--and then, what? Called me?"

"I called you, Michael. I took one look and luckily I've seen enough dead guy pictures that I didn't run screaming out the front door."

"You had presence of mind enough to dial your phone," I say.

"Exactly. You arrived thirty minutes after I called you. I timed it because I knew the police would ask."

"What did you do in the interim?"

"I've been to dozens of homicide scenes. So I kept my cool. I went in and used the toilet connected to my bedroom. Then I came right back here, sat down and lit a cigarette."

"Did you wash your hands after the toilet?"

"I don't—I don't think so."

"The police will want to know why we took so long to call them. The building's closed circuit TV will tell them what time Harrow arrived and what time I arrived. Coupled with your phone log, we paint a perfect picture of elapsed time between your call to me, my time of arrival, and the time we called the police. To delay much longer will only underscore that I was helping you prepare for them."

She stands and shakes her arms to loosen them. She lights yet another cigarette and lays it within the notch on the ashtray. A twist of smoke blows sideways.

"I'm making coffee. You want some?"

"No. Hurry it up. We call them when Marcel returns."

She hurries over to the long kitchen galley where the coffee maker sits silently. She lifts the handle, inserts a k-cup, and pulls down. She pushes a button and coffee begins hissing into a white cup. The sink faucet runs, a quick on-and-off. Minutes pass. The coffee maker goes silent. She adds half-and-half to the white cup then returns to her sofa.

She looks up at me, more awake than she has been since I arrived.

"Okay. So what am I to tell them? I came home and he was already here?"

I frown and shake my head. "Listen to you. You're not hearing what you're saying and that isn't good."

"What?"

I say, "The police will know what time you entered the elevator from the security cameras."

Marcel returns and raps twice on the door. She goes over and lets him back in.

"Interesting," he says. "Security guys didn't hear a gunshot."

"Do they have video of Harrow arriving?"

"Yep. Shows him arriving alone. He doesn't appear drunk or lurching around--nothing like that. Just calmly and coolly shows ID at the front desk and they say they buzzed Mira's condo. She said to let him come up. After that, they didn't see him again."

"But they didn't hear a gunshot?"

"They said they did not."

Mira taps the half-consumed cigarette against the green glass ashtray. Its ember disarticulates. She stabs the butt against the glass and pulls her hand away. She sniffs her nicotine-stained fingers and frowns. "What do I tell them?"

"You tell them nothing. You're advised to remain silent."

"All right. How does our story go, just between us?"

"Well, no one's going to believe you came inside and woke up a few minutes later and a dead guy was found on the floor who hadn't been there when you came inside."

"Highly unlikely," she agrees.

I continue. "So we have a couple of choices. One, you were in a blackout from too much alcohol and passed out. Two, you have some kind of medical condition that rendered you unconscious. Any luck there?"

"I take Ambien for sleep."

"Ambien?" says Marcel, suddenly sitting up on his haunches as he takes close-ups of the victim's entrance wound with his Nikon. "That stuff's all kinds of bad if you've been drinking. How much did you have to drink tonight?"

"One drink at the fairgrounds. I had two, maybe three sips." She looks up, then, and I see she is crying. She wipes her eyes with her forearm.

"You haven't taken an Ambien?"

"No, but I could right now."

"Please do."

She leaves and returns several minutes later.

"Done," she says.

"Good. They'll do a tox screen."

"Of course."

"Where were you when you came to?" Marcel asks.

"Here. On the sofa."

"Were you fully dressed when you came to?"

"Yes."

"Was the TV on?"

"No."

"Was any music playing?"

"No."

"Where was your cell phone?"

The cell phone is lying on the coffee table beside the green glass ashtray. It is a plus-size with the tablet screen.

"Phone was right about where it is. I only moved it to call you then I put it right back."

"How did you feel when you woke up?" I ask.

"Dizzy. Dry mouthed and dizzy."

"How long were you out?"

"That I don't know. Maybe ten or fifteen minutes. Maybe longer."

"Did you make any other calls?"

"Not that I know of."

"Check your phone log, please."

She picks up her phone and presses several keys.

"No other calls."

I turn my attention to Marcel, who is lifting and opening the victim's suit coat with a ballpoint pen. He peers inside the coat.

"His wallet's inside. There's a business envelope in there, too. But I don't want to touch it."

"Won't your gloves protect you?"

He looks at me. "That could be construed as tampering with evidence. Among other things."

He's right, of course. I return my attention to Mira. Tampering-schmampering. This is a client's freedom we're talking about here. The inner lawyer steps up.

"Wash your hands, please," I tell her. "And change your clothes. Maybe put on a sweatshirt and shorts."

She holds out her hands, palms up. The black is gone. "I washed when I made coffee. What should I do with my dress?"

She knows that if she fired the pistol then her dress will register the shot because the gun will have discharged particles of burnt powder. The blowback from a revolver such as hers could easily convict her. A simple soaking and mild scrubbing of the dress will remove all gunshot residue. Washing of the hands--same thing.

"Pour wine on the chest. There's the rationale for washing the dress. Then toss it in the sink. Scrub lightly. Use some detergent and leave it soaking."

She stands and disappears back into her bedroom. While she is out, I pluck the cigarette butt from the ashtray. It is black from her fingers from earlier, before she washed. I drop the remnant into my pocket. She emerges just minutes later, dressed in jeans and a Bears T-shirt.

"The dress is in my bathroom sink, soaking in soapy water."

She displays her hands to me. "Washed up to my biceps this time."

"Your story is you spilled wine and were soaking the dress. But that's for trial if there is a trial. For tonight--"

"Don't say anything. Refuse to talk."

"You're reading my mind."

She forces a smile.

I sit back in my chair and survey the scene. We haven't talked about the upside-down cross above the victim's head. And we haven't talked about the pentagram scrawled on the wall behind the cross. The drawing is evidently rendered in charcoal remnants from an earlier blaze in the fireplace.

"Why were your fingers black?"

"I don't know. They were that way when I woke up."

This is troubling and I'm slowly starting to doubt her story altogether. Which is not a show-stopper; I have been known to defend the guilty before. But here's a twist: the scene says Satanism with the pentagram and the upside-down cross, and yet the body isn't mutilated

as Satanists are known to do. The eyeballs aren't punc-
tured with pins; the throat isn't cut; the genitals haven't
been cut away and jammed in his mouth; organs haven't
been harvested for potions; the fingers haven't been
clipped away--none of the usual Satanic ritualism one
would expect.

"So. What are we thinking? Is someone trying to
frame me?"

"Normally I would say so. But why the drawing on the
wall and the cross above his head? What's that stuff all
about? You wouldn't be expected to be into Satanism.
Whoever did this didn't need Satanism. If anything, it
makes it look *less* like something you would have done."

Mira follows my eye as I survey the scene. She nods.

"It's all about misdirection, isn't it?" she asks, pointing her
hands to indicate the upside-down cross and five-point
star with circle.

I pull out my phone and punch in 9-1-1.

She is right. The tableau is phony. Someone has tried to
make it look like she failed in her attempt to point the
finger at Satanists. Someone is very shrewd.

Satan was never here.

6

While we are waiting for the police to arrive, I send Mira to the shower.

"Use plenty of soap. All over, please."

She disappears into her bedroom and the door closes behind.

Marcel comes in and sits across from me at the dining table as I have moved away from the scene.

"What are you thinking?" I ask him.

He runs a hand back over his dark hair. He keeps it quite long, slicked straight back, and he wears a savvy Italian suit like you might see tooling around Rome on a Vespa scooter in search of romantically inclined females. One long clump has fallen down across his forehead. He continually attempts brushing it back into place, but it doesn't hold and soon returns to his forehead. But it's the middle of the night, so he gets a pass.

"I'm thinking we've obstructed justice, with all of our preparations."

"Oh?"

"Washing hands, soaking dress, hiding the cigarette butt-- yes, I saw when you dropped it in your pocket. Taking of shower, ingesting of Ambien. It's like you're the set decorator in some *Lincoln Lawyer* episode."

"You're saying I'm a Matthew McConaughey look-alike?"

"With that mug?"

My face is scarred from too many plastic surgery revisions. A result of being severely burned two years ago. The face no longer elicits the smiles of women like it did before the fire. Now it draws pained expressions and averted eyes. But luckily I managed to snag a brilliant wife anyway and so that requirement for my life has been met. Notice that I said brilliant wife, not beautiful wife. Men my age are starting to reach the point where they prefer brilliant to beautiful if there must be a choice of one over the other. I think Danny is also beautiful but I'm prejudiced. I'm not alone in that: she also thinks I'm handsome, scars and all.

My wife, Danny, is also a lawyer but tonight she's at home in our bed, fast asleep while I'm out on this house call. I am jealous of her rest but glad for her. She's even given me a daughter, Dania, and a son, Mikey, is on the way. Our world revolves around Dania and will Mikey, too, when he makes his appearance. Nowadays I try case after case after case in the criminal courts of Cook County with hardly a break in between. We are extremely busy ever since our defense of the son of a Chicago priest. Wife Danny all but runs my law office and bears much of the burden of supporting my efforts as a full-time trial lawyer.

"You're saying I don't look like McConaughey's Mickey Haller?"

"You look like Frankenstein's older brother, truth be told. Sorry to have to break the news, Michael."

I shrug and smile. "My wife adores me. That will have to do."

"You're a lucky man."

"What do we tell the cops we have accomplished since arriving?"

"Let's talk to Mira about that."

Just then, she returns. She is wearing a terrycloth bathrobe and pulling a wood-handled brush through her damp hair.

"Please, sit," I tell her.

"Story time?" she asks.

"Yes. Again, you will say nothing. You will defer all questions to me and I mean all questions. Same with you, Marcel: you answer nothing, all questions are passed off to me. Everyone understand?"

"Does that make us complicit in the lies you're going to unload on them?"

I smile. "Not at all. I'm taking the fall on this one."

"They're going to vacuum."

He means the carpet under and around the scene of the crime. We will have left hair and fibers in the crime scene, but that's to be expected.

"We've been careful. But even if not, we're in close quarters here. It would be reasonable for you to lose a long hair or two in the middle of the scene. Easily explained."

"What about the writing on the wall?"

"Handwriting expert? Sure, they'll try that. We'll have to cross that bridge when we come to it."

"What about the gun and my purse?" asks Miranda.

"For one thing, call the credit card issuers."

"What about the gun?"

I start to respond but she cuts me off.

"I can say--"

I raise my hand. "No, you don't do anything. Listen, Mira. Your first inclination will be to answer the questions they ask you. You're verbal, like me, and you will want to explain. It comes naturally to you. But you're not going to say one word while they're here. And you're taking off next week to get your head together. We can work out your next moves then."

"I'm thinking they'll put me on leave until this mess gets sorted out."

"I would expect that. Which works for me: it will keep

you out of the office and away from casual questions and cops. It's a good thing."

She nods. She gets up from the table, puts down her brush, and goes to the coffee maker.

"Anyone?" she asks.

We both shake our heads. There's still a chance we'll steal some sleep tonight if we lay off the coffee. She won't and she knows it, so why not?

Repeated buzzing startles us as the cops assault the doorbell.

"Let me get it," I tell them. "Remember, not even 'hello.' Understand?"

Heads nod. I believe I have made my point.

I cross into the living room, giving Darrell Harrow wide berth, and I open the door. Two uniforms lead the way inside, followed by a plainclothes dick and several CSI's. They are all notepads and evidence kits. The techs shoulder past me and arrange themselves around the dead guy. The dick lingers.

"Your name?" he asks.

"Michael Gresham."

"You live here?"

"No, I'm Ms. Morales' lawyer. She is seated at the dining table. She has orders from me not to speak with you. Please don't speak to her."

"Anyone else?"

"My investigator, Marcel Rainford. Also at the dining table. He won't be speaking to you either."

"Nicely done, counsel."

"You would do the same if you were in my shoes, detective. So let's not play any games, shall we?"

He looks me up and down and shakes his head in disgust. I return the look.

"Names?"

"He's Marcel Rainford. She's Miranda Morales."

"Morales? I've worked with a Miranda Morales out of the DA's office. Mira. That her?"

"Yes."

"Any weapons in the residence?"

"She carries a gun in her purse. She's licensed to carry. The gun and the purse are in the master bedroom."

"Has anyone touched it?"

"Hey, you're the police. Why don't you tell me?"

"I need more than that."

"All I'm going to say is that she's licensed to carry a gun."

"She is if she's the Miranda Morales I know. Homicide prosecutor, right?"

"Right. My investigator will be carrying a gun, too."

He sighs and records a note on his smartphone.

"Please join your friends," he next says and looks up, bored with me.

I leave without a word and go into the dining room. I take my seat and ask for a cup of coffee after all. It's going to be a long one and tomorrow's Sunday so I can sleep in. Coffee is definitely indicated now that the excitement has begun.

The dick comes into the kitchen. He looks over our trio.

"Miss Morales, hello. I know you won't speak to me but I'm wondering if you or anyone can ID the body?"

I speak up. "He's a prosecutor from the District Attorney's office. Name of Darrell Harrow. I'm surprised you don't recognize him."

"Is that supposed to be funny?"

"Not at all."

"Why was he here tonight?"

We all look straight ahead.

"Mr. Gresham, it would help me better understand this case if you would tell me a few things."

"Such as?"

"Why was he here? Hell, why are you here? Who called you? How long were you here before you called us?"

"Those matters are confidential. What else?"

"Have you people walked through the scene? Am I going to find your fingerprints in the scene, hairs, fibers, whatever?"

"I doubt you'll find one iota of interference."

"You doubt I'll find it or you doubt it exists?

"Both. I doubt you'll find it and I also doubt it even exists."

"For all our sakes let's hope you're right."

"Anything else?"

"Are you aware of any other evidence around this condo that is maybe connected to the dead guy? Or the shooter?"

"No."

"Is there anything else you can add that might help me?"

"No."

"We would like to swab your client's hands. Gunshot residue test. Would you allow that?"

"Help yourself."

"What about a blood draw?"

"Draw away."

"What about the clothes she was wearing tonight?"

"She spilled wine on the dress. It's soaking in soapy water right now."

Huge sigh of disgust. "All right."

He turns and leaves us to ourselves. I know he's in there traipsing through his crime scene right now, moving things, spreading his own prints around, crouching just outside the camera's lens--all of which will be cured, by the time the actual lab reports and glossies go to print. Every report, every witness, every investigation will say the same thing: "Nothing was moved."

Of course not. After all, police are sworn to tell the truth. We believe them.

"How long will this take?" Mira asks me.

"All night. They won't leave until they've removed a large part of the carpet under the dead guy. They won't leave until they've taken apart the traps under your sinks and saved the glop. But you know this, you've worked crime scenes before."

"I guess I've never stayed till the bitter end."

"They should be out of here by nine in the morning."

"Do I have to wait here? I've never been a suspect before."

Just then a CSI comes into the room and swabs Mira's hands, wrists, and forearms. The samples are placed into a plastic evidence bag and the CSI thanks her and leaves.

Then another arrives and punctures her arm with a long needle. Blood is drawn, capped, and initialed.

We continue our talk.

I say, "You're not a suspect now, Mira. Are you not telling us something?"

She ignores that question. She goes to the counter and slides open the top drawer. She withdraws a checkbook and pen.

"How much?" she asks and nods at me.

"Well, there's no case filed and we don't know if there will be. So why don't we wait for that until we see which way this is going to go."

"But I need to pay you something. Confidentiality."

"Five thousand, then."

She stoops over the dishwasher and begins writing out the check. Two minutes and she hands it to me. Five thousand dollars, payable now. I fold and put it in my shirt pocket.

"Now, where should I go tonight? Obviously I can't stay here or they'll pounce on me after you're gone, asking everything they can think of to trap me."

Danny and I have a solemn pact that we'll never again have a defendant on our property. So inviting her over to our guest room for the night is out of the question. I just return her stare.

Marcel says, "Hotel? There's a dozen good ones within two blocks of where we're standing."

It's true. Her condo is less than a mile from the Lower Loop.

"Can one of you drop me at the Marriott?"

"I can," Marcel says, stepping up. "Which Marriott?"

She leaves with Marcel; no explanations to anyone, no phone numbers, no objections: everyone knows I'm here and it's from me only that they're going to hear. Even the detective hardly looks up as they pass by and out the front door.

I decide to photograph the after-scene while the police and CSI's are doing their work. First the guest room, where I find one uniformed officer and one CSI going over the room with ultraviolet lights. Next is Mira's bedroom where there is one uniform searching for evidence. He abruptly leaves the room when I enter, but not before I snap his picture. He grimaces but says nothing. Then I am back in the living room, where two CSI's and the detective are examining the body. A third uniform stands guard at the front door. No one is being allowed in and of course no one is going out, not since Mira and Marcel left. I snap off several pictures of the dead body details, the workers, the detective, the penta-gram wall, and finish up with the uniform at the door.

Then I approach the detective.

"My client is going to need access in the morning for clothes to wear to work."

"Someone will be here."

"You're not just going to walk away and leave her door chained, are you? Don't forget, she's one of you."

"Naw, I'll leave someone here until she's in and out. Officer," he says to the uniform at the door. You saw the woman who just left? Let her back in when she returns for clothes. Clothes, that's all she takes out of here."

"Got it. Will do," says the uniform.

I am relieved. I've now done all I can to help my client tonight.

I say, "Thanks. I know she'll be relieved to at least get some clothes out."

"You taking her home with you tonight?"

"Nope."

"Hotel?"

"Can't say."

"But it would be under your name anyway, right?"

"You're very creative. Let me make a note."

"Fuck off, Gresham. Time for you to leave, too."

"I was just going. By the way, officer, I never caught your name."

He fishes a card out of his badge case. Handing it to me, he flashes the detective shield as well.

I look it over. "Okay, Jamison Weldon. Thanks for the card. Don't stay up too late."

I glide past him, past the uniform at the front door, and I am gone.

Funny thing, no one asked us for one fingerprint. How

else are they going to know whose prints are whose when they start comparing things?

They didn't ask; it's almost like Detective Weldon knows something I don't. I realize part of the answer: Mira's fingerprints are officially stored on police computers because of her work as a DA. They already have her prints and they knew that.

Downstairs, the parking garage is empty and the light is very dim. A good place for a killer to lurk. I shiver and double-time to my Mercedes.

Once inside, I quickly lock up and get the engine turning.

Then, my mind is racing along.

Darrell Harrow. He's a jack-of-all-trades in the District Attorney's office, a trial lawyer so experienced that he can cover any type of case on a moment's notice. Every large-city prosecutor's office has several of these floaters on staff.

Except Darrell Harrow is different from all those other prosecutors. He is stretched out on a colleague's floor, the back of his head in pieces on the wall.

While he remains dead, his colleague is checked into a world-class Marriott hotel, her Jacuzzi releasing steam in sheets while she soaks. It is a difficult sell, that she was unconscious when the shooting occurred but then awoke with no signs of attack on her own body, no knots on her head, no knockout drops, nothing that would explain the lapse in consciousness. The Ambien might help, but it's a weak explanation. We need something stronger to convince a jury—something compelling.

Which comes to me. Finding something compelling is my job. It is always my job to find the compelling.

Even when it doesn't exist.

7

D enise Harrow is a woman with high-cheekbones and blue veins along her hand where she's clutching a tissue wet with her tears. Everything about her says she is a widow with money, yet she was married to an Assistant District Attorney who wasn't making over probably a hundred-fifty grand.

As I come up the aisle of All Saints-St. Thomas Catholic Church, I nod at her, and Danny, at my side, walks on up and squeezes her arm as she says something into her ear. My wife is like that, always able to say the exact right thing at just the right moment. The widow nods and touches Danny's forearm in exchange. Then she looks away and we move into a vestibule where several of the city's lights are standing and whispering under the organ's somber tones.

Mayor Tanenbaum is there with his entourage of body-guards and bag boys. He is all suppressed smiles that flare into reelection grins when the widow and her group turn away, which diminish when she turns back and might see. Next to him is Able McCreedy, a reporter from the *Sun-Times* who has an inside track with the mayor's office, always spilling the ink of a good drama twelve hours before all other media. Next to Able is a woman wearing a black dress, long gloves, and the mandatory pearls, who, I am guessing, is the mayor's wife. I know this because she is eviscerating me with her eyes, recognizing me as the lawyer who defended her daughter's killer.

I am immediately sorry I have selected this vestibule and I almost pull Danny away but she's already patting the seat next to her just two rows up from the mayor. I sit and can already feel their hatred heating up the back of my neck. To my great relief, Jimmy Carson, a prosecutor out of the District Attorney's office with whom I am on good terms, takes the seat next to me and leans back to introduce his wife. Then Danny and the Carsons trade hushed helloes while I glance over the small remembrance sheet passed out at the entrance to the sanctuary. On the cover the iconic praying hands suggest that Harrow was a praying man, while inside is a short bio, his favorite Bible verse and favorite hymn. We send off even the guilty ones wearing such disguises, perhaps to trip up the God who will judge us. Jimmy nudges me with his shoulder.

"Hear you got the call from Mira Morales."

"I did. What's the word around the District Attorney's office?"

Jimmy is a thick-necked linebacker from Alabama who will forever be more comfortable in a forty-year-old's touch football game than the Art Museum. He is plainly uncomfortable at the funeral of a colleague and probably uncomfortable talking to me, a defense lawyer, the avowed enemy of the District Attorney's office, but there's a wrinkle. While I'm seeking the DA's insider dope, he can always claim that he laid hold of my thinking, too, when he gets back to the office and gets pumped for what he learned from me about their colleague's defense. It's a two-way street and we both know it.

He leans near and whispers.

"The word is that she had a thing with Harrow."

"As in romance?"

"Uh-huh. What you got?"

"Unconscious. Came to and found a dead man in her living room."

"That'll never fly."

"I couldn't agree more. That's why she called me."

"The great smoke-and-mirrors man, Michael Gresham, now setting up his tent in the northeast corner of the sideshow. Come one, come all and be ready to be amazed and perplexed. For he will walk and he will talk and he will spit wooden nickels while he slides on his belly like a reptile."

"You make me sound like a herpetologist."

"Whatever," says Jimmy and he vacantly pats his breast pocket for a cigarette. Like me, he probably quit eons ago.

Old habits in uncomfortable rooms. It goes with the territory.

I look over. "So. Who's ramrodding the investigation since the District Attorney's Office yelled conflict."

"Assistant Attorney General. Woman by the name of Nora Wigins."

"She's all that good," I whisper. "I've definitely heard good things."

"Better than good. Teaches Evidence at UC."

University of Chicago. My old stomping grounds and the name stamped on my juris doctor diploma. So, she's got court cred. It figures they would send the best they have from the AG's office. I swallow hard. I expected no less.

Just then a thunderous voice booms from behind. I turn; the face behind the voice belongs to his Honor, the mayor himself, Abraham Tanenbaum.

"My wife had to leave," his voice roars.

"Oh, yes?" I respond.

"She can't be in the same room as you, Mr. Gresham. If I didn't have to be here, I'd be following right after her. So let's compromise. How about you move to the other side of the church?"

Jimmy Carson leans forward, distancing himself from me.

"I'm fine right here, Mister Mayor. Given the solemnity of

today's gathering, you'd do well to forego turning this into an event, this hatred you harbor against me."

"I'm waiting. I can have my security people clear this part of the church or you can go peacefully," he hisses.

The hairs prickle along the back of my neck. He's too damn close and I can feel his hot breath. Then Danny stands and takes my hand. Wordlessly, she crosses in front of me, pulling me to my feet. I excuse myself as I step past Jimmy and we make our way to the end of the pew and move left, back toward the entrance. We then come up the far aisle and sit quietly behind three large black men in suits and grim faces. I am sure they are cops and I feel safe here.

Safe with cops around?

Of all things.

8

T hree mourners pay their respects to Darrell Harrow from the lectern.

The first is a black woman who was Attorney Harrow's paralegal in the District Attorney's office. She worked for the man some fifteen years and knew Darrell and Denise as family. She recounts the Christmases and other holidays they spent together. She describes Harrow's dropping in on her when she had a surgery that kept her home for two weeks while her shoulder healed and how he brought in food and groceries for her kids. And she talks about his exceptional career as a prosecutor, a man who wanted to see justice done, who abhorred revenge and refused to go down that path no matter how hard he was being pressured by victims and their families to mete out excessive punishment. Then she returns to her seat and Harrow's sister speaks. She talks about their childhood; his butterfly collection; his learning to swim by falling into the Chicago River when he was five while playing where he shouldn't have been; his time in the army as a JAG officer; and his yearly efforts to keep the peace around the family's Thanksgiving table when the kids were younger and celebrating the holidays in a home not always filled with good cheer. Then she steps back and the widow, Denise Harrow, comes forward to talk about her husband. Her words are few and uttered from a place of brokenness and despair. The kids watch their mother from the first row in the church as their mother's two brothers sit among them, giving comfort.

Danny and I watch and hear all of this from our seats far enough back from the front of the church as to be among the anonymous mourners who don't know each other and can quickly depart after the service, signing the guest book on the way out.

Then it happens. While Denise Harrow is speaking, Mira Morales enters the church. There is a pause as the widow grapples for words, rendered mute by a sudden discomfort. All heads turn to look at what has stopped her cold. Then they see.

Mira takes five steps and stops, looking for a friendly face she can sit next to. She is not yet charged with any crime, as ballistics reports are outstanding and the murder weapon missing. If they find the killing bullet came from Mira's gun she will, of course, be immediately indicted for the crime. But as of this moment when she enters into the church, she is legally innocent. The detectives have warned her not to leave town; of course they never have the legal right to do that. Still she has obeyed, remaining at home on paid leave while the crime lab does its protocol.

Then the widow collects herself.

"Please," she cries out, "someone make her leave!"

"What is she thinking?" Danny whispers. "Why would she come here?"

"Maybe she is innocent," I say. "Maybe to pay her respects to an associate."

"Not likely!" Danny retorts. She knows Mira's sleep-around proclivities and has already decided that the decedent was having an affair with Mira Morales.

Then we are completely stunned as Denise Harrow suddenly steps around the lectern and breaks into a full run right at the latecomer. Mira spots the widow, perceives her intent, and glances around in desperation. A man stands up from his seat and steps in front of her, evidently to protect the women from each other. Another man joins the first. Together they form a half-wall in the aisle. However, Mrs. Harrow is not to be denied in her effort to effect instant justice. She simply dances around the men, bearing witness to the spin moves of the NFL tricksters and ending up face to face with Mira Morales. Denise Harrow leaps at Mira and grabs a handful of perfectly coiffed blond hair. She yanks and a bouquet of blond hair with gray roots comes loose from Mira's head, which causes the victim to wail in pain. The men turn and pursue the women back up the aisle and now pull at them, trying to separate them, encircling waists with arms and leaning away from the fracas, each one with his angry, flailing combatant. Chaos erupts: exclamations of horror, or anger at Mira Morales daring to come here, of pain as the blond hair is ripped free, and half the mourners are now standing, pointing, leaning in or away, looking to all the world like the community witnessing the Last Supper. Indeed, the pastor commandeers the microphone and calls for peace and calm. The worker at the soundboard cues a hymn and *The Old Rugged Cross*, listed in the memorial brochure as Darrell's favorite, rumbles over the loudspeakers. But the pastor persists in trying to talk them down and, with the aid of additional hands from additional volunteers, the women are separated. Soothing words are spoken. Calm is restored. In tears, and pulling her veil down across her eyes, the widow is helped to the back of the church where she's led away into a side room. Meanwhile, Mira Morales, stunned and totally alone in all this, darts her eyes around and just happens to catch my gaze as Danny and I are moving across the row toward her. I reach the scene of the melee and firmly seize Mira by the elbow and begin steering her back out of the church. Danny runs interference, and without thought or plan we walk the woman over to our Mercedes and seat her in the passenger seat. She is softly crying and digging through her bag for tissues and wiping her tears and noisily blowing her nose. She shakes her head again and again, and Danny reaches forward from the back seat and rubs her shoulder.

"I tried to pay my respects," the wounded prosecutor says with all alacrity. It clearly hasn't sunk in why she was attacked and struck by Denise Harrow.

"I thought I asked you to stay home," I say to her, referring to the talk I give all my clients about sticking close to home while under investigation.

"He was one of my favorite men. And the best prosecutor among all nine hundred of us. By far and away."

As if any of this justifies her showing up.

9

"I put myself through law school by waitressing and cleaning offices," Mira is telling Danny and me. We are sitting in a Drummond's Cafe in Evanston, drinking coffee and eating pancakes after the funeral. Mira followed us here, upset with herself for showing up at the funeral and in need of a friend. She had been drinking before the funeral, and, while intoxicated, made the decision to pay her respects to an old friend and colleague, Darrell Harrow. Her situation was blotted out by the drink. "My grades suffered because I had to work," Mira says, "but I was still number three in my class."

"I did paralegal work," says Danny.

They are in full commiseration mode, recalling the sacrifices it took to survive the financial puzzle of law school without support from anyone. Mira is guzzling coffee and Danny keeps it coming.

Mira leans forward and speaks confidentially. "My

parents disinherited me when I got pregnant my senior year of high school. I had my baby but couldn't afford to keep her, so I gave her up for adoption. Someday we'll meet; I'm going to make sure of that, but it hasn't been the right time so far."

"Do you know where she is?" Danny asks her.

"I do. And her parents let me send her birthday and Christmas presents plus a letter once a month. I also send support checks because I know they need the money. They're blue collar workers but have huge hearts. I picked them out of a dozen adoptive parents in a book Social Services brought me the same afternoon she was born. It was the best and the worst day of my life."

"Did you get to hold your baby?" Danny asks.

"I did. One time. For a half an hour. I held her on my chest while I was still in the hospital bed. She slept and I kissed her head. I held her tiny little hand in mine and tried to memorize her fingerprints in case I lost track of her. But that was part of the adoption, that I would get to stay in touch and she could contact me after she turned eighteen if she ever wanted. So far, no contact but she's only fourteen. I'm hopeful."

"Have you ever thought of having more children?"

Mira looks out the window. In huge white letters the glass advertises pancakes, eggs, and bacon for $6.99. I can read all this in reverse as I try to distance myself from Mira's very painful story. I can't even begin to imagine the pain of giving up a child. It's probably one of the worst things any human ever has to endure. She's got tears on her cheeks now as she describes the days after giving birth, when she returned to high school and so many students made fun of her. It had been no secret she gave the baby up and the cruelty of the other students about this just astonished her. She recalls them putting a life-size rubber baby in her gym locker with a note telling her she hadn't lost her daughter after all. Danny comes unglued on hearing this. She wonders out loud how Mira kept from killing herself.

"Actually I did cut my wrists that same day," she says, pulling up her shirt sleeves and showing us her wrists.

She painfully continues.

"I didn't want to live anymore. The trauma of losing my baby girl was quadrupled by the attacks my own class-mates were making on me. Girls who I thought were my friends were deserting me and joining in the hate campaign. The school counselor met with me just about every day that last semester. I'd go into her office and she'd close the door and I would just sit there and cry. It's a wonder I graduated at all."

Danny reaches over and places her hand on Mira's hand. She leaves it there.

"So college must have been a huge relief."

"I got my student loan in August and bought a used VW. I moved from Brooklyn to Chicago and enrolled at Roosevelt U. I worked full-time and went to school full-time. I was still heartsick over my baby and refused to go out on a date until my junior year. I was determined not to ever get pregnant again and so far I haven't."

"Why not? Couldn't you leave that all behind and start a family now?"

Mira shakes her head and watches Danny pour coffee into the cup Mira is holding. Mira adds in a dash of cream. She slowly stirs the mixture with her spoon.

"I think the fear of losing another child kept me from having another. As a lawyer I can think of too many ways a parent can lose a child. I don't want to ever, even for a second, face that prospect. So, I had my tubes tied. Never going there again."

"Well," says Danny, and she runs out of words.

We sit silently, reflecting on Mira's story and reflecting on Darrell Harrow's murder. We quietly begin to discuss the implications for Mira's life. We are both thinking the same thing, Danny and I: anyone but Mira. Mira didn't deserve to be facing a murder investigation. She deserved happiness and joy in her life. Her dues were all paid up but now Harrow's death will take her down again. We're all lawyers; we all know how difficult her life is about to become. Finally, Danny squeezes Mira's hand and pulls her own hand away. The time has come to talk about Harrow and our approach to her defense.

We begin going over the past six months of her life, her relationship to Harrow, and a minute-by-minute replay of that night, starting with getting dressed to go to the Democratic fundraiser.

What we don't go into is my previous affair with Mira. It was before Danny came into my life and by tacit consent Mira and I do not speak of it.

Some defenses are better left unmade.

We finish up and get up to pay the ticket. Mira and
Danny hug goodbye and then Mira comes to me. We hug
and I smell an ancient fragrance. I am immediately
caught up in the memory of a long time ago with her,
nude on her bed, talking until the sun came up the next
morning. We were five years younger, and we both knew I
was much too old for her and that we were just having a
fling. But two nights later we did it again; talking until
five a.m., when I quietly got up, dressed, and went to my
home. We never met again in her bedroom after that
night. The agreement was mutual that whatever we were
doing had run its course. Since those days I have
defended against three of Mira's cases and I have always
had the feeling that she was giving my clients extra
breaks and easier pleas than I might have gotten
elsewhere.

We break our hug and she walks out of Drummond's to
her car. She looks small and bent as if under a great
weight. I want to go to her and put an arm around her
shoulder and tell her that we're going to beat this thing,
that her life is going to be returned to her. But of course I
can't do that. As I watch her back out and begin pulling
away, I notice a new model Ford, black in color, fall in
behind her.

For just a moment I am certain there is a uniformed
police officer driving the car that followed her out. I
watch until they reach the light at River Road and her
blinker indicates a right as they wait. Before the light can
change, she turns right and accelerates. The Ford jerks

out into traffic and falls in behind her. They disappear behind a row of buildings and I look back to count my change from the cashier. I will call her cell to check on her momentarily.

Danny catches my eye.

"What was that all about?" she says.

"What was what all about?"

"You had a thing with her, didn't you?" It isn't really a question. It is an affirmation.

Danny and I don't lie to each other. As lawyers we are very different at home than we are in courtrooms and office buildings. No lies, period.

"Yes," I say. "It was a long time ago."

"I saw it when she hugged you. It lasted a second too long."

"Did it?" I say.

I almost add, "I didn't notice."

But that would be a lie.

I call her to check in. The car that followed her has me concerned. But she says there's no problem. She pulled into a gas station and, while she was filling, watched other cars coming and going. She's quite sure no one followed her from the station.

I'm not entirely relieved but I let it go.

Mira is a smart lady and she'll call if she needs me.

10

The next morning, Marcel is driving me to work while I work on a trial brief in the backseat of my Mercedes.

"Boss," he says, catching my eye in the rearview mirror. "We've got lights."

With his eyes he indicates I should look behind us. I twist in the seat and there, twenty feet behind my car, is a late model black sedan with red and blue lights hidden in its grill. They are flashing and Marcel is pulling over to the side of Lakeshore Drive. There is no safe place to come to a full stop so he slowly proceeds almost to the corner of the block and there turns into a strip mall parking lot. He brings the car to a rest and puts it in park. We wait.

I watch as the passenger in the police vehicle exits his car and strides up to my window as if he owns this part of Chicago. He knocks on the glass beside my head. I roll down the window.

"Mr. Gresham, would you mind stepping out of your car?"

It is Jamison Weldon, the same detective that answered
the call I made from Mira's apartment several nights ago.
He looks more rested now and a slight smile plays around
his lips, clearly the cat about to toy with the mouse he's
caught up to.

I do as asked and climb out, finding myself standing toe
to toe with the detective, who's considerably taller than
me. I don't remember that height advantage as I'm
fairly tall and he peers down on me. In the light of day,
I can make out a scar across his face, running from
below his left eye and traveling starboard across the
bridge of his nose, fading off below his right eye. It's a
hell of a present some bad guy or other has left him
with and Weldon wears it like a badge of honor, putting
his face right next to mine and fastening me with his
eyes.

"Mr. Gresham, would you please come with me to my
car?"

I start to protest but he reaches out and grabs my
shoulder and begins moving me back to his vehicle. I
don't resist; to do so would quickly land me in jail facing
a resisting arrest charge or worse. At his car, he pulls
open the rear door and pushes me inside.

"Move over," he growls and I slide across the seat. He
crawls in beside me and pulls the door shut. All this time,
Marcel is watching helplessly from the driver's seat of my
car, but he's keeping his cool and not getting involved.
Were he to get out and protest he would probably be

arrested on some trumped-up charge and we both know that. So he is left to wait for me.

Weldon leans back against the seat and the air whooshes out with a sigh. He is a big man whose knees press against the back of the passenger seat. He turns to me and I can feel the heat of his anger from three feet away. To my amazement, the guy is in a rage.

"You are going to need to listen to me," he says. "You are going to need to listen or your life is about to go south very quickly."

"So what am I listening to?" I ask. "So far you've only committed false arrest and battery against me. Do you have more?"

He grimaces and his partner turns around from the driver's seat. He is a swarthy, bald man with a fringe of hair and a crooked grin surrounding crooked teeth. He leers at me but says nothing.

"Mr. Gresham, don't think for a minute I don't know you interfered with my crime scene at Ms. Morales' house. It quickly became evident to me that you had moved things around and even removed evidence from my scene."

I am stumped by this. "What evidence did I remove? And how do you even know I removed something if you never saw it?"

"There was an ashtray full of ash. But no butts. Someone removed them and I'm thinking that someone was you. I'm thinking it was probably ashes from your own cigarette. Maybe you had been there for much longer than you're telling us. Maybe you were involved in Darrell's death. Lots of maybes, Mr. Gresham."

I am speechless. The entire logic--for purposes of argument--is ludicrous. However, he is much brighter than I at first thought. Moreover, I don't remember what I did with Mira's cigarette butt when I did remove it. It hasn't crossed my mind or my path since that night.

He reaches across and jabs a thick finger into my ribs.

"You sandpapered your client and you sandpapered the scene. You had her wash her dress so we wouldn't find gunshot residue. You had her take a shower so we wouldn't find gunshot residue. And we know you had her drop an Ambien so you could argue she was passed out. You probably had her drink alcohol, too, I'm guessing. And I'm going to prove you did these things and I'm going to send your ass to jail for ten years when I make my case against you. But I'm a nice guy and I'm giving you a one-time chance to come clean. If you do, we'll go much easier on you. The next move is yours, Mr. Gresham."

"Sorry, but I don't have a move," I tell him. "I have no clue what you're even talking about."

He scowls at me and jabs his knuckles into my ribs, striking me several times in rhythm with his words as he says, "Get--real--sir!"

"I'm as real as I can be. I would never interfere with an official police investigation. I know better."

"You spent thirty minutes inside that condo before you made the call to us, Mr. Gresham. We've got the video of you arriving at her door. It's thirty minutes until you dial us. So cut the horseshit, Mr. Gresham, we both know you were inside making arrangements. I'm going to ask you one last time. Come clean. Cooperate. Save yourself ten years in prison. You've got sixty seconds."

"Sixty seconds or sixty days--it makes no difference. I have no idea what you're talking about, Detective Jamison. But I will tell you what I'm willing to do. You open the door and let me leave this car and I won't press charges against you and I won't personally sue you for false arrest. You have sixty seconds to decide."

The man up front snorts and slaps the steering wheel. "The fucking nerve!" he cries out. "Where do they get you assholes?"

Jamison glances at his partner and then slowly reaches over and opens his door. To my great relief. He climbs out and I follow.

"We aren't done here," he says as I begin walking back to my car. "I'm coming for you, Mr. Gresham."

I stop and turn back. "Well bring your best game, detective. You're going to need it because I'll be waiting for you. You're going to be lucky not to lose your freedom and your assets if you come for me, as you put it. So I'm expecting your best shot."

With that, I turn and stride back up to my vehicle, shoulders thrown back, head high, taking my time to let him know I haven't been frightened by his confrontation.

Which is a lie. Actually, he has seen right through me. I

did do all the things he rattled off. I did my job and just a touch more.

My brain begins to speed up as I climb back into my car and quickly begin the checklist of what he would find out about me if my client turned on me. Marcel begins to speak but I hold up my hand.

"Give me a minute," I say to him.

He turns back around and begins driving us out of the strip mall.

"We need to talk," I finally tell him.

"They're on to you, Boss. We knew they would be."

"They'd rather make a case against me than against Mira."

"You sound surprised. Don't be. You're a high-visibility criminal defense lawyer. You've got a target on your back, Michael."

I look out the window and see my reflection in the glass. I am all frown lines and frightened eyes. My hands shake. These encounters with the police--I've been down this road many times. Always with the intimidation.

With me, it doesn't work.

It only makes me that much more determined.

11

M arcel and I long ago decided that the best
defense to any criminal charge is a smash-
mouth offense. It is Monday and we are headed to Mira's
condo tower in downtown Chicago on the river front. We
are going there to speak with condo security and find out
whatever we can about the security video. Of course the
police will have beaten us there, which is fine, because
with all videography now being saved to hard drives, no
police agency and no defense firm ever gets the "original"
of any "tape." It's a simple matter of obtaining a copy of
the mp3 files contained on the hard drive and plugging
into our own computers and watching the show. Whatever that turns out to be.

We park underground in the visitors' section and take the
elevator up to three, where the security office is housed.
Elmer Gentry greets us there. Mr. Gentry is the agent in
charge of building security for the security firm with the
contract. He oversees all staffing, he explains to us, data

acquisition, storage, and distribution, and he has already provided the police with the same video files we're now seeking.

"July Fourth. We need the twelve hours leading up to the time of the shooting until all police and forensic staff clear the area," Marcel explains to Mr. Gentry, who is more than willing to help.

"In fact," Mr. Gentry says, "I've already had my staff prepare the same mp3 file for you that we provided to the police. Fair's fair."

"I appreciate that," I tell him. "We are sure Mrs. Morales is innocent of any wrongdoing here and can only hope the video will shed some light on the ID of the true killer."

"You can only hope," says Mr. Gentry, "and I'll tell you what. I haven't had either the time or the inclination to review the video myself, but if you find it helpful, I will be glad. Good luck to you and to Mrs. Morales. She's an exemplary resident, never a problem or a complaint lodged against her, no loud parties, no visitors over-staying an acceptable number of days in her condo--nothing remarkable about her at all."

"Say that again," I ask.

"What part?"

"The part about visitors overstaying their welcome. There's a limit on the number of days she can have visi-tors? Why is that?"

"Because all residents are carefully screened by the condo board before any condo sale is finalized. Visitors haven't undergone this screening so, while they're never regarded as suspicious by us, the board does have its regulations. Overnight visits are okay over a reasonable time. Whatever that means. It's a case-by-case basis which effectively gives the condo board full control over visitor stays. All condos have a similar clause in their CC&R's."

"I'm sure," I say.

"Is this a continuous loop?" Marcel asks, referring to the CD he's been handed. "Any breaks?"

"Yes. You'll find all cameras are included, which means you're getting front entrance, elevator, stairways, confer-ence rooms--any area accessible by the common visitor."

"Hallways?"

He shakes his head. "Discretion there. Most of our tenants prefer no record of their visitors. We're a young crowd in this building and there's quite a bit of sharing going on. It's what the board wanted."

"One question," says Marcel. "Was Darrell Harrow accom-panied by anyone when he entered the building?"

"I haven't reviewed the video. I can't answer that."

"If he had been accompanied or later joined by a second visitor--would that show up on the video?"

"Definitely. The CCTV is a continuous loop. You'll find everything on it."

"So, the players are all recorded."

"If 'players' is the proper term, yes. Frankly, I'm thinking it was only one player, but I don't know that for a fact."

"Why do you think it was only one player?"

"It had to be your client who fired the gun. No one else came or went from the condo but police, according to what I'm told."

"Who told you that?"

"The detectives. They called back wanting to know whether there was any other way for a visitor to leave the condo other than elevator or stairs. I told them no."

"Did anyone leave after Harrow arrived?"

"Police came and went, but that was after you must have called them."

I will check the time when I made the call to the police against what the video timestamp shows. If anyone is seen leaving the twenty-fifth floor after Harrow arrived but before I arrived, we will try to identify them and question them.

Exactly what the police are doing right about now.

12

I n my office on the whiteboard we have laid out the floor-plan of Mira's condo. We have placed the dead body exactly as it was aligned in the living room. A photograph of each room, taken from the doorway, wide-angle, is taped beneath each room's drawing. We have received a list of items seized from the condo by the police and we have listed those items under the room from which each item was removed. The whiteboard is four feet tall by five feet wide and our rendering covers its entire surface. This is our typical approach to criminal cases of all manner: set up the scene and the exhibits and witnesses, if any, so we understand the setup and our analysis can be based on fact. In this case there are no witnesses, but we have placed a figure representing Mira asleep on the couch at the time the gun was fired killing Darrell Harrow.

Mira is late joining us, arriving at ten-thirty instead of her appointment time of ten. I am going to be miffed about this until she starts talking. She prefaces her explanation by handing me three pages, stapled. I scan through them.

"So," I say, "when did you get this?"

"A uniform brought it to my condo just as I was putting on my face to come down here."

I read through the pages, a legal document.

"You have been indicted on one count of first degree murder," I tell her, as if a lead homicide prosecutor wouldn't understand her own indictment. The telling comes with the territory; I will treat her exactly like I would any other client because I never try to guess at a defendant's mental state. For all I know, she is too upset to even read and understand the documents, so it falls to me to explain them to her. Which I do, also going over the lesser-included-offenses to first-degree murder, which are the lesser-in-degree charges that are incorpo- rated by implication. For example, if you are charged with first degree murder, the jury can find you guilty of first, second, or third degree, or manslaughter, voluntary or involuntary, or battery, or assault. It cannot find you guilty, however, of one or more lesser included offenses *and* the offense charged in the indictment. I go over this with her, painstakingly explaining how it all works, while she sits and looks at me with a blank look superimposed over the slightest of smiles. Finally, I wind it up and ask her for questions.

"Just one," she says, "what do we do if I'm guilty of none of these charges? That's the part I am unfamiliar with--the not-guilty client."

"In that case, it is incumbent on us to prove *why* you're not guilty."

"I thought the state had to prove me guilty. I thought I didn't have to prove anything."

I smile at her. It is a kindly smile for I am taking her question as if asked in all sincerity, which I believe it is.

"If you're not guilty, we must prove why, no matter what the law says. The innocent person who doesn't prove his innocence--even though the law says he needn't--is playing with fire. We will prove you not guilty. That's the only way to proceed."

"What is our evidence?"

"The Ambien, the lack of GSR, the fact the bullet wasn't fired from your gun--"

"Wait, how do you know it wasn't fired from my gun?"

I spread my hands and lean forward in my chair.

"Because. You've told me you are innocent. That means it's not your gun."

Two hours later, my words are proven partly wrong. The forensics report is delivered to my office by the District Attorney's runner. The gun that fired the bullet that killed Darrell Harrow was the same caliber as Mira's gun. I keep reading. There's no reference made to any tests run on Mira's gun—which is exceedingly strange. The absence of any reference totally stumps me. They do talk about the bullet, however. The Harrow bullet was from the batch of bullets found in a box she kept inside her closet. I feel the air going out of our case. I call Mira with the news. She drops back in at my office.

"My bullet?" she sounds as if in a dream state. "But I didn't fire my gun."

"Of course. I really don't think you shot Darrell Harrow. I've believed you all along."

"Is that why you had me wash off any GSR and take an Ambien?"

"No. I asked you to do those things because I was already in the process of proving you not guilty. Both of those steps would give us indicia of your innocence if the cops did a gunshot residue test or a toxicology blood draw. My requests were made only to confirm your innocence."

"Smart man. I appreciate that. Now that I've been indicted, I need to pay you. How much will you charge me for this defense?"

"My usual charge for a first degree murder case is two-hundred-and-fifty thousand dollars. The publicity I'm going to earn by defending you, however, is priceless. I would do your case for free."

"Uh-uh. I've paid you five thousand already. My dad is taking out a second mortgage for another hundred thousand. Would you take an IOU for the balance?"

"Yes, I will," I instantly say, which violates every rule of getting paid known to criminal lawyers. Criminal lawyers never, ever, under any circumstances, agree to get paid on the other end, after the finding of not guilty. If they did, ten times out of ten they wouldn't ever get paid. But I am violating that most sacrosanct of rules because I really meant what I just told her: the publicity I am receiving for defending the county's chief homicide prosecutor on a charge of homicide is priceless. Already the papers and TV reporters are hounding me for an interview. That will come, in good time, and with it will come an influx of good clients with cash to spend. It's a win-win for me. The incoming hundred grand won't hurt things, either. Much of it will go to expert witnesses to be called by me in her trial. It usually does.

"So, how are we looking, Michael?"

"I think fairly good even with the bullet matching your box of bullets. There's still no gun to match up, which is baffling. I cannot explain it but we're in touch with the police department about it. Also, we'll need to have your Ambien doctor testify about why you're taking Ambien and potential side effects when mixed with a little wine, and that will go a long way toward explaining why you weren't aware there had been a murder inside your own condo when you woke up. So that's a good witness for you. We'll also use a toxicologist to keep the emphasis on your unconscious state and that will undergird what your doctor says and keep the focus on the mental state you were in--which is going to be very important moving forward. Because without intent or motive the state really has nothing against you. If we can do that, you'll walk seven times out of ten."

"And the other three times?"

"That would be negative evidence from something we don't know about yet. An eyewitness to something or

other. An ear-witness who heard you arguing in your
condo before the shot was fired--those kinds of things."

"Well, there isn't anything like that."

"At least not yet. We need to really be open to turning
over all the rocks at this point in our investigation. If it's
out there and has the potential to hurt you, we must find
it and learn how to defuse it. That's my job."

"You have the CCTV video? Has it been reviewed?"

"Marcel watched every minute of it. We've got Harrow
coming to your condo. There's a time lapse, then me,
then Marcel, then the cops."

"Anyone seen leaving my condo?"

"We've got two people leaving on the elevator on twenty-
five. One of them was a cop and the other was the
daughter of a woman recently moved in. Marcel has
questioned the daughter. He's looking for the police
officer but identification is almost impossible."

"Why is that?"

"For one, his hat blocks the view. We can't make out his
face."

"What else about him?"

"He's not wearing a name tag. And we can't make out the
badge number--no good shot of it."

"But he's a cop?"

"Far as we can tell."

"What about any gunshot?"

"Video has sound. But no gunshot."

"No surprise there."

"Well, we've just scratched the surface. We have lots to do yet."

We part company, and Danny comes into my office. As an attorney, Danny is succeeding beyond what I had even hoped for her. She is taking on preliminary hearings and misdemeanor trials and even felony trials here and there where the risk of incarceration is low. I have purposely kept her away from major felony assignments in the office despite her repeated requests for more high profile cases. Those things will come, in time, but for now we have to satisfy ourselves with her assignments as a work in progress.

She sits across from me, absently finger-combing her blond hair across the top of her head and returning my loving gaze with a smile.

"You want the case, am I right?" I say to her.

"More than anything," she says.

"You know I can't do that. Not with Mira looking at life in prison."

"How about second chair? I would love to sit through the trial with you."

I smile.

"We can do that. Tell you what, how about you take on our medical experts?"

She leans forward in her chair. She's really wanting this, I see, and I'm thinking she's ready for it.

"Who would that be?" she asks.

"Mira's physician, the one who prescribed the Ambien. And a toxicologist. I need you to find someone who has expertise in cases where the patient has mixed Ambien and alcohol and had a blackout or passed out because of it."

"I know where to begin looking. That much I do know."

"Where would that be?"

"Local universities. Starting with the University of Chicago. Maybe a professor of toxicology in the med school. Someone who's published a lot and who has experience testifying in court. Someone who's not wishy-washy but who can really commit to a defendant and not waver from their opinions."

"I'm liking what I'm hearing. Welcome aboard."

She gives me one of the wide smiles I adore about her. My heart aches at how crazy about her I am.

"What about your pregnancy?"

She shrugs. "I'll have delivered by the time it goes to trial."

"I know that. I'm asking about continuity in your workup? Will you be able to care for a newborn and cover your responsibilities here as well?"

"My," she says, "aren't you the chauvinist!"

"Why do you say that?"

"Because we will *both* be involved with our baby's care, that's why. We'll use Dania's nursery and keep them both here with us. I won't be out of the office but a week or so that way. I'll be right here."

"All right."

"Besides, Mister. It's a fifty-fifty undertaking once the baby is born. It's not all on me."

"I expected no less, to tell the truth. And you know I want to be there with you. It's my baby too."

I've been chastised and I've taken my best shot at looking accountable. But we both know deep down that I'm old-school when it comes to family duties. I'm trying to get over that, to modernize my mind, as Danny puts it, but old habits and all that.

"We're not special snowflakes, either of us," she reminds me. "Remember, we decided long ago that we want to live our lives like we want to live our lives and we want others to have the freedom to live their lives like they want to."

"Which is why we fight so hard for our clients."

"No judgment, only support. Not the crime, but the person."

"Everyone deserves a second chance."

Even old-fashioned, old-school, chauvinist husbands.

Now I know why we've just had our little talk. She had

the entire agenda in mind before she even entered my office.

And I'm wondering whether she's ready for the rough-and-tumble of major felony cases.

Spare me.

13

"Mira Morales received a standing ovation after her speech at the Cook County Democratic Fundraiser," says Elmer Bancroft, the state chairman of the party.

We are sitting in his office at Worker Stedman, a tech fund on Lower Wacker in Chicago. Bancroft is the managing partner and a jovial politician who knows the first name of just about every precinct worker in his county. He is a large, big-boned man with heavy jowls, a bulbous nose, and eyes perpetually road-mapped with eyestrain from party business at some tavern or restaurant where plans were made, candidates selected in back room deals, and Cook County politics guided by the heavy hand of the chairman as they have been for a hundred years. Predecessors' party politics have resulted in assassinations: Anton Cermak in 1931; in nationally televised riots: Richard J. Daley in 1968; in demonstrations too many times to count now: from Richard M.

Daley until 2010. It continues today. The Cook County Democratic Party is a volatile mashup of every conceivable economic, religious, and social interest group out there. And Elmer Bancroft is the front man for it all, the man who agreed that Mira Morales would be the party's candidate for District Attorney in the first place.

Danny and I are loyal contributors to both political parties in Chicago and it isn't from any deep-seated need to see any agenda furthered. No, we contribute so that, when we are picking juries, we have access to both parties' databases in order to get additional background information about prospective jurors. Everyone with a brain does this in Chicago, criminal lawyers and civil litigators alike. After all, jury panels come from voter registration rolls. It's only good business that we remain active so we have access to citizen demographics and likely social tendencies.

I ask him, "Did anyone notice Mira having words with someone? An altercation of some kind?"

Bancroft leans back in his deep leather chair. He places his fingertips together and shifts some imaginary weight between them. A red toothpick protrudes from the corner of his mouth. He switches it to the other side as he thinks.

"Well, I didn't see anything. Not that I would have even noticed, Michael. I get pretty wrapped up in what's happening on the dais to ever notice anything else. You might ask some of the precinct bosses who were there. I'm thinking in particular of Natty McMann."

"And who is Natty McMann?" asks Marcel. He has come here with me today as we try to put together a list of names among the party functionaries worth talking to.

"Natty is our sergeant-at-arms. He would likely have noticed if anyone got out of line."

"He has people roaming the crowd with their eyes open, is what you're saying," says Marcel.

Bancroft nods. "That's exactly what I'm saying." Then he changes the subject. "So what do you fellows think? Do we need to replace Mira on the ticket and not look back? Or is this going to wrap up and go away pretty soon? What do we do?"

The question is mine to field.

"It's not going to evaporate, if that's what you're hoping. Prosecutors going after one of their own are very, very careful, very circumspect. They know they will be in for the fight of their lives whenever they indict another prosecutor. No, this case will be around for a while. But that doesn't mean you should dump Mira. I'm strongly convinced she's not guilty."

Again with the toothpick. Other side of the mouth.

"That may be, but this case will be dragging on into the fall, am I right? Hell, boys, the election's in November. I think this pretty much gets her kicked out."

"We've had our initial appearance, Mr. Bancroft," I advise him. "The judge put this on the fast-track calendar. We have a trial date of October thirty-first. That's a firm date. So you'll know her status before the election. Everyone will. And if you dump her now it will look like you're admitting she's guilty of something. You'll also be dumping your best chance of beating out Lamont Johnstone in the general election. I would caution you against dumping her. In fact, as her attorney, I'm begging you not to. It would really hurt her case for the public to see her party pull away from her."

"There is that," Bancroft allows. "There is that. Tell you what. I'm going to sit on this through August and keep my ear to the ground. If it is looking good for her, I'll know by September one. We can still field a new face at that time if need be."

"Elegant," I say, suddenly hot under the collar. "A betrayal that's not. Because if you don't like what you're hearing in August or September, you're going to dump her and that's going to make choosing a jury very difficult, considering that Cook County juries run four-to-one Democrat in their makeup. A fallen star won't sit well with those folks. You'll make my job twice as hard."

He smiles and leans forward in a rush. He withdraws the toothpick and points it at me.

"That, Michael Gresham, is exactly why you get paid the big bucks. Because you can make wine out of water, pull rabbits from hats, and slay dragons in the courtrooms of Chicago. I know, I've watched your star rise. Especially since you left your old firm. Where, I believe, you were asked to leave."

He does know everyone's business. I *was* asked to leave my old firm, and it really *was* my old firm since I started it. But because my book of business had all but ceased to exist, I was voted out. Since then, my business has come roaring back like a tornado. Bancroft knows this too, but I don't push the point. No reason to defend or justify myself, not with this opportunistic hack.

"Where do we find Natty McMann?" asks Marcel, sensing that I'm about finished up here.

"Natty works in the County Clerk's office. He's second-in-command there. But catch him early in the morning. After lunch he's usually oiled up pretty good and you wouldn't want to put all your marbles on what he might tell you then."

"Will do," I say, and extend my hand.

We shake across the desk and turn to leave, when he stops me in my tracks.

"Michael, there was one thing you should know about the fundraiser."

I turn back around. "Yes?"

"Darrell Harrow showed up that night. My sources tell me he was in hot pursuit of Mira."

"What's that mean?"

"It means they were an item. So I am told. Don't take my word for it."

"Whose word should I take?"

"Talk to Natty. He's my source."

Maybe--I am hoping--Mira avoided having anything to

do with Harrow in public that night. But knowing Mira and her bent for married men, I'm afraid I know what I will hear. Truth be told, I'm not eager to talk to Natty, though I must. Besides, I am certain beyond a reasonable doubt that the District Attorney's investigators--democrats in an office of democrats--have already been to see him. And, I'm equally certain they have his recorded statement and will add him to their witness list, a witness against Mira.

Cook County politics, Cook County government.

It is what it is.

14

M arcel drives us up to Daley Plaza in his truck and we find underground parking at only fifty bucks a day. A steal, given where we are. A dash across the street and into the Daley Center, where we enter the County Clerk's office on the East Concourse and ask for Natty McMann. Who is asking? Michael Gresham, the attorney for Mira Morales, I reply. The clerk turns to page Mr. McMann. Moments later, she returns and leads us into the second office from the last down a long, wood-floored hallway. There are ancient radiators along the walls and the windows at the end of the hall look like they have been painted shut for a century or more. A reminder that not all Cook County tax dollars go for infrastructure.

There, near the end, she opens a door with opaque glass on which is stenciled,

Nathaniel J. McMann

Assistant County Clerk
Cook County, Illinois

We step inside and find ourselves in an outer office with an empty desk. So we take a seat as the clerk directs, and we wait.

Five, ten, fifteen minutes crawl by.

Finally, the inner door opens and a swarthy, bald man with a stubby nose invites us into his office. "Natty McMann," he says once he shows us to the two visitors' chairs. He takes his seat behind his desk without offering to shake our hands. "I'm very busy and have a lunch date in fifteen minutes, so let's cut to the chase. You're Mira's lawyer and you must be the associate," he says to Marcel, who lets it slide. "What can I tell you about the fundraiser that you don't already know from Elmer?"

"You've spoken to him?" I ask.

"He gave me a jingle. Said I should take extra good care of you. Which of course I will. But about Mira Morales. I don't know much about her. She's never really had much to do with the County Clerk's office. She's mostly in the criminal courts. But I do know her when I see her and I saw her the night of the fundraiser. She was standing off to the side of the stage when this Darrell Harrow fellow comes up behind her. He wraps both hands up around her eyes and says something into her ear. She slips out from under and pushes him away. Her look is anything but friendly. I'm watching all this from the stage as I'm not ten feet away from her."

"Were you able to hear any of what either one of them said?" I ask.

"Yes. I heard Harrow say he had come to make a donation in her private place."

"Swear to God?"

Marcel and I lean closer.

"Swear to God."

"Did she respond?"

"She did. She said, word-for-word, 'You do realize you're speaking in public, Mr. Harrow?'"

"Meaning?"

"He had a full load on. He was rocking up and back on his feet and reaching for her. I think he was trying to keep his balance."

"Was there alcohol being served at the fundraiser?"

"Naive, are you? This is a Democrat fundraiser. Of course there's booze. The micks and the grease balls can't pull a voting lever without a good load on. You know that, Mr. Gresham. You're Irish."

"Actually the name is Irish. But my lineage is English. Long story. So how long were they having their say at the fundraiser?"

"She was introduced and went up on stage probably ten minutes later. During that time, he kept saying rude things to her, crude things, out loud where everyone around them could hear. The gist of it seemed to be that she had once had a thing with him and had recently called it off and he was mad as hell about that."

"Did she ever turn on him? Threaten him?"

"Naw. She kept her cool. Elmer told me Mira's like that. She's been around the block too many times to lose it to someone like Darrell Harrow."

"How did they leave it?"

"Right before she goes onstage she finally agrees to meet him after the fundraiser. She tells him in the meantime he should go find the coffee bar and try to sober up. She wasn't going to talk to him if he didn't."

"What did he say to that?"

"He just laughed and had to grab some guy next to him to keep from falling down. She turned away in total disgust and pretended not to hear him again. That was how she left it with him: coffee then talk."

"Mr. McMann, have you spoken to the police about what you saw?"

"Sure. Two detectives came around a day or two after she killed Harrow. They asked me all kinds of things."

"Such as?"

"Where was I sitting, what did I hear, describe their relationship, describe their affect, whether they had been drinking, what I saw--that kind of stuff."

"Had she been drinking, by the way?"

"I never saw it if she was. She was fine when she spoke at the mike."

"Did you see anything at all that led you to believe she might shoot him later that night?"

"Like I told the dicks, nothing like that. They asked me the same thing as you. I didn't see anything to indicate she was going to plug the guy."

"Mr. McMann, would it be okay if I sent Marcel here back to record your statement?"

"No. I don't like that because you'll use it to trip me up in court if my words change even one syllable. I know lawyers, brother, and I ain't going there."

"All right. Well, I guess we're done here," I tell him, and he looks away dismissively.

Marcel and I gather our notepads and load up to leave.

"One last thing, Michael," he suddenly blurts out. "You didn't ask me what I heard around the courthouse. The big rumor."

"Which is?"

"That Lamont Johnstone actually took the guy into Mira's living room and shot him while she was passed out. He drugged her and then shot her lover."

"This is a rumor? Seriously?"

"Mira has a lot of friends around here."

I say, "Evidently Johnstone doesn't. You know, that's so far-fetched that I'm not even going to honor it with a serious reply. Lamont Johnstone is an honest prosecutor. He would never do something like that."

The assistant clerk spreads his hands.

McMann says, "Hey, I said it was rumor. Frankly, I'm not buying it either. I've got my own ideas about what happened."

"Such as?"

"Such as he shot himself."

"Won't work. No suicide weapon found nearby. Sorry."

"Well, I'm still working on it."

"If you come up with anything else, please give a call. I don't bite. And by the way, I wouldn't have used your statement against you in court. I just wanted it to show I've done my job in talking to everyone. Due diligence."

"That's all?" he asks. "Then send your guy back around. I'll give you what you want."

"Can't thank you enough, Mr. McMann."

"Just be sure it's before noon. I'm very hard to get ahold of in the afternoons. That's our busy time."

"We'll do that," I say, remembering what Elmer Bancroft has told me about Natty McMann's drinking habits.

So we leave the clerk to get back to whatever it is county clerks do. I've never really known, never had need of their services, and would be bored to death working in that particular office.

Even the air smells stale.

Outside, the sun is shining and I am happy to be alive and free as we dart back across Washington Street to our DayPark.

15

Assistant District Attorney Brianna Finlayton was distressed. She was prosecuting Tory Stormont now that Darrell Harrow had turned up dead. When an ADA went after a cop, suddenly she became the focus of all cops' hatred of lawyers. The eyes were watching and they were very unfriendly and totally unforgiving.

Worse, Stormont was a cop with political connections. He was said to be on first name terms with the District Attorney himself, Robert Shaughnessy. But even that hadn't stopped Stormont from being prosecuted for the murder of an unarmed black youth. First-name friendships went only so far around the courts of Chicago, especially when an all-black neighborhood was in flames.

Friends and contacts of the officer had called her and recommended dismissing the case against their man based on this or that flimsy reason, but, like all good prosecutors, Finlayton had resisted. She was going to secure a conviction and ask the judge to retire the guy to prison for his final two shots. It was her job, and Brianna was an honest and true prosecutor. Tory Stormont was in deep with the Chicago powers-that-be when juror rolls were made up. Obtaining a verdict against him would be difficult. Just one "Not Guilty" vote from a member of the jury would wreck her case. She had a strong case on the facts but it was against a defendant who was connected and who could even resort to violence if he gave the word to the right people.

The mayor's office had called Finlayton to check up on the progress of the case. Finlayton had tried to lower the mayor's expectations but so far she had been largely unsuccessful. The mayor believed that a conviction was a slam-dunk certainty just an easy jury trial away. But Finlayton knew better. Defense counsel was one of Chicago's brightest stars in a silk-stocking, white-collar defense office. Defense counsel was ever-anxious to go to trial and make more and more of a name for herself. To further cloud the case's prospects, Brianna had inherited the case only recently after Darrell Harrow had been murdered. The District Attorney himself had dropped it on her desk the morning after Harrow's death without a word. It was her responsibility from that moment forward. Initially, she had found the file wanting in its thin investigation, thanks to Harrow and his notorious battle with drink. Further review confirmed the file was a hit-and-miss mess. So this morning, as Finlayton toweled off after her shower, she looked at herself in the mirror and saw a frowning, distressed Brianna Finlayton staring back.

As she stood nude in front of the mirror blow-drying her

hair, she turned her face side-to-side, looking for the first wrinkle she expected any day now. Maybe it was time to leave the District Attorney's office and get into a boutique criminal firm where the hours were less and the stress was halved. Maybe it was even time to get out of law altogether. Maybe write a handbook for new prosecutors, see if something like that would sell and support her. Her needs were meager; it was just Brianna and two cats, Ace and Jack, who were pretty much okay with whichever way she turned, she thought with a smile. As long as there was Chicken-of-the-Sea in their bowls twice a day, they were happy.

No wrinkles in the face. Not yet, and that was good. There had been a man or two over her first ten years since law school. One of them had been disbarred for dipping into client PI settlement monies and been carted off to jail; the other had turned out to have a family downstate--which explained why he was too-often absent on weekends and holidays. God, how naive had she been? She cursed him as she slipped into her underwear and swung hangers in her closet looking for the perfect outfit for the first day of trial. She settled on a pinstriped suit with a pale blue button-down shirt and short red necktie--something to warm up the otherwise dark look. It was important for the look not to be too warm, however; opening day of a white-collar criminal trial called for serious and solemn, the two S's of trial theory and presentation.

She didn't hear the intruder come in through her condo's front door. She didn't hear him glide across the hardwood floor in the living room and stop at the edge of the hallway to listen, hearing the blow-dryer doing its work.

She heard nothing of the gun being drawn from the holster on the police utility belt and the slide working to guide a bullet into the Glock's .40 caliber chamber.

The intruder listened when the blow-dryer suddenly went silent. He waited for the possible appearance of the Assistant District Attorney in the hallway, perhaps coming into the kitchen for coffee or toast after showering.

But there was no sudden interruption as the intruder crept along the hallway to just outside Brianna's bedroom door. There, the intruder paused, bringing the gun up to his chest and checking it one last time. It felt heavy even against his body armor. He knew he was ready to pounce.

Stepping around the doorframe, he found Brianna posed in front of her open closet, picking through the day's footwear. She never heard him coming.

The intruder crept up behind Brianna and suddenly jammed the gun's muzzle into the prosecutor's back.

"Don't fucking move," the intruder hissed. "Don't turn around."

"Whaaat--" Brianna murmured, her air catching in her throat. "What-what--"

"Here's what you're going to do," said the intruder, who still hadn't been viewed by Brianna.

"What?"

The prosecutor had come upright and kept her hands extended so as not to alarm the intruder. She froze, looking neither right nor left, her lungs screaming for air while she dared not even take a deep breath out of fear of alarming whoever was behind her with a gun.

"You're going to dismiss the charges against Tory Stormont this morning. You're going to dismiss the case with prejudice."

"All right," said Brianna. "I'll do that."

"And you're going to know this. I know where your parents live out in Barrington. I know your father is a dentist and your mother owns a jewelry store. I know everything about them. I know about your sister's two girls and your brother's enlistment in the navy. I know where they live and I know their schedules. Are you beginning to understand your predicament?"

"I'll do whatever you say. For the love of God, leave my family alone."

"Tory Stormont's case has the attention of some very nervous people who don't want to see Tory in prison. Your job is to make sure that never happens. Are you following?"

"Yes. I'll *nolle pros* the case this morning."

"If you fail to dismiss, your mother will be dead before noon and your sister's children will be kidnapped from their elementary school and never heard from again. They will be sold as sex slaves. Your father will be dead before dark. Everything to make all this happen is in place and waiting for a call from me. Do you understand now?"

"I understand. The case will be dismissed before noon."

"Noon today?"

"Noon today."

"Dismissed with prejudice?"

"With prejudice. They won't be able to re-file it. I'll lose my job for this."

"That's a small price to pay for your family's safety, isn't it?" It truly wasn't a question.

"Yes."

"Good. We're done here. Now you go into your bathroom and close the door behind you. You remain inside the bathroom for ten minutes. Then you may come out and you call no one, including the police, including the DA's office. You will go on with your day as usual and dismiss all charges against Tory Stormont. If you come out after only nine minutes, I make my call and family members start dying and kids start disappearing. Are we clear?"

"We're clear. It's done."

Without another word, the intruder jammed the muzzle against the prosecutor's head, propelling her in the direction of the bathroom. He watched as the door opened and closed, then he turned and calmly made his way back to the front door of the condo. He holstered his weapon in his utility belt.

Minutes later he was riding downstairs on the elevator, a young woman with a cell phone jammed to her ear riding down with him.

As the elevator doors whooshed open at L, the woman nodded at the intruder and smiled.

"Have a safe day, officer," said the woman.

The police officer nodded. "You too."

Then he was gone, down to the street corner, turning right, leaping into a waiting van without markings, and then pulling away into the early morning traffic along Clark Street.

Two hours later, the charges against Tory Stormont were dismissed and Assistant DA Brianna Finlayton was in her office at the District Attorney's, cleaning out her desk. She refused all questions and looked neither right nor left as she finally left the office without a word to anyone. There were tears in her eyes and her heart was pounding as she carried the small box of personal belongings in the direction of the elevators.

Downstairs, on the sidewalk, she whipped out her phone and speed-dialed her dad. He was with a patient. She made the receptionist interrupt him, then he came on the line.

"Dad, are you okay?" asked Brianna.

"Yes, honey, why?"

"Mom's okay? And Norma and her kids?"

"Yes, why?"

"Just checking in. I just quit my job."

"Come by the office. We'll talk."

She was crying now.

"All right, Dad. I'm on my way."

She stepped up to the curb and began waving frantically for a cab. She quickly found one willing to pull over and give her a ride, and she climbed through the sliding door on the curb side.

"Barrington," she told the driver.

"It'll be expensive," said the young black man into the rearview mirror.

She nodded.

"I know. Everything's expensive today. But it's okay. Just drive."

"Hang on, lady."

"I am. I am hanging on."

16

Natty McMann's rumor mill made me wonder whether Lamont Johnstone was somehow involved in Darrell Harrow's death. Johnstone is running on the Republican ticket. He's the stiffest competition that Mira could possibly face. Johnstone has a solid rep; he's a blue ribbon prosecutor, a gifted professional, and he's long ago paid his dues in the District Attorney's office.

So, Marcel and I drop by his campaign headquarters on the off-chance we might grab a few minutes with him. We've heard that he works out of there full-time since leaving the District Attorney's Office to mount his run.

The Office to Elect Lamont Johnstone is a setback building along Jefferson Street. As we pull up to park we see that the outside window is all red-white-and-blue bunting, American flags, campaign posters, and a portrait of Ronald Reagan. We pull open the double doors and enter into a clutch of maybe a dozen workers manning phones and keyboards, none of whom acknowledge us. So, Marcel walks up to the nearest desk and says to a young Asian woman, "We need to talk to the candidate. We have questions we'd rather ask in private about his campaign."

She raises up one finger and continues holding her phone to her ear. Either someone is going on and on in her ear or else she's on hold. Whichever it is, her face is drawn tight and her eyes cold. "Does not like being disturbed," Marcel says to me as he turns to whisper. "Put that on her report card."

She finally hangs up and looks at us with a scowl.

"Yes?"

"We're here to see Lamont Johnstone. I'm Michael Gresham and this is Marcel Rainford, my assistant."

"Are you from the press?"

"Nope, lawyers."

"Can I tell him what this is about?"

"It's about the death of Darrell Harrow. We just have some questions."

"Wait one," she says, and takes to her feet. "I'll see if he's in his office."

Just minutes later she returns. "Follow me," she says without expression. I am convinced the campaign must be in dire trouble if the candidate's workers are all so put off by visitors.

We're shown into Johnstone's small, unpainted office where the drywall still shows pencil marks and the quarter round stands uninstalled in a corner. Evidently things have happened in a hurry here and on the cheap. Rather than spend money on painting the walls, it appears as if campaign funds have been diverted to yard signs and bumper stickers--that's my take, for what it's worth.

Lamont Johnstone gives us the candidate's smile as Marcel and I take the two visitors' chairs. The dental crowns are evident--refrigerator white. I mean, no one has natural teeth that white and if they do it makes the rest of us look calcium-deprived. He is a lean, fortyish man, red hair and tortoiseshell glasses with a pouty mouth surrounded by a scruffy goatee. The look is anything but electable--just my opinion. But I should talk, when it comes to looks, given my own desperate physiognomy.

"We're here about Darrell Harrow," I tell him.

He brightens, then his face falls.

"Darrell Harrow?" he says sadly. "We did Friday night cards. Poker, usually, but occasionally pinochle. He was a shark, that guy. Too damn bad. Darrell left a wife and two college-age kids, if I'm not mistaken. So you have Miranda Morales? I know her even better than I knew Darrell. Lots of us know Mira," he says with a wink.

I don't dive right into the reasons for the wink. I'm guessing I already know, but I'm put off that this guy would use it against her with a wink. Smart people don't usually admit to affairs with murder defendants. But, still, anyone running for public office isn't necessarily one of those--a smart person--either. You'd have to be crazy, in my view. These things run through my mind, but I say, simply, "Lots of you knew Mira? I hear she was very well-liked at the District Attorney's office."

"Not exactly what I meant, but yes, she was very well liked. The women hated her, but the guys thought she was one of them. A total hoot, teller of dirty jokes, world-class drinking partner, and great in the hay--you know all about that, I'm sure."

If he only knew how close that hits to home. But I maintain my poker face and the moment of potential self-revelation passes. I keep my secret and my promise to Mira. But, I'm thinking, if you insist on going there, lead on; I was going to finesse you into it, but let's do it your way.

"So she was one of your conquests?" I say with a pretty decent smile of my own.

"Conquest? I would say we were more like equals in that department. With Mira it was always hard to say who was the pursuer and who was the pursued. I'm sure Darrell would tell you the same thing."

"Give me your best guess: did she shoot him?"

He frowns thoughtfully and leans back. "We're off the record, Michael. I know you and I know you'll respect that. Same for your friend here?"

Marcel holds up both hands. "Hey, I'm not writing any of this down. Go ahead."

"My guess is she probably didn't shoot him. Of course her indictment has all but handed me a win in the general election, all else being equal. So I don't need for her to be guilty in order for me to win. Still, I'm betting she's innocent."

"So who would have done it?"

"Hard to say. But I'm betting she wasn't in on it. Did the cops pick up any physical evidence linking her?"

"Her bullets match the bullet removed from Harrow," I tell him. "But no DNA, no prints, no hair, no marks, nada."

"Her bullets? How's that work?"

"They haven't found the gun—so they say. Which is baffling. But they have matched the Harrow bullet to the same batch of bullets they found in Mira's condo. So there's that."

"Any idea where the gun is? Did they ask you, Michael?"

"Me? Why would they ask me? I'm not in the habit of hiding evidence for my clients."

"Just wondering. Someone would have to be pretty stupid to make off with the gun but leave behind the bullets. Major blunder there."

"Tell me this, Lamont. Were Mira and Harrow working a case together? Would you know anything like that?"

"Be very unusual. We manned our own cases and very, very rarely would try a case in tandem. You probably defended the last case where they had more than one

lawyer on the State's side of the aisle. Mayor Tanenbaum's kid."

"Yes, the DA had two, maybe three assistants at trial."

"And still lost it. You walked a guilty kid out, Michael. You
guys--how do you even live with yourselves?"

I shrug. "Good question. Nobody ever said it was easy."

"Well, at least that's good to hear. Now, what else did you
want to ask me?"

I've gotten what I came for, so I decide to fire off the
cannon.

"I'm wondering whether you were involved in Harrow's
murder. Like you said, the fact of Mira's indictment puts
you on the throne at the District Attorney's office. You've
won already and there hasn't been one vote cast."

I'm waiting for him to explode and throw us out. But he
doesn't. He's too canny for that.

"Nice try, but no. Sorry, but I'm not your bad guy. I was at
the Republican fundraiser the same night as Harrow's
death. I spoke to the crowd for about twenty-five minutes.
Way too long, but I needed to raise some dollars for my
war chest."

"I saw you on the news that night. You're an excellent
prospect for the job. Chicago should be so lucky. But so is
Mira."

"Thank you. Coming from one of the Democratic Party
faithful like you, Michael, that's very flattering. But you're
still barking up the wrong tree. I'm covered. After the

fundraiser we all went over to Representative Atkinson's home on the lake. Drinks and snacks, lots of cigar smoke, back-room stuff. Plans were laid and votes prematurely counted. You know how that goes when everyone's had a little too much to drink."

"I'll take your word for it. Your alibi is airtight and I was half-kidding when I asked. You're out from under, in any case."

"Too bad for Mira."

"Not really, Lamont. I've always liked you and thought you were an excellent prosecutor. I'm glad you're clean and alibied."

"So who're you gonna lay this off on? You defense lawyers always need a fall guy."

"I've got a couple of candidates in mind," I say with a big grin. Then I turn serious. "Not really. We're very new to the case. Just talking to people, trying to get that first break. It's a very strange case."

"I saw your press conference. She said she was uncon-scious, somebody spiked her drink?"

"Something like that."

"And she woke up and found a dead guy in her house? That seems like a hell of a way to spend the morning after, trying to explain the party to the cops."

"It wasn't morning. She wasn't out all night."

"And you say there's no link between her and poor Harrow except the bullets? That's not an easy case to make, on either side. Maybe I'd better start making more speeches. I know you, Michael, and it would be just like you to walk her out a free woman a month before the election. You bastard."

I smile; I just can't help it. "Now you know my strategy. My cover is blown."

He raises a finger pistol and cocks the hammer and points it at me.

"Good luck to you with that. Who's prosecuting?"

"Brianna Finlayton. At least she was until she quit the DA's office."

"Bri quit? Since when?"

"Just happened, I guess. Not a word to anyone. Just dismissed the case against Tory Stormont, walked back over to the office, and packed her stuff and walked out."

"So Brianna's gone and Mira's on leave? That's quite a dent in the homicide staff. It's a small staff to begin with."

"Yes. We don't know her replacement yet. Still waiting to see who files their appearance."

"I could make some calls."

"Don't bother. We'll find out soon enough."

"Well, good luck, Michael. And nice to meet you," he says to Marcel. "Let me give you a card. Consider voting for me."

Marcel takes his card. He tosses it back down on the desk.

"Sorry, I never vote."

"You don't pass the good citizenship test if you don't vote," says Johnstone.

"Not that. Just that the candidates don't pass my candidate test."

"Read my website. I've got a hundred years of experience in the cases I've prosecuted. Seriously."

"Thanks again," I say to Johnstone and we shake hands. "Oh, one more thing," I say and turn back from the door. "Why would the District Attorney be protecting one Chicago cop? Dismissing the case against officer Tory Stormont? Can you help me there?"

The color drains from his face and his eyes don't meet mine.

"I have no idea what you're even talking about," he says. "Nobody was off-limits when I was working for Shaughnessy. We were equal-opportunity prosecutors, whether we were after cops or convicts."

"Not even police officers accused of gunning down unarmed black teens?"

He stands and leans over his desk. "What do you want from me, an affidavit?"

"No. I want your testimony. At trial. I want you to testify that Ronald Shaughnessy never allowed any prosecution against the Chicago Police Department. Can you give me that?"

"You're asking me to commit perjury, then."

"No, I'm asking for you to tell the truth. If you won't agree to do it, I'll hold a press conference in the morning and tell the world you refused prosecutions against the cops."

"That would be a lie, Gresham."

"That would be politics, Johnstone."

Color has returned to his face. He is livid, red.

"You wouldn't dare."

"Be watching the news tomorrow then," I say, and turn abruptly for the door.

"Wait! There's something you should know."

"What's that?"

"It hasn't got anything to do with protecting anyone. Shaughnessy never prosecuted cops because those guys are thick. They stick together. Prosecuting just one of them could cost the DA ten thousand votes in the next election. Shaughnessy wouldn't risk it."

"So there was a policy?"

"You'd have trouble proving it."

"Let me ask it this way. Did Harrow's indictment of Tory Stormont get him killed?"

"That's a more difficult question. I wasn't in on that. I was long gone."

"Best guess?"

"I don't have a best guess. But I know this. If you crossed a line with Shaughnessy he would leave you dangling. Everyone knew better."

"All right."

"So what about the press conference?" he asks.

I wasn't really serious about holding a press conference, but this guy is too close to the pile to know when I'm shoveling shit and when I'm not.

"What press conference?" I ask.

Outside in the parking lot, Marcel turns to me.

"We're having a press conference?"

I have to laugh. "You too? What is this, Gullible Day?"

"You had me going."

"Had him going, too. That bit about Shaughnessy not throwing cops under the bus. That confirms what I've always heard."

"So he does protects the cops?" Marcel says as we load into his truck.

"His office just dismissed all charges against the killer of an unarmed teen. That killer is a cop."

"Yes, but that prosecutor who dismissed the case is now gone. Resigned."

"Truth telling time? I'll bet even money that Shaughnessy gives her a written recommendation when it's time for her to go out looking for a job."

"Whatever," says Marcel. "Bottom line is there's a killer

out there. Two of them, counting Stormont. The other one killed Darrell Harrow. You wouldn't think they're the same person, would you?"

"Stormont? As in killing Harrow too? Interesting speculation."

"I'm going back over the video. This time I'm looking very hard at the cops who come and go."

We both settle back as Marcel steers us into the fast-moving traffic.

At that moment it really does come into focus for me: there is a killer on the loose.

And it's not Mira Morales.

17

The District Attorney's black Suburban with smoked windows picked up Lamont Johnstone from his campaign headquarters at seven-thirty p.m. It was earlier that day that Michael Gresham had come into Johnstone's office and confronted him about DA Ronald Shaughnessy. Gresham had told him he believed the DA was protecting the Chicago PD, especially police officer Tory Stormont.

"Thanks for coming by," Johnstone said to the large black man occupying half the back seat of the SUV.

Ronald Shaughnessy, huge like an NFL tackle with a scowling face hidden behind sunglasses nodded but didn't reply. Then he said, in his trademark growl, "Gresham's a smart guy. Been around a long time, knows too much about too many people."

"You have any ideas how he's to be handled?"

"It's a done deal."

"As in how?"

Shaughnessy turned to his protégé. "You just gonna have to trust me, Lamont."

Shaughnessy nodded to the driver and turned to look out his own window. The Suburban began pulling away from the curb, flashing its red and blue police vehicle lights to gain a foothold in the evening traffic jam. Then he leaned back against the seat, working the pleat in his trouser legs between thumb and finger. He was like that, Johnstone had noticed long ago: alway fiddling with his attire, trying to look every inch the important public official he actually was. Johnstone had been there through four of the DA's campaign slogs. He had officially gone on the record as the office's ranking Republican staffer as someone who, regardless of party politics, would be voting for Shaughnessy the Democrat and supporting him. In a city manned at all four corners by diehard Democrats, Johnstone's support of the Democrat was unequalled in the recent memory of most Chicago pols. He was effectively abandoning his own party in his cross-overs every four years, which made it all the more remarkable that now he had received his own party's endorsement for DA. He had abandoned them--but only in the DA race--but they had come around and gotten on board with him. They had had to; he was the only truly electable Republican on the primary ballot.

"What about Tory Stormont? What's going to happen with him now that his case is dismissed?"

"Have you seen the news? South Chicago's been on a rampage every night since--burning buildings, lootings, patrol cars being shot at, undercover narcs being outed. The religious leaders are calling for a boycott of all white-owned businesses. The blacks are calling for a lynch mob to come after me. My guess is there won't be many Democrat Party voting levers being pulled in South Chicago come November."

"So my chances against Mira are looking really good?"

"Not so fast. The black community knows all about you, Lamont. They know you and I are joined at the hip. You might not be a Democrat on the voter registration rolls but you sure as hell have hitched your star to one. Namely, me. They won't forget. Without Mira's mess dragging her down she would be looking very good to those voters about now. But Harrow's untimely demise has effectively shut her down."

"But if she's found not guilty? From what Gresham tells me her case is very defensible. The Attorney General is going to have a hard time convicting her."

Shaughnessy smiled for the first time that night. He turned to Johnstone and laid a huge paw on his friend's shoulder.

"Didn't I tell you we've got that covered?"

Johnstone pressed it.

"Mind telling me how?"

"Just read the papers tomorrow evening. Turn on the news. It'll become very apparent in its own time."

By now the DA's official SUV had reached the East-West Kennedy Expressway.

"Let's go to Schaumburg," the DA said to his driver. "I'm meeting the wife and kids at Jungle World for dinner. I'll drop you at the Niles train and you can head back to your house."

Johnstone nodded. He was still anxious to know what his ex-boss had up his sleeve for Michael Gresham. He decided to pry.

"Gresham told me Mira isn't the shooter. She didn't kill Harrow."

"Mira? Naw, she wouldn't shoot anyone. Screw them maybe, but never shoot them."

Both men chuckled. They both knew whereof the DA spoke. Her rep just wouldn't stop following her around. But it was her own damn fault, thought Johnstone. She had never made any attempt to hide her private business; her sexual couplings were as open and notorious as a hooker's.

"He also told me that Mira's box of bullets matched the one that killed Harrow."

"So I'm told. So I'm told," said Shaughnessy, suddenly tiring of the game. He knew that Johnstone was going to try to guess his way into whatever Shaughnessy had planned for Michael Gresham. But he wasn't about to let that happen. He had held public office long enough to learn the number one rule of getting re-elected: trust no one. It was a rule he followed assiduously, so he wasn't about to spill the beans to Lamont Johnstone. Besides, it would all go public tomorrow anyway. Johnstone--and the rest of the city--would find out soon enough.

"Gresham also told me the murder weapon hasn't been found. The gun is missing."

"That so?" smiled the DA, his eyes opening wide. "That so? Maybe it's time that gun turned up."

Johnstone sat back against the deep leather seat.

So that was it, he thought.

Tomorrow was going to be a red-letter day for him and his campaign.

He could expect to rise at least ten percentage points in the polls.

Ten? Hell, might as well make it twenty if what he thought he had just caught a sniff of was in fact cooking on the stove.

Gresham was about to be served up to the public.

And it couldn't happen to a more deserving guy, thought Johnstone.

He had it coming.

18

T rue to his word, Detective Jamison does, in fact, come after me.

I'm sitting at my desk in my office, reviewing the order of dismissal in the Tory Stormont case. Marcel has copied the order from the court file, as I am trying to understand what rationale was used by Brianna Finlayton to dismiss. There must have been some comment or reasoning she would have thought would be acceptable to the public, some predicate that the court found compelling enough to allow her to dismiss and that the public would accept.

Which was, of course, impossible. The black community is outraged. The skinheads are delighted. The Nazis are —you get the idea. America is as splintered anymore as there are ethnic groups times one hundred. Some applauded the dismissal of the charges against the white cop; some were outraged. Sometimes there just isn't a good answer. There is only palliative care.

Which is when my closed office door suddenly comes flying open, rattling on its hinges as it is thrown back against the wall. Close behind is Detective Jamison, his sunglasses perched on top of his head, a wicked grin lighting the way. In his hands are papers that can only be the search warrant he has talked some judge into issuing for the search of my office. I am half out of my chair when he rushes across the room and gleefully scatters the papers across my desk.

"We'll need you to leave the office, counselor," he says in his command voice. "We're here to execute a search warrant. You need to get up and go into the outer office and wait there until we're finished in here. Don't bother going to your car. It is being searched as we speak. Same with your home. Have we covered everything?"

The man is wicked, but I don't engage.

"Let me see the warrant first," I say.

He pushes the papers across my desk. "Read away. It's all copacetic."

I leaf through the paperwork. It's signed. The affidavit, while about half-bogus, is also about half-correct. He's done a good job at reconstructing the steps I took to protect Mira the night of Harrow's death.

So I come upright and silently go into my waiting room and plop down in the chair closest to my office door. Mrs. Lingscheit is pushed back from her desk while a technician copies her hard drive onto a drive he's brought along. I know that he'll be in my office next copying my own hard drive; my heart leaps into my throat. What's there? I'm wondering. Are they going to find a smoking gun they can use to put me away for ten years?

I'm very paranoid for several moments while I calm my racing heart and logically go through what they might uncover. Probably "uncover" is not the best word. It indicates I might be hiding something, which I am definitely not. I am congratulating myself for my honesty in how I defend my criminal clients when a shaft of pure conviction suddenly lights up my mind: the cigarette butt. The one I took away from Mira's condo after she stubbed it out in her ashtray. The butt was blackened from the charcoal on her fingers, the charcoal she or someone had used to draw the Satanic pentagram on the wall above Harrow's body. I had, in fact, taken the butt with me in order to hide the fact that when I first spoke with her I'd had to ask her to wash her hands. To wash her hands because I was concerned they would be examined by the detectives or the CSI's. But the cigarette butt: I had all but forgotten I had just dropped it into her file after I returned to my office later that morning. I'm hoping they don't realize what it is. But that's the slimmest of hopes. These guys are pros; they're going to catch on in a hot second: the butt will be examined and it will have her DNA on it. There's the first presumption it came from the crime scene. Otherwise, why would I have it?

How incredibly stupid of me, I'm thinking, and I'm chastising myself. What the hell was I even thinking, memorializing the fact that I had removed evidence from a murder scene? A chill passes up my spine and I am stupefied I could have done something so randomly ignorant. It just isn't like me to remove evidence from a crime scene. On the other hand, I had done it without a plan. I hadn't thought through to what I planned on doing with it. Forgetting it was in my file, ready to be seized by the police, was definitely not what I had in mind. But, here I am and here they are.

Any minute now Detective Jamison will come out and pounce on me, announcing his find and waving a plastic evidence baggie in my face, one containing a Salem butt. I want to jump up and run downstairs to my car and drive away, but I fight to restrain that impulse, fight to stay in my chair, in Mrs. L's office, and face the music. Besides, my car has also been removed from my control. I am trapped.

Marcel's office is next, evidently, because he joins me in the reception area, taking a chair across from me.

"What the hell?" he mutters to me. "How did they ever get a judge to authorize this?"

"I saw Jamison's affidavit on the search warrant. The key is that a confidential informant has told him that I am secreting evidence of Darrell Harrow's murder in my office, in particular inside Mira Morales' file."

"What the hell does that mean? Confidential informant? In our office?"

"Yes. Someone turned me in."

"But there's nothing to be found. You're not hiding anything."

"I'm not?" I lean forward and whisper, "Did you not see me pocket her cigarette butt?"

He looks at me. It is a look of dismay.

"You're joking, right, Michael? You didn't get rid of it?"

I spread my hands. "I didn't get rid of it. We hadn't done our case review and I hadn't been back inside her evidence file since that night."

"So you saved it?"

I nod. "Sure as hell did. Sure as we're sitting here."

"Oh, Jesus, man. This isn't good. This is very bad, Michael. You know this cop already wants your head!"

"I know, I know."

Sure enough. Ten minutes later, Detective Weldon comes bursting into our reception area and approaches me and Marcel. He is almost galloping. He waves the plastic bag under our noses.

"Bingo!" Is all he says. Then he points at me and shakes his head.

"What?" I ask.

"What the hell were you thinking, counselor? Removing evidence from my crime scene? You know that's a crime, of course, because you're a criminal lawyer. So this particular criminal lawyer--mainly you--knew he was committing a crime when he made off with this cigarette butt. But I'm asking myself, why this cigarette butt? Why would the defense attorney remove this from the crime scene? And then I'm seeing the black smudges on the cigarette paper. And I'm putting two and two together and I'm thinking the crime lab's ultraviolet spectrographs will connect up the dots."

"What's that supposed to mean?" I ask, though I already know the answer--I'm afraid.

"It means we will very likely find out that the black smudges on the cigarette butt are the same stuff as what we scraped off the wall in Ms. Morales' condo. The black pentagram someone drew there. Let me say, counselor, you have the right to remain silent. Anything you say can and will be used against you. And blah blah blah. I won't go into the whole *Miranda* thing right now because I'm not running your ass in right now. I'm going to wait until the crime lab confirms what it is you've removed from the scene of a homicide. Then I'm going to run your ass in."

"I--I--" I want to argue, but Marcel interrupts--thank God.

"Don't," says Marcel. "Let it go. He has zero idea what he's talking about."

"Oh don't I?" Weldon says with a smirk. "I think we're very close to solving this homicide and even closer to solving who tampered with evidence at the scene of the homi-cide. Gentlemen, it's going to be a fun couple of days while we wait to hear back from the crime lab. Wouldn't you agree?"

He looks at us: me, then Marcel and back to me. We don't reply, better judgment having overtaken us--me, actually. I keep my mouth shut.

There's nothing to win here and everything to lose.

19

Three hours later, I finally leave the office. It is one o'clock and the search is still underway but I just can't stand to be there any longer. Marcel and I head down to underground parking. My Mercedes is sitting there with all four doors open, its trunk and hood open, and technicians crawling it like ants over a turd. The car is being vacuumed, dusted for prints, and taken apart at every point where separation of interior lining from frame is possible. My car has been stripped. "Who puts this back together!" I cry at the team of four investigators and two cops. One cop punches the other and there's a barely suppressed smile shared between them.

"That's your problem, sir," says a youngish CSI tech. "We don't have authority from the court to put it back together."

Marcel and I stand there, dumbfounded, unsure what comes next. Then Marcel takes me by the arm and steers me down the row of vehicles to where his truck is parked.

Marcel takes the wheel of his truck and we head north on Lake Front Drive. Danny has stayed home today with Dania, who spent the morning watching cartoons before she went in for her checkup with her pediatrician. I've called Danny and told her what is going on and it is actually her idea that I just leave. The police have already been to our house and are gone. I tell her I think that was just intimidation; that they came to the house just to let us know they could. Because they can always come back if they decide they've missed something.

"Hey," Marcel says sideways, "what say you put in a call to Harley Sturgis?"

Harley Sturgis is Chicago's very own up-and-coming female trial lawyer who eats prosecutors for breakfast. She's a no-holds-barred two-fisted brawler who loves to duke it out with the cops. Word on the street is that she'll fight about anything, that there are seldom stipulations on any issue at trial, much to the displeasure of Chicago judges who prefer agreement wherever possible.

"You want me to call her? What for?"

"Look, Boss. We're going to need someone to help us very soon."

"You mean you're pretty sure I'm going to be facing charges and will need another lawyer on staff?"

"Yeah, something like that. And Harley would be a great choice. I've done some work for her on the side and she's amazing. Cops run and hide when they hear she's on a case. Prosecutors buckle and settle. She's pretty damn amazing, Boss."

Tonya Sturgis is known around town as Harley, nick-
named for her last name Sturgis: the name of the town in
South Dakota that is the site of the annual get-together of
thousands of Harley riders. And she deserves the name,
too--from what I hear. Still, whatever else might be said
about Harley, she's almost impossible to cut a deal with,
according to the DA's who've reported back from skir-
mishes on the front lines with Harley. Exactly what I
would want.

"Hold that thought," I tell him about calling Harley. "Let
me think a minute."

So we travel north while I morosely look out the window
at Lake Michigan and the five-million dollar Tudors that
line its banks. Most of them have three or four cars in the
driveways--Land Rovers, Porsches, Mercedes, and the
occasional Rolls. As I watch the evidence of others'
success pass by outside my window, I am kicking myself
for being so damn stupid as to remove evidence from a
crime scene. It was a pure mental lapse; in the last thirty
years I've never even come close to something that stupid
and obvious, but here we are. It's happened and there's
one hellbent cop on the other side of the equation
chomping at the bit to see me in jail. And, truth be told,
there's a good likelihood he'll have his way. I have no
defense. The butt is evidence, it was at the crime scene
and I knew it was evidence, and I removed it. If Mira was
the artist who drew the pentagram, then it only stands to
reason she's the same person that shot Darrell Harrow.
And the cigarette butt ties her to the pentagram charcoal
drawing and that, in and of itself, is huge. It is compelling
evidence that she was the shooter.

Marcel's voice breaks through my reverie.

"You're beating yourself up back there, aren't you?"

I have to admit he's right. I am beating myself up. With good reason.

"I am. It's just not like me, Marcel."

My phone vibrates and I have a look. It is my office, Mrs. Lingscheit.

"Michael!" she cries into the phone. "Are you at home?"

"No, why?"

"Don't go home! The police are looking for you right now."

"What?" I am stunned.

And frightened.

"They found a gun in your car. In the trunk. Weldon is beside himself. He's crowing. He's saying it's the same caliber as the one that killed Darrell Harrow."

"My God, in my trunk?"

"In your Mercedes."

I have her on speaker. Marcel has heard all of this.

"Where to?" he asks, pulling to the side of the road. We are parked beneath McDonald's Golden Arches. I can smell the poison on the air.

"Where to? I don't know."

"You know what?" he asks.

"What?"

"Let's just take you on home. They're coming for you, Boss, and you're not running. We know that."

I am unable to put together even a thought. I can only nod.

Marcel says, "Wait one. I've got Harley's number on my cell. Do I call her?"

I can only nod.

Then the words come to me.

"Yes. Hurry."

HARLEY STURGIS

20

W ell color me overwhelmed! Michael Gresham has just called me and asked me to defend him.

Who am I? My name is Harley Sturgis and I am a recovering lawyer. I'm sprawled on the leather turn-of-the-century chesterfield in my office, lying on my back, my ankle crossed over my knee, lighting one cigarette off another. My pulse is pounding and I want to open the window and scream out to the shoppers down below on Michigan Avenue, "Michael Gresham wants to hire me!"

But I can't. For one thing, the damn thing doesn't open. The builders didn't want us throwing ourselves out of the eightieth floor of the Hood Building whenever we had a run of bad luck on Fall Corn at the Commodities Exchange.

He chose me. Why would he choose me? I'm forty-two years old, tall--but not gawky!—with thick rimless glasses, bottle blond (bleached, actually), and walk with a cane, thanks to a spill I took on my Can-Am Spyder, the three-wheel motorcycle out of Canada. It's a super cool way to tear around Chicago's clogged streets when court lets out and I need to blow off some steam. Anyway, I dumped my Canny--which the company says isn't possible--and it left me with a bum hip and trick knee. I'm deciding whether I want to sue Can-Am. Probably not. There're enough bullshit products liability cases floating around that I don't actually feel the need to pile on. Besides, I make so damn much money that anything Can-Am could payout to me would feel like overkill. I don't need their money. But I do want them to examine my accident. I filmed it with my Go-Pro, which I've sent to Toronto for a once-over.

But back to Michael Gresham. I met this guy in court several years ago. Criminal court, if you weren't aware, consists of five minutes of intense back-and-forth with a judge, separated by an hour of waiting for your next case to be called. I've learned to sleep in court with my eyes open, but that day it wasn't happening. So I found myself sitting next to this sort of handsome guy secretly texting on his smart phone. Judges jump up and down and do the panty twist when they catch anyone using phones in their courtrooms, so Michael was actually hiding the phone behind the *Illinois Rules of Evidence*, a gray, humorless book about--guess what--evidence. Michael's got the book cracked open and pretends to read but he's really texting. Sitting beside him, I start enjoying the conversation he's having with some bimbo named Nancy.

MICHAEL: YOU WERE AMAZING LAST NITE.

NANCY: Not bad yourself.

MICHAEL: Where did you learn that?

NANCY: I lived in Japan and worked as a geisha 4 a year. They taught us so much.

MICHAEL: Amazing. I think Im in love.

NANCY: You get what you pay for.

Pay for? He had me at "Where did you learn that?" But *pay for*? This guy's paying for sex? Naw, too good looking for that. Good looking in a sort of *don't-give-a-damn* ruggedness that more men should aspire too. More Clive Owen than Robert Redford. My two cents.

So I wrote my number on my legal pad and nudged him. I showed him my number. He didn't flinch but started thumb-typing. My own phone announced a new message had arrived. Following Michael's lead, I hid my phone behind my legal pad and appeared to be writing.

MICHAEL: What's cooking?

HARLEY: This courtroom is a drag. Wanna bust out and grab a beer?"

MICHAEL: Don't drink. But I'm up for coffee and a donut.

HARLEY: Starbucks on the corner?

MICHAEL: Gr8. Whats ur name?

HARLEY: Harley. Like the motorcycle

MICHAEL: Im Michael Gresham.

HARLEY: I KNOW. EVERYONE KNOWS YOU.

MICHAEL: DON'T FLATTER ME. I MIGHT FALL IN LOVE WITH YOU.

HARLEY: GOD FORBID. I HAVE ENOUGH MALE ADMIRERS ALREADY.

MICHAEL: COME HERE OFTEN?

HARLEY: A PICKUP LINE IF THERE EVER WAS ONE.

MICHAEL: SORRY, IM RUSTY.

HARLEY: YOU MARRIED?

MICHAEL: NO. HAPPILY DIVORCED. DON'T HAVE ANY MONEY TO ASK ANYONE OUT. THE X CLEANED ME OUT.

HARLEY: SO HOW DO YOU KEEP THE COBWEBS CLEAR?

MICHAEL: ARE YOU TALKING ABOUT HOW DO I HAVE SEX? ARE WE THERE ALREADY?

HARLEY: IM BORED TO DEATH. CUT TO THE CHASE WITH ME.

MICHAEL: IVE GIVEN UP ON WOMEN. JUST THE OCCA-SIONAL BLIND DATE THAT SOME WELL-MEANING FRIEND ARRANGES. THOSE NEVER GO ANYWHERE. WHAT ABOUT U?

HARLEY: SINGLE NOT LOOKING. I MAKE MORE MONEY THAN EVERYONE. MEN COME ON FOR FINANCIAL GAIN.

MICHAEL: LMAO

HARLEY: ME 2

One thing led to another, court muddled on through, and

by noon we both had our cases called and had met at the corner Starbucks. He beat me there and when I walked in he was devouring a sausage and egg muffin. I pulled out a chair and sat down.

"What can I get you?" he said through a mouthful of egg and meat.

"Feeling noble are we? Most guys won't wait on a lady anymore."

He smiled. "Welcome to the nineteen-fifties. Mom would kill me if I forgot my manners."

"You've got a mom? I thought lawyers like you just parachuted down from heaven."

"You flatter me."

"It's the rep, Precious. I'm impressed."

"What's that get me?"

I looked at him and smiled. "That gets you the right to bring me a venti bold, extra cream."

He stood and went up to the cash register. Nice bum. Came back with a steaming cup of Seattle's finest and we smiled at each other and officially introduced ourselves, handshakes and all.

"Don't think I'm not impressed too," he said. "Harley Sturgis is a household name. Chicago's fastest-rising legal star."

"Really? What household would that be?"

He laughed. We were going to be friends.

But back to today.

Evidently the cops executed a search warrant on my
friend. And he told me they found a gun in the trunk of
his car. When he called he was waiting for charges.
Expected an indictment any moment. So we agreed to
meet. My office, four-thirty.

"Angelina," I buzzed my paralegal.

"Right here, Boss."

"Bring me your brief on accessory law."

"We're defending someone charged with being a criminal
accessory?" Angelina asked. She sounded interested,
which was a good start with Angelina, my perky twenty-
five-year-old paralegal/night law school student. Minutes
later the brief appeared on my screen.

I began reading. It was my guess that Michael would be
charged as an accessory to the murder of Darrell Harrow
since nobody would be claiming he was actually present
at the shooting. Criminal accessory law is very interesting. In criminal law, contributing to or aiding in the
commission of a crime can get you charged as an accessory. Accessory is one who, without being present at the
commission of an offense, becomes guilty of such offense,
not as a chief actor, but as a participant, as by command,
advice, instigation, or concealment; either before or after
the fact or commission.

Concealment. That's Michael's problem right there. Or so
I was thinking.

At four-thirty sharp, Angelina showed him into my office.

I called him over to my conference area, which was really nothing more than four Eames chairs arranged around a glass coffee table. Angelina took our drink orders and scurried out. (Don't feel sorry she has to fill drink orders. She would be back to briefing cases for night law school on my dime in five minutes, and probably already had been since lunch. Not a bad gig.)

"So, Michael," I start it off. "Sorry to hear about your problem. But that's the trouble with practicing criminal law. Sit in the barber's chair long enough and sooner or later someone's going to get a haircut."

He crossed his legs and settled his coffee cup and saucer on his knee.

"It's a sham; they planted the gun in my car. That's all," he said.

"But aren't they all innocent? I've never had anyone walk in here who was anything but innocent. Not counting the little old lady who was a serial shoplifter of flashlight batteries. It was just her thing and she couldn't restrain herself. The judge committed her to community service and weekly OCD counseling. It must have worked; she hasn't returned to see me. But now, Michael, here you are, telling me you're innocent too."

He shrugged. "That's because I am innocent."

"Why would they plant a gun on you, Michael?"

He looked off in the distance. Michael--I had found from dinner dates and the like--was a contemplative sort, a man who preferred to actually think before he spoke.

Kind of a refreshing trait for a criminal lawyer, most of whom have a line of bullshit a mile long. Then he looked back at me.

"Actually, I believe I have been targeted. Set up, for some reason I can't understand."

"Have you rubbed someone the wrong way over at the District Attorney's office? Pissed off some heavyweight in the detective bureau?"

He set his coffee cup and saucer down on the coffee table. It was only then that I noticed his hands were shaking. He rubbed his hands together like Lady Macbeth.

"I think someone is making a case against Mira Morales and they needed a tie-in."

"What's that mean?"

"It means they want everyone to believe that Mira asked me to remove the murder weapon from the scene of the crime. That way they can indirectly prove guilty mind. Like fleeing from the police."

I had to think about that. If Michael was right, if he was part of a scheme that clever, then he was in for the fight of his life because the mastermind behind something like that would be a genius freak.

But I didn't want to just jump to such a working thesis, and I told him so.

"Let's start with the basics," I told him. "Who had access to your car?"

He again looked away. "Anyone and everyone, I guess.

Marcel drives me into work almost every day and it gets parked in the basement of my building. The entire world has access to it down there."

"When was the last time you had the trunk open?"

"Danny and I took a trip to Saint Louis to watch the Cards last spring. We took two suitcases in the trunk."

"Was there some part of the trunk you couldn't see simply by opening it up?"

"I asked myself the same thing. So I popped the trunk when we got it back a half hour ago. There's a space behind the spare tire. I would never look there unless I was changing the tire."

"So the gun might have been in your trunk for quite some time and you just didn't know?"

"Possible, I guess. But why?"

I lean back in the Eames chair and begin tapping my pen on the leather arm. "Unknown. We're just talking here. Let's try not to ascribe motive to possible scenarios at this point. Motives are always ambiguous."

"Okay. One possible scenario: someone put the gun in there the night of the shooting. Another scenario: they planted it the next day. Another scenario: they planted it on me at the time of the execution of the search warrant."

"You're saying the search team might have placed it in there?"

"Hell, I don't know that it was ever even in there, for that matter. They might just be saying it was in there, for all I know. For all I really know they found it in Mira's condo, put it into evidence, tagged it, and then said they found it in my trunk. The scenarios are endless."

"True enough. I'm thinking too that maybe you put it there. Let's rule that out by logic. If you put it there, that would be the dumbest thing you've ever done, right?"

He looked at me crossly, then his demeanor relaxed. "All right, I'll play that game. Let's say I was helping Mira cover up the crime. Let's say I did remove the gun from her condo. The trunk of my own car would be the last place I would have put that gun."

"The first place being?"

"I don't know. Maybe outside the building, maybe on the sidewalk, a trash bin, or a Dumpster down the first alley."

"No, the nearby trash bins and Dumpsters would have been searched by the cops when they couldn't find her gun in her condo. You would have had second thoughts and wouldn't have put it anywhere near her building."

"Maybe I would drive home by the lake and throw it in. That wouldn't be so hard to imagine."

"Agreed. Do they have metal detectors that work under water?"

"Damned if I know. Why?"

"I don't know. Dumb question, I guess. So. We are expecting an indictment probably for being an accessory after the fact. Or maybe even conspiracy. You conspiring with Mira to complete the crime."

"The accessory angle is my guess. I'm guessing they'll be wanting to make a case against me for being an accessory to murder."

"Or maybe as an accomplice. An accessory may or may not have been at the crime scene. An accomplice was at the crime scene and aided in the commission of the crime somehow."

"Like helping hide the murder weapon."

"Exactly. And we both know these crimes are often charged as obstruction of justice nowadays."

"So there's two counts: accessory and obstruction of justice."

"Three. Don't forget conspiracy."

"Four, hell, they might even charge me with being present when the fatal shot was fired."

"Five, as long as we're speculating, they might even charge you with being the killer, the one who fired the shot."

He shook his head and clamped his hands on both knees. "This starts to run out of control with just a few minutes of plotting."

"It sure as hell does, Michael."

"So I need to retain you. How much do I need to pay you to get you onboard?"

"One-fifty. That'll get my attention."

"A hundred-fifty-thousand dollars. I'll have Marcel swing by with a check in the morning."

I looked at him and we both knew what I was going to say next. We both had said the exact same thing hundreds of times to hundreds of clients.

"Don't talk to anyone about this. Not even Danny. All right?"

"A page right out of my own playbook. All right, coun-selor. My lips are sealed."

"I'm counting on that."

We finished our coffees, talking about the few times we went out together and wondering why that never did go anywhere. Michael quickly became uncomfortable with that topic--he was now married and virtuous--and he set aside his cup and saucer and stood to go.

"Hugs?" I said to him.

We hugged and I could sense him smelling my hair, my Chanel.

We had had our moments. Our times together had twice been rip-roaring successes. That I could recall.

We stepped back from the hug. Chanel can always be counted on to flood a victim with old memories of sweet times.

Exactly why I reapplied it after he first called. He had gotten away. But I'm a sore loser. I don't quit and I never give up. Which is not to say I'll be pursuing him; I won't.

But if he ever came snooping back around, I certainly wouldn't turn and run away.

Who could, with Michael Gresham? Even now, with his face all burned and scarred. The Michael I knew was much more than some skin deep hunk.

He was Michael Gresham.

21

M ichael called me three days later. He had been arrested and they were taking him to jail. So I dropped everything and headed for the Cook County Jail on California Avenue. CCJ is the last place anyone with a pulse would ever want to spend the night. Full of piss, vomit, shit, and other unmentionable bodily discharges too unpleasant to even think about. I jumped in my Jag and headed out.

My offices are located on Michigan Avenue, so I headed out and hit Wacker, connected up with the 90 South, and then west on Garfield to 2600 California Avenue. It was normally about a thirty-minute drive in my Jag. Today, the traffic was fairly light, and I made it in just over twenty minutes flying low. No cops, no tickets, the Eagles blaring over my Bose, while I was thinking about Michael Gresham and trying to understand why anyone would want to implicate him in the murder of a District Attorney. It just didn't make sense. Except it made it look like

Mira was complicit in having the gun removed from her condo by her lawyer. More fuel for the fire.

I parked next door to the jail and headed up the sidewalk. This was a complex that housed a small city of men and women while they awaited trial in the main courthouse, next door to the jail. While the courthouse was old and dim, the jail itself was modern but choked with humanity. Too damn many bodies crammed too closely together.

My bar card got me to the head of the line and I stepped through the scanner without a peep. Then it happened. A male deputy maybe fifteen years younger than me pulled me aside.

"You're a lawyer?" he asked. "Are you Tonya Sturgis?"

"That's what my mother calls me. I'm Harley to everyone else. How can I help you?"

"Your client Michael Gresham is in the infirmary. He started a fight with four cops and got the worst end of the bargain. Please follow me."

We passed back through security, back outside, and headed into the infirmary next door.

We hurried back up the block to 2800 California Avenue. The address belonged to the Cermak Health Services, the jail's medical clinic, where we bypassed security and headed back to the ICU. Sure enough, the deputy brought me alongside Michael, who was lying flat on his back, his right arm elevated in traction and his face badly bruised, one eye swollen shut and the other puffy, a mere slit yet visible.

"Get me out of here, Harley," he whispered. "They attacked me."

"Who attacked you?"

"The two cops bringing me in. They stopped a block away. Worked me over. I'm pissing blood."

"All right. Can you give me their names?"

"I never got them. They came into my office. Walked right in and cuffed me. I was talking to a client. They didn't give a damn. Handcuffs, threw me up against the wall and searched me. Threatened me on the way over. Then one of them turned around. Pointed his gun at my face. Then laughed."

"We need names, Michael. I'll have a Civil Rights action filed against them before the end of the day."

"I wish you. Would."

He was wheezing, trying to catch his breath.

"Ow-ow-ow. Ribs broken in two places. Kicked in chest and face. Mean fuckers, those cops."

He then lapsed into disconnected words and phrases, crazy talk, delirious, coming and going and having great difficulty putting words together. Some of what he said made no sense.

"Has anyone called Danny?"

I told him I didn't know. So he tried to recite her number but couldn't remember it. There was memory loss because his brain had been injured. I called his main office number and got connected to Danny. With me holding my phone to his ear, he was able to mumble at her for several seconds. Then he broke down and cried, muted moaning wails that sounded like an injured animal. Tears came to my eyes as I saw how much pain my friend and client was in. And rage settled over me. I immediately was flooded with a drive for revenge against the cops and the CPD in general. Not to mention the assholes that planted a gun on him. Because I knew Michael would never remove a gun from a crime scene. That's just not something Michael Gresham would ever do.

"It's time to hit back, Michael," I told him. I gripped his free hand and gave it a small squeeze. "I'm going to let you sleep--"

But it was too late. The painkillers had taken him away and he had fallen unconscious. Morphine does that.

I sat down at his bedside and began drafting a Civil Rights lawsuit. Ten minutes, thirty minutes, and the complaint was shaping up. I was just about to text it to my office for filing with the federal court when a nurse appeared. She checked Michael's vitals. She flicked the morphine pump and watched it deliver another dose.

"Who did this?" I asked her.

"They never tell me that kind of stuff, Miss. I'm just a shift nurse. I've got nothing to do with who did what. Friend of yours?"

"Client. I'm his lawyer." I handed her my card. "Do me a favor. If any cops come in here and try to talk to him, would you show them this card? I don't want him talking to anyone."

"Sure, Miss."

Just then, Danny Gresham came rushing through security and joined us in Michael's ICU cell. An orderly led the way and stopped, pointing out Danny's husband. I introduced myself and she immediately realized that I was the lawyer who Michael had hired to retain him on the search and seizure gun case.

"Oh my God!" she cried upon getting her first look at her husband. "Who did this!"

"He was awake when I first arrived. He managed to tell me it was the cops who arrested him. Evidently they stopped about a block away and worked him over."

"Just like that? Just beat the hell out of him? Is this America or what?"

I was struck at her naiveté. Police beat-em-ups happen every hour in America. Police-citizen shootings happen every day. This was anything but unusual. Especially with Chicago cops, who are known to be Neanderthals when it comes to making arrests.

"Heads are going to roll!" she cried. "I'm suing everyone involved in this!"

"Relax," I told her. "I'm on it."

"Really? What do you have in mind?"

"The first thing I'm going to do is find a federal judge. I

want him moved to a neuro hospital. He has head injuries."

She stopped and looked up at me. "Really?"

"He couldn't remember your phone number, Danny. Anytime the cops get someone down they go for the head. It's an unwritten rule. More often than not it causes memory loss and the victim can't recall what happened. Which allows the cops to make up all kinds of shit. That's what they had in mind for your husband, Danny. Unfortunately for them, they didn't give him the Full Monty. He remembers bits and pieces of what happened."

She straightened up from looking at her husband. Tears spilled out of her eyes.

"Well, I'm going with you. We're doing this together."

"Fair enough. Your car here?"

"No. I caught a cab over from court when they texted me. I continued my hearing and came over without stopping at the office."

"I've got my car in the lot. Come on if you're coming. I'm leaving right now. This cannot wait."

"I'm right behind you."

Michael was still unconscious when we left. Danny kissed him tenderly and turned away. Her shoulders squared up and she said, "Let's go get these bastards."

She took the words right out of my mouth.

Twenty minutes later we were back in my office, Danny

and I. I called in Angelina. She had typed up my Civil Rights complaint against John Doe I and John Doe II and against the Chicago Police Department and against other entities and individuals to be named later. Danny and I both proofed it, her reading over my shoulder.

Thirty minutes later, Danny and I walked the complaint over to U.S. District Court. We also brought along a motion for TRO *ex parte*, which asked the court to order the Cook County Sheriff to immediately deliver Michael to University of Chicago Medicine.

The judge we found in chambers was Manfred J. Maxwell, a twenty-year jurist who had directed the Chicago ACLU before being appointed to the federal bench by President Clinton. He was a black man with a wide, sloping nose and startlingly white teeth and an inquiring manner that left no questions unaddressed before he would rule. Plaintiffs prayed for his assignment to their cases, which were done by rotation in the federal courts, but that day he was the emergency judge. We had filed our case with the clerk and been directed to his office.

His chambers secretary said he would see us immediately after reading our motion.

Ten minutes later we were shown in.

"Come right in, Ms. Sturgis, and who is this?"

Danny said, "Dania Gresham, Your Honor. I'm the plaintiff's wife and one of his lawyers as well."

"Well, I've read the complaint and read the motion for

temporary restraining order. The gist of the motion seems to be that the plaintiff, Michael Gresham, was arrested and while being transported to California Avenue he was violently assaulted by the transporting officers and he is now in Cermak ICU. That about it?"

"That's about it, Your Honor," I spoke up. "Michael complained to me of being kicked repeatedly in the head by the cops. He was rendered unconscious and came to when they started working his body over with their saps. His wife--my co-counsel--and I wish to see him receive expert neurological care in the Neuro-ICU at UC. He has been previously injured and warned that another head injury would be extremely serious. We would like him transported there immediately."

Judge Maxwell nodded violently. "Totally agree. Here, let me sign this and get you on your way."

With that he signed his name to the TRO with a huge flourish and sent us packing for Cermak Health. Traffic was heavier this time; we burned an hour getting back. I led Danny into the Sheriff's Office and plopped the order down on the receptionist's desk.

"Here's an order requiring immediate transport of Michael Gresham to UC Neuro-ICU. Please deliver this to the sheriff."

The receptionist, a sleepy-eyed gal dressed like Betty Boop, lip-read the TRO.

"You don't need to read it," I implored her. "Just hand it to the sheriff."

"Honey," she said with a surprising drawl--Illinois is Yankee land--"I need to see if that's the appropriate thing to do, first. Please try to cool your jets."

"Jets-Schmets," I said. "This is a federal court order. Do I need to get Judge Maxwell on the phone to talk to you? If I do, it won't be pleasant. And if I do, I'll be adding your name to the lawsuit."

She immediately stood up and disappeared down a brightly-lit hallway. We could watch her only so far, but she entered the door at the far end without knocking. No more than five minutes later, she returned.

"Well?" I asked her.

She said with just the hint of a huff, "The sheriff will have your client over to UC-Neuro by five p.m. Is that soon enough, Ms. Sturgis?"

"You really want to piss me off, lady?" I shot back. "Because you're about to get that done. In fact, why don't you just give me your name? If he's not there by five, I'm amending the lawsuit and adding you in."

She swallowed hard and pushed back from her desk.

But she gave me her name. I even made her spell it twice.

"J-O-N-E-S," she said, flustered and toned way down. "My name is Jones."

By FIVE O'CLOCK we were sitting at the University of

Chicago's Neuro-ICU glassed-in room where they'd placed Michael. He wasn't even cuffed at this point.

First there was a battery of CT scans and other machines, which took a good hour. Then they brought him back. He was more awake and said he was relieved we had him moved to UC. The University of Chicago's Neurosciences Intensive Care Program is world-class and is known throughout Chicago as the place you want to be. UC is staffed 24/7 by neurointensivists and that makes it the only facility of its kind in the area. We brought my brother here when he fell from the second floor of a building under construction. He survived and is back on the job today, thanks to UC-Neuro. So I felt like I'd made a good start toward representing Michael and it was a day well-spent so far.

Michael's eyes shut when he realized he was safe, and he didn't wake up again until just after seven. Danny and I were waiting, talking quietly, laying plans for his defense and the pursuit of the Civil Rights case against the CPD. Michael was in terrible pain the moment his eyes opened and continued that way until the morphine load took him away again. That was close to seven-thirty. Danny and I then took turns going downstairs to the cafeteria and grabbing a bite. At nine o'clock I left for the day; Danny was committed to staying all night, as the hospital had provided a rollaway, a blessing given her pregnancy discomfiture. Their daughter Dania was spending the night with her nanny.

At 2:25 a.m., in the middle of that first night, Danny called me in a panic. It was time for his twelve-hour neuro exam and they couldn't get Michael to awaken. They had tried all the usual tricks with him and, while his eyes moved around, the lids wouldn't open. His doctor was called and it was decided to let him sleep through the night and try it again in the morning. Danny, however, was beside herself, crying and reaching out for support. I couldn't stand that she was alone, although she said Michael's investigator Marcel had arrived and stayed after work. But I felt like Danny and I had connected woman-to-woman and I knew deep down that she needed me. So, up I jumped, dressed, grabbed a protein shake, and left for the hospital. Despite it being three a.m., traffic was still a tear. Somewhere along the way I decided it was time to hire a driver. I called Angelina and left her a message, tasking her with locating a full-time driver. Chicago law was stressful enough and my work load had almost doubled in the last three months, so it was time.

Michael's initial appearance had been scheduled for the morning but now that was impossible so I told Angelina she would need to notify the court about Michael's condition.

Then I lit up a Tareyton, opened the sun roof, and let my bleached locks blow in the night air. I needed space to think about Michael's case. The indictment that had been served on him was still in my briefcase, riding in the backseat of my Jag. I hadn't even had time to get up to date on the charges against him, so I decided I would use the long early-morning ahead to get into it.

On the way, I found a Jungle Joe's all night coffee shop and hit the drive-through. Danny would at least have the macchiato she requested when I checked with her. That would be a good start, the kind of thing friends do for each other. Which we had become, friends.

Back at the hospital, we had our hugs, got her relaxed in her bed after a few sips of her drink, and I took the recliner. It would be me staying awake to watch over Michael. It would be me reading the indictment, too, and getting up to speed with it. I had Westlaw and Lexis-Nexis on my laptop and that made legal research two clicks away.

The next time Michael and I discussed his case, I would be ready.

22

Hospitals, in case you've never gotten to stay overnight in one, are desperately noisy and interruptive places. As a patient you may get some shuteye but that won't be because of your normal sleep patterns; it will be because some medication has rendered you unconscious. And so it was with Michael. At four a.m., the nurse came in and did vitals. She talked out loud to me like it was noon the entire time. Michael soon opened his one operating eye and peered around.

"Where am I?" he asked.

"UC Neuro-ICU," I told him.

"What?" Danny said, coming awake.

"Go back to sleep, both of you," I said. "It's Harley, Michael, and I'm sitting in the visitors' chair in your ICU station. You were sleeping until this lady--" she was still poking and prodding--"came in to take your temperature and see if your heart's still beating."

The nurse shot me a glowering look. "Smart tonight, aren't we?"

"Why do you people act like it's broad daylight and everyone else should be awake just because you have to be?"

"Comes with the territory," she said. "It's routine."

"Well, please pipe down and let my client sleep, okay?" I said.

"Client? You his insurance agent?"

"Cute," I said. "I'm his lawyer and I'm just pissed enough to add someone to the lawsuit I filed on his behalf today. Care to give me your name?"

She stood fully upright and shook her head. "I'm only doing my job," she allowed.

"I could say the same thing," I said. "I'm trying to see my client get the help he needs, including mine if that's what it takes for him to try and sleep. So let's all pipe down and let our patient get some shuteye, what do you say?"

"I'm sorry," she said. "We are pretty thoughtless on graveyard."

"And call it something besides graveyard. That's very morbid, all things considered."

Which went right over her head. She finished and moved away to the next bed, where yet another patient's family member--presumably--was on night watch. She smiled at me across the dim light and nodded. She gave me a thumbs-up and we connected.

The thing about being quiet went for her too, her movements said.

And I then got back into Michael's indictment.

Here's how it stacked up, none of which was easy.

First, they had charged him with being an accessory to the crime of murder. The allegations said he hadn't been at the scene when the shooting occurred but that he had arrived after and had helped to cover up evidence.

Keep in mind that these allegations are pled in the alternative, meaning that the DA can say one thing in the first count against Michael and then say the opposite thing, or something quite different, in the second count, and so on. I only mention this because several counts down the page the DA alleged that Michael had not only been present when the trigger was pulled but that he had actually been the gunman who pulled that trigger.

This pleading in the alternative had been used in no less than nine different felony charges against Michael Gresham, defendant.

Having read through the indictment, I then began collecting up the cases using online legal research. I wanted to have a compendium of law and evidentiary rules ready for Michael for when he was able to talk again.

Which was when two detectives unexpectedly showed up. It was just eight a.m. and I was sitting at Michael's bedside, nursing a fresh cup of coffee from the thermos of the good stuff that Danny brought from Starbucks

when they opened. I planned on staying around the
hospital until noon when I would go back to my office
and check in. My cases for that day were being attended
by my staff attorneys--I had a staff of three attorneys--so
my time out of the office was covered around the court-
houses in Chicago.

The first detective through the door was Jamison Weldon.
He was wearing a light gray suit and white shirt with a
narrow black necktie, Florsheim's scuffed all around, and
Ray-Bans. A toothpick was kept moving from side to side
in his mouth as he positioned himself at the foot of
Michael's bed, looking down at my semi-conscious client.

"So, Michael," he said, totally ignoring me and Danny,
who had been sitting on her rollaway, studying her
Kindle, "you might remember me, Jamison Weldon. I was
at Miranda Morales' condo the night Harrow was
murdered. Can I ask you some questions?"

The hair along the back of my neck prickled up. Was this
guy serious?

"Hey," I said, "I'm his lawyer. Why don't you ask me if you
can talk to my client? No, on second thought, no need to
ask. The answer is hell no he won't talk! Not only that,
thanks to your friends down at CPD who almost killed
him, he can't talk even if he wanted to. So why don't you
address your questions to me, Mr. Weldon?"

"Detective Weldon," he said, wheeling on me.

"Whatever," I said and stifled a fake yawn.

"We need another set of prints. The idiots out at California Avenue smudged his right hand. Possible you can help us there?"

"Not possible," I said. "Get a court order."

"Well that's not very cooperative. I can get that order, you know."

"Be my guest. Now leave my client's area on the floor, please. You're not an approved visitor and you're not family. Shoo!"

"Shoo you, too," said the smaller detective who had accompanied Weldon into our area of the floor.

"Oh, what's this?" I said. "Do I need to call security and have you bodily removed? I'm more than willing to oblige, mister."

Weldon raised his hand. "No need. We'll get our court order and then we'll be back."

"Like I said, be my guest. But if there's any form of cooperation you're hoping for at any point in this case, you can forget it. After what your men did to Mr. Gresham there will be no cooperation and no deals. So you run along and put on your big boy pants, detective. You're going to need to be dressed like a big guy from here on."

"Yeah and fuck you, sister," said the smaller man.

"Why don't you give me your name, asshole," I said. The night had been long, I was in a rage over Michael, and I just didn't like the little guy's looks. I was ready to go to the mat and have it out. Which was when he took a step in my direction. So I reached down and clicked Michael's pager. In less than a minute, his nurse had appeared from two beds over.

"These men aren't visitors on the list and they aren't family. Please call security."

"They said they were family," the nurse began.

"Well they lied to you. They lied because they think they have that right. Now you call security this minute and get them out of here or else the hospital itself is going to be looking at a serious medical malpractice complaint that you really don't want to see. Should I begin counting? I know my way to three before I dial 911."

With the mention of 911, the dicks began removing themselves from our area of the neuro-ICU floor. It was a large area, open on two sides, consisting of four beds. Right down the hallway was another four-bed unit, and on around the entire floor. The detectives had no place to hide or lurk and no other direction to go but toward the elevators. I followed them over to the open hallway and watched as they made their way past the main nurses' station and across to the elevators. They turned back to see whether I was watching. I was, and their faces fell.

"Sons of bitches," I told Danny. "Tell you what, I'm hiring a security service to keep Michael undisturbed while he's here. I'll get someone on that right now."

"Go for it," said Danny. "I was thinking the same thing for when you left. When my bulldog leaves I'm going to be feeling very vulnerable here all alone."

Two hours later, we had armed security at Michael's bedside.

Now the game was evened up. The guys I hired were ex-FBI and weren't afraid of anyone.

We were manned up.

23

At noon I left the hospital, went down to the visitors' lot, and climbed inside my Jag. The air was warm, the sun was bright, and I was ecstatic to be out of the hospital. They are not my favorite places.

I was cutting up the parking lane toward the exit when I noticed that a luminous black sedan had pulled around my parking row and was rolling up behind me. With the addition of the two probing detectives in my life I was being super cautious and noticing things I would ordinarily pay no attention to. So the car caught my eye and I watched it keep back a respectable distance as I turned right at the short row that paralleled the street. Another stop sign, another left turn and I was on the main drag, headed downtown. The black car stayed right on me. So I decided to run a test and find out whether I was, indeed, being followed.

At the first traffic light, I suddenly swerved from the center lane to the far right lane and hung a right on Rockaway Avenue. Pulling into high speed traffic, I jagged left to the center lane went up one block and took a sudden left on a stale yellow light. No longer attempting to keep a nonchalant distance behind me, the black car sped up, hung right on my rear bumper and went through the yellow with me.

Now there was no doubt it was cops on my tail and, worse, they were making no attempt to cover-up the fact they were following me. It looked like they meant to harass.

But what they hadn't counted on was this: When I hired the security service to come to the hospital and watch over Michael, I had hired an extra service on their menu: vehicle monitoring. Now, behind the cop car, was a third car. This was a tan Chevy Suburban transporting my own bodyguards. And they were filming everything the cops were doing with me. So when the cops lit me up with their emergency lights and I pulled over and the cops tucked in nice and tight behind me, who should also pull over but my men. Without waiting for the cops to make it up to my window they suddenly lurched ahead, intercepting the cop who had been driving, as he walked up to my window.

The Suburban stopped in the right lane almost up with my Jag and turned on its hazard lights. Following traffic was forced into the center lane and made to go around. The roadway had suddenly become crowded and horns were honking and middle fingers displayed. There were cops and security and together they were impeding the flow of traffic. Which my forward-reverse rearview camera was recording as the moments ticked by.

"Hey, Officer," yelled the Suburban driver loud enough that I could hear. "Before you confront my client, you should come see the video we've got of you following her. She violated no traffic laws since leaving the hospital lot, yet here you are, pulling her over in this busy traffic, with nothing more on your minds than harassment."

Which was when I got a good look at the cop's face in my outside mirror. It was Jamison Weldon, rumpled suit and all, his trouser legs flapping every time an eighteen-wheeler flew past. He was obviously uncomfortable as he stood there deciding between coming up to my window and attempting to frighten me or returning to his vehicle and forgetting the whole thing. Luckily, he chose the latter, suddenly spinning on his heel and returning to the black sedan. He hadn't said a word to my security team, but he didn't have to. They pulled up ahead of me and pulled into the curb lane. Now they were directly ahead of me and they led me on the way down the street. The last time I looked, the cops were still pulled over to the curb, unmoving, evidently giving up on the game.

LATE THAT AFTERNOON, as I was sitting in my office taking assignments off my calendar for the remainder of the week, my phone buzzed.

"Harley? Danny Gresham here."

"Hey, how are we doing?"

"We just heard from Michael's doctor. Evidently his tests are looking normal although he has suffered a concussion--the doctor called it multiple concussions, actually. But he gets to go home in the morning."

"Great news!" I tell her. "And it's great for another reason, too. Michael's arraignment got moved to Monday. The judge's clerk called me for an update and I told her Michael would in all likelihood be able to come to court Monday. I had put in a call to Dr. Rudiger myself for an update as soon as I got back to the office. He had told me Monday would probably work, so I was ready for the clerk's call. So it's good news."

"Has bail been set?"

"It's covered. Bail was set at one million, Mrs. Lingscheit made a trip to the jail and posted the hundred grand. Michael's free to go home when he's cleared by Dr. Rudiger."

"You've been very busy," Danny said. "That means everything to me, Harley."

I smiled. "That's what I'm here for. You and Michael."

"How did you get bail set without an initial appearance?"

"Let's just say a certain judge with a certain case assignment was agreeable. I called him up and reminded him that I had chaired his committee to reelect over the past eight years. He hadn't forgotten, tit-for-tat, Chicago style, and here we are. Michael gets bail, it gets paid, and the patient goes home. All neat and tidy."

"You're a genius."

"I keep the odds low by staying involved in the legal community down here. Anything I can do to buy influence with the judges and police, I'm all over it," I told her. "And there's one more thing. I've got an appointment with the chief at nine tomorrow morning."

"With the chief of police?"

"That's right. We're going to be discussing some of the tactics his officers have been trying out on me. I've got video to show him as well. They followed me from the hospital and I had my camera crew along. Busted, you might say."

"Incredible."

"That's why you pay me the big bucks," I laughed.

But deep down my laugh was superficial and short.

The fight had only just begun.

24

"What the chief is saying," the chief's administrative assistant was telling me, "is that Michael Gresham has a conflict in the Miranda Morales case."

We were sitting in the office of the Chicago Chief of Police and the chief had just unloaded on me the DA's objection to Michael continuing as Mira's lawyer.

"The conflict being?" I asked but I already knew. He couldn't defend Mira and be a defendant in the same case.

"The conflict arises from the fact your Michael Gresham is now a defendant in the same case as Miranda Morales. He cannot defend her and claim his own defense isn't entwined with her defense. He can't defend himself by claiming she was the shooter at the same time he's defending her and claiming she's not the shooter. It's simple conflict math, Harley. Do the numbers, please."

"I'll recommend he withdraw from the Morales case, with this caveat. I'm going to file a complaint with an objection with the court to Michael's indictment. Michael has been charged by the DA with a crime only to force him to withdraw from the Miranda Morales case as her defense lawyer. A very slick move but you're not going to get away with it."

The Assistant District Attorney, Martha Reddy, smiled from ear to ear. "While you're at it, why don't you also explain to the judge how the murder weapon wound up in the trunk of Michael's car? Doesn't that fact seem to make him more involved in the murder case than as a simple chess piece?"

"Obviously planted there. I already know you won't find his fingerprints on the gun."

"How can you be so sure?"

"Because he told me so. He's told me Marcel saw Mira's gun the night of the shooting. But it wasn't touched. And I happen to believe him. My guess is you already know his prints aren't on the gun but you're just not turning those findings over to me until the last minute when you absolutely have to. No, we'll be moving to dismiss the charges against Michael on the grounds they were filed simply to create a conflict so he couldn't defend Miranda Morales. Does that answer your question, Ms. Reddy?"

She clammed up. Everyone in the room knew the prosecution stunk. Everyone in the room knew that Michael Gresham was too far along the road to defense attorney success to ever let himself get involved as an actor in any client's case. It just wouldn't happen. Plus, if they were anything like me and knew Michael personally they would have also known it wasn't in Michael's DNA to ever shoot anyone or hide evidence of a crime. That just wasn't Michael, either.

"It answers my question," said Ms. Reddy, "in form but not in substance. We're just going to have to agree to disagree. So you file your motion and I'll file my response and we'll have a hearing."

I next directed myself to the chief.

"Two of your detectives came to my client's hospital room yesterday and attempted to question him while I, his attorney, was there and without my permission. Prior to that, one or more of your officers beat Michael merci-lessly, causing concussions, broken ribs, and other injuries to him. As you are aware, I have filed a Civil Rights action against the City, the officers, and against you, sir, and I'm going to make you an offer to settle on that case."

The chief, a grandfatherly white-haired man with a bulbous ethyl alcohol nose mapped out with thick blue veins, looked to the city's lawyer. Nothing was said but it was apparent to me they were interested.

"This is a joke, right?" said the Chief. "Your client attacked the officers dispatched to arrest him. While subduing him to take him inside the jail, he was injured. It's too bad but it's your client's own damn fault, Ms. Sturgis."

"Michael will accept the city's check for ten million dollars to make the Civil Rights case go away. And he will require that the criminal charges against him be dismissed with prejudice. Counter-offers will not be countenanced."

The cops and DA and city attorney looked at each on and, as if on cue, began laughing uproariously.

"And here's the good part. I'm hiring a firm to represent me in a Civil Rights action against the two cops from yesterday who followed me and harassed me as well. Now we're all on the same page. Got any charges you'd like to manufacture against me to get me off the case? Well, your agents were trying to do that yesterday and probably would have claimed I attacked them if my own security hadn't caught them with their pants down. Score one for the good guys. So I will take twenty-five thousand in full settlement of my claim."

"Come on now," said the chief, a forced look of disbelief on his alcohol-ravaged face. "Get real, counsel."

I stood and collected my things, then I said, "Chief, you want to see real? Leave those charges pending against my client in criminal court. Then walk down to federal court and watch me nail your asses to the wall in our Civil Rights case. I promise, sir, you will see 'real' more than you ever dreamed."

"Counsel," the chief replied, "if I were you I wouldn't write a check on what you're going to get out of the City of Chicago. If you do, you'll be looking at a citation for issuing a bad check. Just another charge against another phony lawyer."

"What?" He just called me a phony. I was stunned. "Chief,

I might be lots of things, but I'm no phony. I guess you're going to learn that the hard way. I'll have you stuffed and mounted in my reception room by the time I'm done with you and the criminals on your force. Consider this your final warning!"

"Please, please," the chief said, making himself sound as bored with and tired of me as he possibly could. It wasn't lost on me. Such derisive words, attitude, and behavior were wonderful because they fueled the fire in my belly.

It was on.

25

The very next day after my meeting with the chief of police, I stumbled into Lamont Johnstone's press conference. Taking advantage of Chicago's rare good weather, Johnstone was meeting with the press in Daley Plaza, a public area just outside the Daley Court Building. It is a large expanse of concrete and modern art and is often seen adorning the front cover of travel brochures and websites. The key attraction in the Plaza itself is the fifty-foot steel Picasso, the iconic representation of the City of Chicago. Johnstone was backed up to the Picasso with his microphone, lectern, and gathering of maybe two hundred onlookers and press. I stopped at the fringes of the crowd to listen and then flipped on my recorder.

"—Miranda Morales has demonstrated her guilt in the murder of Darrell Harrow. How has she done this? By colluding with her lawyer to hide her gun. Why hide her gun? Because the crime lab testing and evaluation has proven beyond all doubt that it was Ms. Morales' gun that killed poor Darrell Harrow. For this reason, it is our campaign's position that the campaign of Miranda Morales is finished. She should be removed from the ballot, at the very least. At the other end of that spectrum is justice crying out for her to go to prison."

A member of the press, her microphone and TV camera extended toward Johnstone, asked, "How can you be so sure that she was the shooter? Wasn't the gun actually found in the possession of her lawyer?"

"That's a very good point, Ms. Downey. But consider this. If her gun somehow wound up in the possession of her lawyer, how did it get there to begin with? The question begs this answer: she gave it to him. What, are you thinking maybe she gave him her gun so he could shoot Harrow for her? Well, consider the legal consequences of that theory. At the very least, she would be an accessory to the crime of murder. She would also be guilty of conspiracy to commit murder. No, the fact that the gun was found in her lawyer's trunk doesn't let her off the hook. Anyone else?"

A *Tribune* reporter by whom I had twice been interviewed piped up, "Do you really think the Democrats are going to keep her on the ballot? Won't they just announce her withdrawal then put the name of some other high profile attorney on the ballot?"

"A good question, Abe. But consider this: Any candidate selected at the last minute won't have my experience. I'm the only candidate with the experience it would take to execute the office of the District Attorney for the benefit of all the people. Any last-minute competitor would be a

candidate selected by the Democratic Party's inner circle
and not selected in a primary race such as selected me.
That would be unfortunate and, my research tells me,
illegal for the Democrats to do. I doubt that any judge in
Cook County would allow the ballot to be changed like
that at the last minute under our current circumstances.
Anyone else? Nancy Jardin? What's your question,
Nancy?"

"Mr. Johnstone, there's a mountain of gossip floating
around that you were somehow involved in Harrow's
death. That you somehow arranged the murder in order
to ruin your opponent's candidacy. How do you answer
these rumors?"

"Thank you, Nancy. I'm really glad you asked that. I want
all rumors on the table so we can pick them apart. First,
as to my involvement: I can assure the people of Cook
County that, after my twenty years of meritorious service
as the first assistant to the Cook County District Attorney,
that I didn't just suddenly have a complete personality
exchange with Richard Speck. I'm just not that person
who would do such a thing and anyone who looks at my
record will instantly know that. Second, the police have
spoken with me. My office has made all personal calendars, phone records, office calendars, and all documents
and bank statements available to the police detectives. I
was completely exonerated by that investigation. But
third, and most impressive, is the fact that on the night of
Mr. Harrow's murder I was attending the Republican
fundraiser from early evening until after midnight, even
after the police responded to the call from Ms. Morales'
attorney to the police. Making a long story short, it was

impossible for me to have been involved. But thank you for the chance to get these facts out in front of the voters, Nancy."

At that point I was wondering what dupes these voters would have to be not to have the wits to imagine a scenario where Johnstone was the puppet master pulling the strings behind the scenes of the most spectacular political murder in the history of the city. But, much to my dismay, no one challenged him with that proposition. So, all else being equal, I decided to do it myself. I raised my hand.

"Yes, Ms. Sturgis," he said to me, forced to call on me since I had raised my hand during a lull in the questions, leaving me the only attendee with an upraised hand.

I began, "How do you answer the multitude of voters who, increasingly, believe that the gun found in Mr. Gresham's trunk was put there by the same police who searched the murder scene? People all around the city are increasingly coming to believe this was an inside job by the police. And that you are in bed with the cops and even helped pull this off."

He was clearly treading water the first few minutes while he stammered and hem-hawed in an effort to gain footing on the slippery slope I had laid before him. Finally, he said, "Moreover, there isn't a single shred of evidence that proves the police somehow planted the gun. Do you know of any, Ms. Sturgis? If you do, please give it to us now."

I stepped closer. "Yes, I do. The fact that my client's fingerprints are nowhere on the murder weapon. That is compelling evidence that he didn't place the gun in the trunk of his own car."

"That is ridiculous!" cried the candidate. "Anyone who watches TV for even one night in America knows about wearing gloves in order to avoid leaving fingerprints. Anyone else with a question?"

But I was finished. I had done all the damage I could do short of running up and tackling the guy.

He was damn lucky I decided against that.

26

The Chicago PD had its own set of rituals and customs. One of those was the *12:1 Rules* of detective work. I knew all about the Rule and all about Stuyvesant's. All defense lawyers knew.

A swinging dick by the name of Edward Ngo invented the *12:1 Rule*. His *Rule* said that twelve minutes at his desk in the homicide bureau was equal to one minute at a crime scene. Sixty minutes in the office went by in five minutes at a homicide. The point was, the crime scene was what the detectives lived for, the opportunity to apply all of their experience and training to the resolution of some horrible murder or other. So when the CPD shift changed at six p.m., the robbery-homicide dicks who'd been stuck in the office headed for Stuyvesant's Tavern on Clark Street. It was time to let out the frustration that always grew from being cooped up without a callout while on duty. By midnight at Stuy's the murders had all been compared, theories had been exhausted in long, heated exchanges, and all the bad guys were under arrest--so it was time to go home for six hours of sack time until the day shift fell in again the next morning.

But the same night that I met with the Chief of Police I did something I'd been known to do before: I met with the homicide dicks. Except--are you ready for this?--they didn't know who I was. Nobody recognized me in the smoke-filled tavern where the lights were low and my mascara was heavy. Plus, I was wearing a brunette wig to hide my bleached flag.

But I knew them.

Especially Jamison Weldon, for I had seen him at the hospital. And, just as I hoped, he didn't realize, when he bought me my first drink, that I was the one who had confronted him in Michael's ICU room and demanded that he leave immediately before I called security on him. That never made it through his alcohol-haze, because it wasn't until just after eleven that night when I entered the tavern, heavily made up, brunette wig in place, a cigarette hanging from the corner of my mouth, wearing a short black skirt, high midriff top, and fishnet stockings. I was to all the world turned out like a hooker, but one with class: I was wearing a wedding band and huge diamond rock. Gifts from some long-forgotten suitor whose name I couldn't even recall.

I had edged in beside Weldon and leaned across the bar to order. My ample bosom was laid out on the bar, certain to attract Weldon's attention, whose right hand was proximal to my left boob by four easy inches. He didn't flinch, though, and neither did I.

"Vodka martini," I called to the bartender when I caught her eye. She gave a curt nod and turned to her bottles.

"Put that on my tab, Marie!" my target called to her. I smiled and turned my pretty face to Weldon.

"Why, thank you," I said through a fog of cigarette smoke. "The lady is grateful."

"What is the lady's name?" said Weldon, oozing confidence and interest.

"The lady's name is Grace and Peace."

"Well, Grace and Peace, my name is Jamie."

"I like that. Jamie. It fits you--so sunny and friendly."

He smiled like a Cheshire cat. "That's me, always sunny, my friends say."

"So what do you do, Jamie? I mean besides hang in Stuy's. What do you do?"

"Law enforcement. You call 'em in, I come get 'em."

"So that's how it works. You make arrests?"

"Yes, Grace Peace. I make beaucoup arrests. I'm a cop. A detective who works homicide."

"Well how about you arresting me? I'm looking for a high hard one."

"Can do, Grace Peace, can do. However, I'm separated and my wife has our place. Do you have somewhere we could go for a drink?"

"Why not my condo? It's not far from here at all."

"Now that's what I like hearing. A sweet girl named Grace
with a condo just down the street from Stuy's. My dad
told me you'd come along once in my lifetime."

I smiled like the Cheshire cat this time. "And here I am,
Jamie. So we're both in luck tonight."

"I'll drive," he announced.

Ordinarily, I wouldn't give a dude like Weldon--bad
breath and thin hair--a second look. But tonight he
understood he was getting a chance to role play above his
class. He was exultant, ready to drive, ready to buy a
vodka bottle to go from Marie. It looked to be a long night
until we could drink ourselves to sleep, screw ourselves to
sleep, or a lot of both. For me, I was all in.

I was about to catch a rodent.

He drove; two blocks north, four blocks east.

My condo is a trap. It consists of hidden CCTV cameras
that cover virtually every square inch of the place. Along
with omnidirectional microphones that are so sensitive
they can sometimes pick me up unrolling the bathroom
TP.

I unlocked it and we went inside. Like all first-timers to
my space, his eyes bugged and he froze in his tracks just
inside the front door.

"Holy shit!" he said. "This is all yours?"

He was incredulous. Witnesses always are when I lure
them into my web.

The decor made words like "subtle" and "sublime" imme-

diately irrelevant. The place was a garden of delights, a
decorator's playground, a rich female lawyer's every
whimsy made real. The first thing to sock you was the
zebra rug spread on the floor in front of my ten-foot
leather sofa. Fake zebra, real leather. Above the sofa was a
bedspread-size modern painting of two nudes, women,
one sitting, one lying on her back, staring at a male figure
with his back to the viewer. As in *awaiting*. The coffin-
sized glass coffee table was peppered with black and red
candleholders and red candles, plus a small stack of the
mandatory *Architectural Digest* magazines. At the far end
of the cantilevered room was the galley kitchen, all
marble and chrome and toned down by its indirect
lighting for dining occasions. Which is exactly what
Weldon had in mind as he took it all in: hunger. Not the
food kind, either.

We headed for my bedroom and, like most drunk men,
he was quick to paw and slobber.

Normally a total turnoff, of course, but for just right now
I took him on. I needed his confession and I would have it
before he pulled up his pants and left that night.

Foreplay, rejected advances, then entreaties to proceed
followed by more rejection, less enthusiastic but rejecting
nonetheless. And then, just as he figured he was about to
gain admittance to the holy of holies, I asked him,
"What's the worst thing you've ever done as a cop?"

"No, you go first," he said. He was lying on his back, his
pants down to his ankles, staring up at my bare breasts.
He belonged to me just then. I could do with him as I
wanted.

"The worst thing I ever did with a man? The night I took on the Chicago Bulls starting five."

"You screwed five NBA brothers at once?"

"I did. And even walked away from it the next day. But trooper, I was so sore! Now you. What's your worst?"

His face puzzled up. Cops aren't known for fun times, necessarily, so I knew it would be downbeat, serious. I was waiting.

"Planted evidence. That's right. I planted evidence on a guy."

"Oh, you rascal! What did you plant, coke?"

"Naw, nothing so mundane. I planted a gun on a lawyer."

"I never heard of that before," I said. "He must have really pissed you off."

"Hey! You're not recording this, are you?"

I pushed my breasts into his face. "Do I look like I'm recording?"

"No," he gushed, "no, you're not recording. Sorry I asked."

Just then my cell phone chimed. I had set its alarm while I was in the bathroom before we got down to it. I climbed up, walked over to the dresser, and placed the cell phone to my ear as if I were taking a call.

"Hello? What, you got back a day early? Of course I'll wait up, honey. Hurry now!"

I tossed the phone on the dresser and turned to my

victim. He was drunk but not stupid. The pants were already up around the waist and the belt was being tugged into the third hole.

"Husband?"

"Sure is. He's an Army Ranger. Supposed to be deployed this week, last three-day leave."

"Oh, my God. An Army Ranger? Why the fuck didn't you tell me that?"

"Because your name is Jamie and you're a darling man. I wanted you."

"OMG," he mumbled.

Then he ran out into the night without so much as a goodbye kiss, much less a hug or a handshake.

Gone, kaput, fled, flew off.

So I went into my office and played it back.

My CCTV is a twenty-thousand-dollar movie system that can focus down on a gnat's hairy ass.

Which it did. In less than one hour I had edited the full one-hour version of Weldon's visit to my home to less than five minutes. I had even bypassed the bare breasts.

What I was left with was golden. Just for safekeeping I stored the video file on the cloud.

Sweet dreams, I told myself after I had checked the locks on all exterior doors.

Sweet dreams.

Married? Of course not. How could a woman like me be expected to manage a husband and a bedroom of witnesses who came and went at all hours of the night.

Besides, I didn't want to pay alimony ever again.

Been there, done that.

27

M arcel decided it would be a good idea to take Michael and his staff--and me--out on Michael's boat. The whole idea was to get out, get some fresh air, and take a look at the case against Michael and the case against Mira. I had filed a motion to dismiss in Michael's case, alleging a police conspiracy as the basis. We were going to look at evidence we could pull together to support this claim.

So we met up at Michael's boat club on Saturday morning, prepared and supplied for a day on Lake Michigan. Those coming aboard were Marcel, Michael, Danny, me, my paralegal Angelina, and two of Michael's friends that I wasn't acquainted with. It turned out that one of them was Michael's new neurologist who had been working with Michael to open new pathways around the injured part of his brain. The other was a woman from the *Chicago Tribune* who did investigative reporting. We were going to include her in our case review, I learned from

Michael, because she was doing a behind-the-scenes workup on the police conspiracy angle.

The crew consisted of a rent-a-captain who was brought in to free up Michael to meet with the rest of us and because even Michael wasn't comfortable with his ability to captain his boat--yet. Plus, we had a galley-slave. A cook. What could be better than having a dedicated cook? We were set.

An hour north of Chicago, we all gathered in the salon for our show-and-tell. Marcel went first, playing the key footage of Mira's condo video. He had edited down seven cameras' hours and hours of video to a fifteen-minute presentation. This would be the video we would use in the Mira case. But it also could be much more than that. It could also possibly impact the case against Michael.

I say that because the video focused down on one police officer. Here's his setup. As near as we could calculate, the actual shooting occurred at 10:59 p.m. on the night of the Democratic fundraiser. We were able to pinpoint Mira's arrival home at 10:49 p.m. thanks to three different CCTV cameras. When we saw Marcel's exhibit of who came and went at what time, the whole truth of that night suddenly exploded on all of us, as Marcel knew it would.

Because--check me out on this--at ten o'clock almost on the button a stout youngish man arrived in the building, wearing civvies and a hat and toting a shoulder bag and he proceeded upstairs and exited the elevator on Mira's floor and disappeared down her hallway. We didn't actually have footage of him entering Mira's condo because the HOA didn't allow the taking of video of guests coming and going from tenants' private residences. Video of who was coming and going in the elevator vestibule was considered sufficient--it being a choice the HOA made based on input and a vote from all tenants. Fair enough, I got that.

We study the guy in the hat who is carrying the shoulder bag. Bottom line: it *looks* like Stormont. Is it for sure? Anybody's guess.

We've learned that Stormont worked out of downtown on the four-to-midnight rollout. Stormont the unarmed-kid-killer. Marcel quickly associated him with the Ballantine Street shooting of Johnny Washington. His fame had preceded him and, to say the least, we were shocked that he was even on the premises. Why? Because he was suspended at that time, with pay, but suspended none-theless.

Marcel had spread some money around and obtained departmental records on Stormont. His rank was patrol-man. It turned out he was still suspended the night of the shooting. It was a short leap to connect Stormont with Darrell Harrow, who had been prosecuting him for the murder of Johnny Washington.

We reviewed the video several times. The figure we're guessing is Stormont arrived before the shooting and departed after the other police and CSI and detectives had arrived on the scene. He arrived wearing civvies and left wearing his police uniform—that would be our contention. *How was that for strange?* we all wondered. During the interim, Michael Gresham came and went, leaving after Stormont had already left; Marcel came and went; Mira came and went. We had no actual video of Stormont at the scene because of the restriction against hallway video cameras, but we could guess.

Was Officer Stormont inside of Mira's condo at the time of the shooting? We couldn't prove this either way. However, what we could do with this information is we could suggest/infer that he had been inside and that he was involved in the shooting maybe even as the shooter himself. Who had a better motive to shoot the Deputy DA who was prosecuting him than Tory Stormont? When you give a defense lawyer the opportunity to push the blame off on someone other than his client you've just handed him a huge weapon. Even better, in this case the weapon was double-sided. On the one hand, it raised the definite possibility of a shooter other than Mira. But-- more importantly for the case I was defending against Michael himself--it gave rise to an inference that if the police would engage in criminal conduct such as a shoot-ing, maybe they would also engage in planting the murder weapon in the trunk of Michael's car.

So now we were getting somewhere and I was loving our retreat on the lake.

The video rolled for the tenth time. This time, partway through, Marcel hit pause and enlarged a still portrait of the guy wearing the hat. His face was partially visible at the exact frame where Marcel paused. This time Michael sat bolt upright on the salon's leather sofa.

"Oh my God!" he exclaimed. "That face. Now I recognize that face!"

This was a moment of breakthrough. Michael's memory banks had been cleaned out by the multiple concussions. Now the memory of at least one pre-beating event was returning. For one, I was very excited.

We all looked at him, anticipating what might come next. We weren't disappointed.

"He was at the condo. He assisted with the search of Mira's bedroom and took over for the original cop who had been stationed at the door!"

"You're sure of this?" I asked. We were on very dangerous ground here, ground that the police witnesses would violently oppose.

"Sure of it? Wait one."

Michael pulled out his smart phone and began swiping pictures across the screen. Then his face brightened with excitement.

"Look," he said in the voice of the astonished, "here he is!"

We all passed around Michael's phone. Sure enough, the face of Officer Stormont was clearly framed there, standing inside Mira's bedroom. He was leaning forward slightly, his face caught in the frame as one who has been surprised by the sound of a camera lens clicking like smartphones replicate. I flipped through the several pictures before and after it when it came my turn to examine Michael's shot. There were three other, less clear, shots that included parts of the same officer.

"I took these pictures to memorialize the scene before and after the cops arrived," Michael told us. "It's becoming clearer to me and clearer. Anyone who knows me knows how little credibility I give your usual cops' claim on cross-examination when they're claiming their glossy crime scene photos accurately portray the scene as they found it. More often than not, I've found they don't do any such thing, that the first responders all too often traipse through the scene, moving or kicking this or that aside, lifting objects to look at them more closely, and all the rest of the dumb-shit stuff that goes on."

"You've certainly recorded that fact with your camera in Mira's case," I said. "This is definitely the same guy Marcel showed us from the CCTV video. But this tells us who that guy actually is. We've seen his face plastered all over the newspapers."

Michael nodded vigorously, his face lit up and smiling. It was a breakthrough moment for him, the most invested in a meeting that I had seen him since his release from the hospital.

Michael, I could see, was coming back to life.

"Marcel," I said, "I'm wondering. Can we re-play Stormont as he's leaving the condo?"

"Sure," said Marcel. "Here we are, let's watch."

We all turned our attention back to the flat screen TV mounted on the bulkhead amidships.

The time on the video feed when Stormont rounded the corner from the hallway and came into view at the elevator vestibule was 1:14 a.m. Following after him a little later on their way out were Mira, Marcel, and, later,

Michael. No other person came or went in between the three civilians and the cop.

"Let's watch it again," I told Marcel after the initial screening.

Marcel obliged, playing it at full-speed three times: the officer rounding the corner, looking neither right nor left but proceeding directly to the buttons at the side of the doors and pressing the down arrow repeatedly as if impatient and as if repeated pressings of the buttons would actually help.

"Half-speed this time, Marcel," I requested. "Please."

This time, just as the figure came around the corner leading to the hallway, I yelped, "Stop! Right there!" and Marcel stopped the figure's movement in mid-step.

We leaned to the screen and all of us examined it. We weren't sure what we were looking for, but it became apparent that the officer's right rear trouser pocket was perceptibly bulged out. He was carrying something inside that pocket.

"Is that the gun?" I asked Marcel.

He replayed it again then stepped through the video frame-by-frame.

In the end, we couldn't be sure. The bulging pocket was inconclusive.

Then Michael had a different idea.

"Let's look at his backside as he exits the elevator downstairs," he asked Marcel.

Marcel stepped the video forward and presto, there was the same cop leaving the elevator downstairs in the parking garage.

And guess what? His right rear pocket, when Marcel focused down on it, clearly showed the print-through of a revolver. A pistol. We could all agree we could make out the grip, the cylinder, and the length of the barrel. I also knew--as did Michael--that by sending the gun images to the right technician, we could obtain the exact length and probably even the style of the gun. At least we would have the length to compare to the actual length of the gun ostensibly discovered in the trunk of Michael's Mercedes.

Michael rubbed his hands together gleefully.

"So there you are, friends and family. There's the non-smoking smoking gun. Officer Tory Stormont of the Chicago Police Department is seen leaving the crime scene where a homicide by firearm has just occurred, secreting a firearm in the pocket of his uniform. I rest my case."

We were excited. A round-robin of exclamations and thanks directed toward Marcel and his video skills erupted. We were elated.

Then the galley chef called us to lunch. Out on the fantail we enjoyed rock lobster, grilled of course, brown rice, grilled asparagus tips in butter, and iced tea. He followed up with lemon meringue pie and we all fell silent as the plates were cleared away.

Then Michael spoke up.

"I'm ready to come back to work," he proclaimed. "Not just ready to return, either. I'm actually anxious to return. My heart goes out to Bill Grady sitting over there, my incredible neurologist. And to Danny Gresham, my ever steady-in-the-boat spouse. To Marcel Rainford, my trusted investigator, confidante, and sidekick. And to Harley Sturgis, the lawyer without whom I would still probably be locked up out on California Avenue waiting for my turn in front of a jury. Thank you one and all."

We all returned Michael's thanks and comments and the boat grew strangely quiet. Coffee was served as we headed back south along the shoreline.

It was a good outing, at least. It was an incredible outing, at best.

We were ready to present my motion to dismiss.

And we were ready to kick some police ass.

28

M ichael's judge was Peter J. Wang. He walked into court the day of Michael's arraignment carrying an arm-numbing stack of law books and a tall Styrofoam cup. Wang was almost six feet tall, had the thick arms and broad shoulders of a wrestler, and smiled a nice white smile that had the chameleon-like ability to turn into a scowl suddenly and without warning. His emotions were at all times apparent and he didn't care, as he had frowned and smiled and grimaced and eye-rolled his way through a half-dozen of my trials and dozens of my motion hearings before him. So it was no surprise that he frowned and clicked his teeth when he opened Michael's court file and read the motion to dismiss I had filed.

It didn't sit well with him. Beside me, Michael nudged me with his knee and I caught his profile out of the corner of my eye. He looked terrified, like perhaps my judgment had been off and the motion to dismiss shouldn't have been filed. I wanted to reach over and squeeze his arm but could not under the circumstances.

Michael had been home from the hospital less than two weeks and still wasn't a hundred percent. Danny and I had spoken maybe five times since his discharge and it was always worrisome how withdrawn and temperamental he had become after the beating. On the boat he had said he was ready to come back but he was also having serious down times. I had included in the motion an affidavit signed by Danny setting out the extreme personality changes she had witnessed. The Michael whom she had married was no longer available to her; he couldn't be reached no matter how calm and safe she made things for him around the house. He was constantly creeping to the curtains and blinds and peering outside, most often rewarded only with glimpses of the security force Danny had put in place around their home and office. He was suspicious even of these people and would take care not to let them see him in return.

Then there was the crying. Periods of depression followed by bouts of tears and laughter intermingled and impossible for Danny to minister to. She was a lawyer, not a psychologist, and she found that living with the new Michael was grueling if not downright miserable. So they agreed to take it a day at a time; sometimes even an hour at a time. Her affidavit ended with the facts in support of her observation that he had earlier lost all desire to practice law, and that, by extension, the police had accomplished what they set out to accomplish, to-wit: the separation of the attorney Michael Gresham from the client Miranda Morales.

My motion to dismiss the charges against Michael then went into a ten-page presentation of the law--hence the judge's stack of law books. The books indicated to me that he had done his homework and had brought along his own points and authorities for what action he had decided to take.

Judge Wang called court to order and then addressed the litigants.

"Counsel, the State has filed an objection to Mr. Gresham's representation of Miranda Morales in this criminal case, based on an alleged conflict of interest between Miranda Morales' case--a co-defendant--and his own case. The sum and substance of the State's objection appears to be that because Gresham and Morales have each of them been charged, alternatively, with firing the gun that ended the life of Darrell Harrow, and of hiding that same gun from the City of Chicago police who responded to the crime scene, there is a conflict of inter-est. Ms. Sturgis, as counsel for the defendant and the party who filed the motion, do you have any witnesses for the court?"

"I do, Your Honor," I said. "I would call Marcel Rainford to the witness stand."

Marcel came forward, his long black hair combed straight back and tucked nicely behind, as he had humored me and obtained the style of haircut I knew would play best with the court. Moreover, Marcel was wearing a conservative Brooks Brothers suit with a white shirt and club tie. He looked like a member of the bar or a physician, which would impress the judge. Settling into the witness chair, Marcel smoothed his tie and then looked up at me.

"State your name," I requested.

"Marcel Rainford."

"What is your occupation?"

"I am the chief investigator for Michael Gresham and Associates."

"What is your training as an investigator?"

"Four years with Scotland Yard. Six years with Interpol. Two years Chicago Police Department. Five years private investigator licensure. Licensed by the States of Illinois and California. Training includes two police academies, undergraduate degree in police science, master's degree in forensic science. Oh, yes, also served with the British Secret Service, MI5, on special deployment from Scotland Yard. That lasted another entire year."

"So you have investigated numerous homicide cases, I presume?"

"Probably in excess of one thousand."

"Did you participate in an investigation in this case?"

"Yes and no. When I began my investigation, Michael Gresham wasn't a party. But my investigation has continued even now that he is a defendant."

"What has your investigation consisted of?"

"Speaking to witnesses, reviewing and editing certain videos, studying the crime scene, interacting with both defendants, attending court mainly as an observer, and the usual other things PI's do. This includes picking up and dropping off evidence reports, lab reports, discovery documents, photographs, and articles. Plus, I have partic- ipated in pre-trial meetings firm-wide and one-on-ones with both you and Michael."

"Did you have a chance in this case to attend at the crime scene where Darrell Harrow was shot to death?"

"I did."

"How did that come to pass?"

"Michael called me en route to the scene. I responded and arrived there maybe ten minutes after him. I couldn't say exactly how long it was."

"Describe what you saw when you arrived."

"I entered the condo and immediately was confronted by a dead body on the living room floor. Later I would find out this was Darrell Harrow. I paused to get my bearings and to make sure I wasn't contaminating the scene as I moved on into the condo. Michael was there and Miranda Morales was there when I arrived."

"What happened next?"

"The three of us spoke."

"Was Michael acting as Ms. Morales' attorney at that time?"

"Yes, it's my understanding he was. So what they and I said is privileged."

"Objection," said the District Attorney. "Invades the province of the court."

"Sustained," said Judge Wang. "Mr. Rainford, the court will decide what is and isn't privileged. Please continue, counsel."

"I am going to hand you what has been marked as Defendant's Exhibit One. Do you recognize the person in that photograph?"

"I do. This is a photograph of Tory Stormont."

"Is that a true and accurate portrayal of Mr. Stormont?"

"It is. Mr. Stormont is a police officer with Chicago PD and I have obtained his jacket photo and compared it to Exhibit One. It's the same person."

"Did you see Tory Stormont at the scene of the shooting?"

"I did. He helped with the search of the premises."

"Have you seen Tory Stormont since that night?"

"I have, if you include video in that question."

"I do. Please explain."

The witness leaned back and studied the photograph for another moment, thinking.

"All right. I have prepared a video that presents footage of Tory Stormont coming and going in the condominium building where Ms. Morales' condo is located. These are mostly parking garage and elevator camera images, but they do accurately portray Tory Stormont."

At that point I asked the court for permission to run the video. Judge Wang readily agreed and the video was played for him. We also did the still shots and the close-ups and presented Michael's smartphone snaps. When we were done, I continued with my questions.

"Mr. Rainford, as the police officer Tory Stormont is viewed entering the elevators from Ms. Morales' floor, do you notice anything unusual about him?"

"Yes."

"What is unusual about him?"

"He's carrying a firearm in his right rear pocket. I have had the video analyzed and learned that the firearm is the same size as the firearm allegedly seized from the trunk of Michael Gresham's car."

"Do you know, did any police officer or other person claim to have found the firearm at the scene of the crime?"

"No one has made that claim, no."

"And with regard to the firearm seized from the trunk of Michael Gresham's car, is that the same size as the firearm hidden on Officer Stormont' person as he's leaving the scene of the crime?"

"Yes, and there's one other thing. My investigation didn't end there."

"Please state that on the record."

"I also learned from the sources at the condominium building that on the night of the shooting the key CCTV surveillance camera in the visitors' portion of the underground parking for the building was tampered with. It was turned away from Michael's car. All video surveillance was lost in the area where Michael Gresham parked his car that night."

"So you're saying with the weapon in Officer Stormont's trouser pocket that night, there was the opportunity to place that weapon in Michael Gresham's trunk when the video surveillance of his parked car was interrupted?"

"That's exactly what I'm saying."

"Your Honor, that is all."

ADA Martha Reddy attempted to cross-examine but basically got nowhere. Marcel was well-schooled in cross-examination techniques and fielded and answered all questions perfectly. I offered no redirect examination and then told the court my presentation was concluded.

Judge Wang then took over.

"For openers, the Court concurs in the allegation of conflict of interest and for the record finds that such a conflict does in fact exist. Now the question becomes, is the conflict one that arises from the underlying factual predicates of both criminal cases--the one against Morales and the one against Gresham--or is a more troubling picture coming into focus here? A picture of the law enforcement authorities taking matters into their own hands by hiding evidence in Michael Gresham's car, namely the murder weapon, in order to create the conflict in the first instance?"

Martha Reddy and I were both seated, raring to go as soon as he acknowledged us so that we could present our arguments.

But he surprised us both, then, as he continued with his opening remarks.

"So here's what I'm going to do. I'm going to consider the search warrant's sworn affidavit, signed by Detective Jamison Weldon, and I'm going to consider the beating of Michael Gresham, while in the custody of Detective Jamison's employer, the Chicago Police Department, as a continuing act. Here's what this means. In and of itself, the affidavit signed by the detective which prompted me to issue a search warrant would appear to be circumspect on its face. There was no reason to doubt the facts sworn to and offered to me by the police department when I issued the search warrant. But now, a subsequent matter and other materials, namely the senseless beating of Michael Gresham and the video evidence just presented, have come to the court's attention. These developments compel this court to look retroactively at its original issuance of the search warrant."

Counsel Reddy and I looked at each other. Sitting beside me, Michael nudged me with his knee and tossed me a sideways look. I could only shrug when the judge wasn't looking. I was clueless where this was going.

Judge Wang then continued.

"So here is what the Court is going to do. The Court is going to treat the State's objection to representation and the defense's motion to dismiss as part and parcel of the Court's visit back in time to the issuance of the search warrant. The Court, in re-visiting the search warrant issue, finds for the record that the search warrant for Michael Gresham's motor vehicle was issued in violation of the Defendant's right under the Constitutions of the United States and the State of Illinois not to be subjected to unreasonable searches and seizures. Again, this is predicated on what the court has found to be Detective Jamison Weldon's state of mind, which was that he was evidently willing to do or say anything to see Michael Gresham removed from this case. A state of mind that would go so far as to plant evidence on this lawyer and then come into my courtroom and raise hell because he deigned to still remain on the case and represent his client. Accordingly, the search and seizure of the handgun from Michael Gresham's automobile is ruled to have been done in violation of his Fourth and Fourteenth Amendment rights and therefore all evidence seized during that vehicular search must be suppressed and is, and will not be allowed into evidence before any jury or other trier of fact."

Beside me the breath left Michael's body in one long outpouring sigh of relief. He dropped his head to his chest and I could see the tears.

"Moreover, the court will also grant the Defendant's

Motion to Dismiss. The indictment against Michael Gresham is hereby dismissed and he is set free and his bond exonerated. Ladies, have I left out anything?"

"Judge, the State objects! We--"

"Objection noted. Anything from the Defendant?"

"Nothing further, Judge," I said.

The judge then went on to say that he would issue a written opinion in support of the suppression of evidence and the dismissal of all charges against Michael. He then stood and abruptly exited the courtroom.

Just like that.

Michael turned to me and the tears came rolling down his cheeks.

"My sweet God," he said and held out his arms to draw me near.

I leaned into him and hugged him back. Danny came forward from the spectators' section and wrapped us in her arms too.

As she was leaving, I said to the prosecutor, Martha Reddy, "Your client is still facing a Civil Rights lawsuit for money. I'm visualizing a copy of the judge's written findings blown up to whiteboard size and set on an easel in front of my jury. They will read that the judge found that your clients in fact created a case against Michael both with the planted weapon and the police brutality. From where I stand, ten million dollars seems cheap right now.

After five o'clock today let's just double that amount. Have a nice day."

"And tell Jamison Weldon I said thanks for the money," Michael added. "I'm going to use part of it to fund full tuition packages for law students specializing in criminal defense. I might even name the scholarship after him. Something for him to explain to his buddies down at the police station."

For the first time since the hospitalization, his face brightened and he shook his shoulders and arms as if coming fully awake.

"Damn, I could use a cup of coffee. Anybody coming with me?"

Danny and I held hands and skipped up the courtroom aisle—her huge pregnant belly made her progress more like lunging than skipping, but you get the idea. When we pounded out through the doors, DA Reddy was nowhere to be seen.

Oh, to have been a fly on the wall when the chief of police took that call.

Oh, yes, Danny delivered the Gresham's first son at four a.m. the next morning. He was named Michael and came in at eight pounds twelve ounces. Michael called me that morning and said he wouldn't be available for a few days. There was a new son to be welcomed into the family and he wasn't going to miss a minute of it.

I didn't blame him one bit and made a mental note not to

call him. At one moment two days later, I forgot my mental note and dialed his number with a question.

The call went straight to voice mail.

He wasn't kidding about the new son being the most important thing in his life at the moment.

So I left my message and hung up, happy for him, happy for Danny, and happy for having had the luck of drawing Judge Wang on Michael's case.

MICHAEL GRESHAM

29

"**M**ichael Gresham," Danny says to me a week after my case is dismissed, "you're walking around here whistling, playing with Dania and cooing at Mikey and digging in my garden. It all makes me believe you're doing much better. Maybe even better than ever."

I stop what I am doing--spreading mayonnaise on my ham sandwich--and look up at her. She is right. I *do* feel good.

"You're right," I say. "I'm back."

"So I think it's time you did something nice for your staff. Everyone has stood by you and soldiered on even in the darkest of dark days. None of your work went undone and terrific results have been obtained so far."

"This is going to come to something I'm not going to like, right?" I say.

She looks at me. She is a loving wife but she knows I have

her number. Which isn't to say she doesn't have my number too, she does. We are interdependent in a healthy way. In our world it has sometimes been our interdependence that has kept us bound together as a fighting unit even when one of us was badly injured in body or spirit.

"You're going to like it. I'm going to propose you take the staff on a long weekend getaway."

"Okay. Where to?"

"Well, you loved Rosarito when we went there. Why not take them there? It's right on the beach with great food and lobster grills, mariachis, the whole nine yards. The gang at the office will love it."

"I think we take Harley with us too. If she'll go. She's performed above and beyond."

"That would be terrific. Ask her, if you want."

"I do. I owe her so much."

Arrangements are made with our nanny to care for Dania and Mikey while we're away. The nanny and her mother are going to stay in our house with our daughter and son and keep things as normal as possible. So that's a relief and we're one step closer to being on our way.

We charter a small jet. We load up all the lawyers, parale-gals and secretaries, and fly west to San Diego. Along the way, there are card games, a game of craps in the tail of the plane that you can get into if you are crazy enough, and there are TV shows and movies. After changing a pending court hearing, Harley is able to accompany us.

She is delightful, and brings along what Danny and I can only conclude is a boy toy, as he must be at least 15 years younger than her. We're introduced and learn, much to our chagrin, that he is actually her son from a marriage long ago extinguished. He now lives with his father, a pilot for United Airlines.

When we land in San Diego, it's sunny and warm and the outlook is for more of the same. I have chartered five SUVs. We load up luggage, someone's guitar, the cat of one of our paralegals who has been unable to find cat-sitting services, snack food and we head for the Mexican border fifteen miles south of San Diego. Just across the border, the traffic gets heavy and turns into stop-and-go bumper tag. As we inch along, roadside vendors are selling anything and everything that can be made from wood or ceramics. Crosses, praying hands, statues of the Virgin, and all the rest of the religious iconography associated with Latin American populations are everywhere we look. Then there are the modern day icons: L.A. Lakers' shirts, Chargers' hats, Padres' coffee mugs, and Dodgers' sweats. Hundreds of pounds of these items are sold each day at the border, northbound and southbound. Our SUV opts for churros all around and soon we are munching on the sugary donuts as we head into the Mexican interior.

We check into the Rosarito Beach Hotel, all twenty-six of us on the same floor. From our windows we can look out on the beach and the Pacific Ocean, one of the nicest views I've ever been favored with by a hotel. Around three o'clock Mira arrives at the hotel. She has come by a separate air carrier after we cleared it with the court for her to attend.

Then a strange thing happens. At just after four o'clock in the afternoon there's a knock on our door. Danny opens it and I hear her arguing with someone. At least it sounds to me like they're arguing; Danny is quite fluent in Spanish and the words being exchanged are all in Spanish. The door then closes and she returns to me in the living room of our suite.

"What was that?" I ask.

She has a puzzled look on her face; she's frowning as well.

"Hotel security. They're saying that a bomb threat has been called in. The Rosarito police are searching the rooms below us and they would like all of us to go downstairs and gather out on the beach. They were quite adamant that we leave our room this very minute. The chief of security is thinking maybe someone in our group called in the threat. I told him that was impossible, that none of our people would ever do such a thing. He wasn't convinced and we had words. So up and at 'em."

We gather together our wallets and Danny's purse and my fanny pack and head out for the elevators. The hotel takes drink and appetizer orders all along the beach and over the next hour we're all served our favorite beverages and eating finger food. Harley sits with Danny and me; her son is taking his first surfing lesson and we watch as he repeatedly struggles to get up on his board and immediately falls to one side or the other. The waves carry him ashore and then he's immediately paddling out again, where his instructor is waiting beyond the breakers, a huge smile on his face. So that's all good.

"So what about this bomb threat?" Harley says. "I didn't think they had terrorism in Mexico."

"They don't," Danny replied. "I'm thinking they wanted access to all of our rooms for some reason."

"Well, they're searching them as we speak," Harley said. "What do you think, Michael?"

"I honestly don't know what to think. But let me ask. Are you playing with the idea that it might have something to do with Mira's case?"

Harley pushes back in her beach chair and clenches her hands.

"Damn! I want to say no way, but my B.S. antennae are up. There's something bogus about all this."

"Exactly," Danny agrees. "It's just too convenient to have a bomb threat the same day we check in. Almost the same hour."

"Well, we'll keep our eyes open," I'm saying when Marcel comes strolling up the beach. He's found a quiet spot to the north a hundred yards or so, and is spending some time with Mrs. Lingscheit (who's actually divorced, but still prefers the "Mrs." tag).

He plops down in the sand beside me.

"What are you thinking, Boss?" he asks me.

I look at Danny and Harley.

"There is a consensus among my little group that this is just too coincidental. Harley is wondering if Mira's case has followed us to Mexico."

Marcel nods. "I'm with Harley. I'll need to search everyone's room before we go inside again. I'm going to pass the word and get everyone ready to cool their jets while I just give everyone's room a quick once-over. You on board with that, Boss?"

"I am. One hundred percent."

"Who might be behind this?" Danny asks, always the dutifully persistent one.

"We've talked about it," Marcel says, referring to conversations he's had with me and with Harley. "There's a consensus that there was much more to Michael's attack than just some random cop playtime with a prisoner."

"Are you thinking Lamont Johnstone's campaign is involved?" Danny says. "Because I am."

"I don't think we want to rule anything out at this point," Marcel answers.

"So you're going to go through the rooms. What are you looking for?" I ask Marcel.

"Anything unusual. Maybe bugs, maybe hidden cameras--I don't know. But I'll know them if they're there. I brought along some equipment for just this reason."

"That bag you wouldn't check?" Danny asks him. On the plane ride out, he sat one row ahead of us and kept the largest possible carry-on stowed overhead. Anytime another passenger would attempt to get into that bin Marcel would be right there with them, keeping an eye on his small suitcase.

"Yes, that bag," Marcel says. "We can't really let our guard down." He looks at me.

"Spread the word. Tell the gang to stay put on the beach or go inside to the restaurant when the all-clear comes. Michael's orders," I tell Danny and Marcel. They immediately head off to advise the other employees of our firm, leaving me and Harley to ourselves.

I waste no time.

"I've been thinking about us," I say to her.

"I didn't know there was an 'us,'" she laughs. "Am I missing something?"

"I'd like you to join my law firm."

She smiles and looks out at the ocean. Then she turns back. "Well, Michael, that's very flattering, but I've got a firm of my own."

"You still would. But you and I would associate on certain of each other's cases. To make it work, I can offer you five million, paid mortgage and automobile note, expense account, thirty days off plus whatever else you need, and complete autonomy. But the good part is, you wouldn't need to ever take the bread-and-butter cases again, that stuff that sucks up so much time but brings in the overhead money. I'll be covering that for you."

"Probably forty percent of my time goes into those kinds of cases," she says.

"Is any of this sounding attractive?"

"Attractive, yes. Something I'm going to wind up doing, probably not. I need time to think it through."

"Be my guest. We've got the rooms for three days. Just be ready to give me an answer before we fly home, please. If you're up for it, I want to bring you in with me on Mira's case."

"Because?"

"Because there's a chance I might be called as a witness in that case. I don't want Mira to be looking at a mistrial if the DA tries to call me to the stand."

"That would be a conflict."

We are in agreement there. An attorney cannot ethically act as a witness in a client's case. The fact that I had evidence planted in my car and the fact that I was beaten by the cops is pretty strong evidence that we might need to pull a rabbit out of the hat at some point. Probably not, but there's always that possibility. I don't want to leave Mira hanging with a lawyer forced to withdraw from representation should that happen. So I want Harley beside me at trial. It's only smart planning. Plus I've tasked Danny with the medical issues that come up. Even so, she's not ready to take on the entire case by herself. I really need Harley with me at counsel table. Better safe than sorry.

On the other hand, I plan to use Judge Wang's ruling as

evidence with the jury of the police corruption rampant in my defense of Mira Morales. Most likely that will be all that I need because the order also includes factual findings by the court as the predicate for its ruling. Those facts specifically include the court's findings that, one, I was beaten by the police to gain advantage in the case against Mira, and two, that the gun was planted in my car by the same police department that beat me. My own testimony about these things will nine times out of ten be unneeded, but just on the off chance the DA would see fit to have me testify about any of it, I want Harley sitting next to me to carry on.

30

Two hours later, we get the all-clear from the hotel staff. We remain in place, as agreed, while Marcel goes ahead and scans our rooms for listening devices and cameras. One by one he gets word to us when our rooms are all-clear. It's close to eight o'clock when Danny and I return to our room. The sun is just dipping belong the horizon and we pause to watch the reds and yellows crawl across the sea toward us. Then it's lights out.

We have coffee and sweets brought to our suite and buzz up our people, inviting them in for small talk and a good-night cup. Maybe half respond, drifting in and out. Danny and I find ourselves all alone by eleven and we crawl into bed. It's been a long day and we both immediately cuddle up and she begins kissing me. I return her warm kisses and before we even realize it is going to happen, it's happening. For the first time since I was beaten we make love. In a way it's a huge relief for me; I honestly didn't know whether my body still worked or not. I am relieved and happy when we're done. Danny falls asleep quickly and I'm left there, lying on my back, her head on my chest, and I'm thinking about my life.

I conclude that I'm the luckiest man in Mexico. I am.

I don't know how much later it is, but I awake with the absolute certainty that someone is in our room with us. I didn't hear the door open and I haven't heard them moving around, but I know they're there. I look around in the dark but it's useless: the blackout drape is tightly closed and there's no ambient light. All is blackness.

I am lying on my left side, my left hand beneath my pillow. My fingers curl around the grip of my Glock. Yes, guns are illegal in Mexico and yes I could go to jail if caught. But with all that's happened to me, Marcel was insistent that I keep a gun in my room anyway so he brought one along and took it with him during the hotel search. Now I'm glad that he did.

Ever so slowly I slide the gun down and into my right hand. I lift it out from under the pillow. Then I reach across and make sure Danny is still in bed with me. She is. But I don't know who else is or isn't with us, so, while my first thought is for our safety, my second thought is that I don't shoot until I know what I'm shooting at. Not only that, but in hotel rooms the walls are usually not thick enough to stop a bullet and I sure as hell do not want a near-miss traveling into the adjoining room or even the next and killing someone. So here I am, lying half-on my back and half-on my left side, gun in hand, waiting for a noise--anything--to alert me to what in the hell has come to visit.

Then I hear it again. A brushing, as if the palm of a hand is sliding across a wall. Slight but real. I slowly roll fully onto my back and begin inching into a more upright position. Now I am fully sitting up, gun in hand, trying to stop breathing and just listen. Which I do--for a good thirty seconds--during which I hear the sound twice more and I tighten my finger around the trigger.

Then it occurs to me. Turn the damn light on.

Which I do, reaching out with my left hand until I find the twist switch on the table lamp on my nightstand. Then, in one continuing move, I turn the light on and sweep the gun across the room.

There he is.

A huge *raton* is walking across the top of our bureau. He freezes in the light and looks at me, baring his teeth. Then he ducks his head, runs to the far edge of the bureau, and leaps off onto the floor and disappears from my view.

Rats as big as cats are common in Mexico. While the Rosarito Beach Hotel is a very classy place, the room door was propped open while people came and went during all the room searches. I know the room was open in this manner because it was still propped open when Marcel came to our room to perform his first sweep and he told me I should call the front desk and complain, which I did. The clerk profusely apologized and offered to comp our dinner but I told him that wasn't necessary.

The whole experience was greatly unsettling. As I switched on the light, Danny came fully upright in bed, effectively blocking my view to my right, leading into and through the closet/dressing area and back into the bathroom. Had there been someone there I would never have seen them until they were on top of us and finished with us.

I couldn't go back to sleep that night. The next night wasn't much better, but I finally managed to sleep. The next morning we all report to the hotel's private dining room as we have planned. A case review will take place.

A small breakfast buffet is set up so we all make our selections and spread out to eat. An hour later we have enjoyed our firm breakfast.

Now it is time to review for Mira's trial.

I go first, standing up after breakfast was cleared away and reciting what I believe the State's case will consist of when Mira goes to trial.

"Okay, everyone. Here's my birds-eye view of the trial against Mira. Let me preface by saying I hate the timing. The case goes to trial on October 31, a Monday. One week and one day later is the general election where the District Attorney will be elected. We absolutely must have a verdict prior to the morning of the eighth so that the voting public knows Mira was found not guilty. If we don't, she loses the election, plain and simple."

Marcel raises his hand. "Can we get the case tried in one week? I mean you need at least two days to pick the jury, am I right? Then the State drags its feet in putting on its case. Correct me if I'm wrong, but I don't see any way this case goes to verdict before the election."

I nod and indicate my total agreement with Marcel.

"That's why we're going to need to file a *Motion to Expedite*. I'm going to ask the court to give the State three trial days and to give me one. One is all I need and the State will scream bloody hell if I try to give it any less than three. In addition, we'll need two days to pick the jury. So there's our entire calendar. This way the State will have to be done and leave us enough time to put on our defense case and possibly get our verdict before the election."

Danny raises a hand. "Should I get on the *Motion to Expedite*? I'd like to write it."

"You're hired," I say. "Let's get it on file immediately. Remember, everyone, the election is November Eighth. We need to have an article in the *Tribune* and everywhere on TV about our defense verdict no later than the night of the seventh. Otherwise, Mira loses the election and the good old boy network wins."

"Got it," says Danny. "I'll have the *Motion to Expedite* by tomorrow morning."

Then I continue with my guesstimates of how the trial will proceed.

"First they will call Detective Jamison Weldon to set the stage. Then they will call one or two CSI's to explain what evidence the crime scene has given up. They will call a uniformed police officer somewhere in here to testify about the integrity of the crime scene and the identities of all persons coming and going while the scene was under police control. Next will come someone from the Medical Examiner's office to describe the body of Darrell

Harrow and its condition and so forth. The assistant medical examiner who performed the autopsy will then be called to testify regarding cause of death and autopsy findings. A criminalist will testify about the gun used to kill Darrell Harrow, his position and the shooter's position when the fatal shot was fired, distances of both, and placement of gunshot residue and result of finger-print/DNA testing on the gun itself. Darrell Harrow's widow and maybe an older child, if there is one, or a brother or sister if there is not, will then take the stand and talk about the broken hearts Darrell left behind. This will inflame the jury against Mira so that when we begin her defense case we will be working against their rage."

Marcel stands up. "A cigarette butt was seized during the search of your office. It was a cigarette butt that you removed from the crime scene. No crime lab reports have crossed my desk about it. So what do we do about it when they try to use it at trial?"

The beating erased the cigarette butt from my memory. I had forgotten about that portion of the search and the police finding that item. Now it all comes back, the gleeful look on Detective Jamison Weldon's face when he waved the baggie in my face at the search and seizure. I groan and my hands fall to my sides.

Mira's expression when she realizes Marcel is correct is pronounced. A cloud crosses her otherwise calm face and she explodes at me.

"My God, Michael! You removed evidence from my condo and the cops found it in your office? Seriously?"

Marcel shakes his head and sits back down. He has done his job.

"Well, to be very honest, the beating I took must have blocked that memory. Until just now, I had forgotten about it. But there're no crime lab reports in the file, nothing about any testing done on the butt. So I'll argue at trial that it shouldn't come into evidence because, without a crime lab report, it proves nothing. There's no DNA testing or spectrography to tie it to Mira and prove what the smudge substance is."

"Bullshit!" cries Mira. "No judge will keep that out of evidence. You have tied yourself to me as someone who isn't trustworthy. How does the jury view you when it all comes out? How does that make them view me?"

For a moment, I have no answer.

"That's a very weak argument, the one about the fact there's no crime lab report. Because there will be, Michael," Harley says. "This isn't good at all."

I'm flustered. I can't understand how this happened and I've evidently blocked it. I look at my staff for help. Evidently I'm not as together as I had thought coming in here this morning.

"Just erased it from my memory bank. Do you have any idea what we do with it?"

Harley looks from me to Marcel and then back to me. "Honestly? I don't. Except, like you said, there's no crime lab report so we argue like hell to keep it out from in front of the jury. We can also argue that the judge's order suppressing the search and seizure of the gun from the car also should apply to the cigarette butt from the office. But that's iffy and might not fly."

"For the love of God," I say, and the air goes out of me. I'm left feeling very vulnerable. It is malpractice that I removed evidence from the scene. Worse, it is a crime. The fear creeps up my spine and I shudder.

The room has gone very quiet.

"Let's take a break," I say quietly.

We break for coffee as it's been about forty-five minutes since I began. We spend five minutes making small talk, during which time Harley sidles up to me and says good morning. She gives me a funny look, as if she's privy to some secret that I don't know about, but I brush it off as nothing.

WE FINISH our coffee and return to the case review. I lead it off.

"So I'll start with testimony from the court clerk about the data and issuance of Judge Wang's order. Then I'll call Harley to the stand to testify about her motion to dismiss and the substance of Judge Wang's order of dismissal and order of suppression of evidence. Then--"

Harley suddenly stands and raises a hand. "Hold it, Michael, please."

All eyes turn to Harley.

"Don't you think that I should call you and put you on the witness stand for some of this?"

"I don't understand," I begin but then it dawns on me. She has made her decision about my offer and she is grinning ear to ear now. She's in!

"You're in?" I say.

"I'm in. One hundred percent."

Without missing a beat, I plunge ahead.

"Well, in that case why don't we divide up the witnesses into technical and non-technical. You take the technical witnesses and I'll take the non-technical ones, including Mira herself if we decide to call her to testify. If there's any medical stuff, Danny gets that."

Harley adds, "Ordinarily, neither of us would call the defendant to testify, but where the defendant is a lawyer-- and a criminal lawyer to boot--my normal reservations and precautions will probably be set aside in favor of her getting to tell her story. I have no doubt she can handle herself on cross-examination against whatever they might throw against her. And the simplicity and believability of her story and her role as a witness will go a long way."

"True," I add, "especially since she was a law enforcement officer as an assistant DA when the shooting occurred. That will carry some weight with any jury."

Harley sits back down.

"Hey, everyone," I say, "Harley has just today joined our

law firm. Let's give her a big round of applause and do everything we can to make her feel welcome."

Applause follows and Harley waves off all cries that she make a speech. Finally she does a three minute introduction of herself and an impromptu history of her career and life.

"And that guy you've seen killing himself on the surfboard every day this week? That's my son, Tom. He's no surfer, I'm thinking, but my God he's got game!"

We all laugh. Casual employees are dismissed, free to enjoy the beach and the shopping. The rest of us now find ourselves alone, huddled together around one table, ready to start in on the real business of trial law practice: the strategy and, ultimately, the defense.

Then it's back to San Diego and back to Chicago. A short trip, but a great one, as most of us have worked out the city kinks and blurry eyes from too much law.

Now to make ready for Mira's trial.

31

Time passes and witnesses are subpoenaed and jury instructions are dictated and typed up for the judge just like he's ordered. Everything is finally ready and the weekend before trial is suddenly upon us. Are we ready? One final review and we'll know that for sure.

Most important, though, is that we get a verdict before election day. We want the voters to know that Mira has been found not guilty. We are pulling for her to win the election for District Attorney and return triumphant to her office. The Democrat Party has relented and agreed not to replace her on the ticket, mostly based on our great success at getting the charges against me dismissed and getting the vehicular search suppressed.

Danny and I are meeting with Mira Morales in our conference room. Today is Sunday, October 30 and trial begins tomorrow. This is our last chance to really talk in-depth before jury selection begins and opening statements are given.

We go over the trial schedule we need the judge to order if we are to have a verdict before election day. Three days for the State's case; one day for the defendant's case; two days to pick a jury. Mira knows the timing of the situation and she tells us that her campaign has been going along in starts and sputters. Her biggest adversary hasn't been Lamont Johnstone and his party; her biggest adversary has been uncertainty. Her constituents are all saying, "Well, I could promise to vote for you if I knew you weren't going to be found guilty of murder. But with that hanging over your head...."

So I try to assuage her as best I can and promise that I will do everything within my power to guarantee her a verdict before the last edition of the *Chicago Tribune* hits the streets before voting begins. Without that, she can kiss it all goodbye. Then we turn our attention to the trial starting tomorrow.

Harley is late for our meeting, so Danny and I start in without her. We're doing a plausibility interview. Our job is to develop the story that we will try to sell to the jury. If we're successful, we win. If not, Mira goes to jail. This is the most important meeting we will have.

Mira is very understated today, very calm and collected. She is wearing a Fall tweed outfit and her hair is down and breeze-blown. No lipstick, no eye shadow, just plain good looks. Danny and I are both exhausted; Dania had the twenty-four-hour flu and we were both up with her last night, me pulling the first watch, Danny pulling the second. Dania and Mikey are in her play room two doors down from us, Dania sleeping the sleep of the innocently exhausted, Mikey sleeping because that's still mostly what he's all about.

"So," Mira says, "we all know about Brianna Finlayton quitting the District Attorney's office. She dismissed all charges against Tory Stormont then packed her personals and walked out. Not a word to anyone."

"District Attorney protecting a cop, Tory Stormont?" Danny asks.

Mira smiles. "Somebody sure as hell is."

I step in. It's my turn to update Mira.

"I wanted to brief you on Marcel. He's canvassed your neighbors. Your floor and the floors above and the floors below. No one heard a gunshot. And many of them were home, most sleeping, but a number were awake and would definitely have heard."

"I might have been passed out but I think I would've heard a gun going off."

"It happened. Harrow walked in. He was wheeled out on a gurney deader than a rock."

"The video shows him walking in?"

"It does. Did you open the door for him?"

"I don't know. Maybe. What about the gun? You've seen the actual firearms report?" Mira asks.

"Yes. Definitely your gun."

"Someone else did the shooting and they used my gun. That's scary to think that I was unconscious and some madman was wandering around my home with my loaded gun ready to kill. Makes me need to throw up just thinking about it."

"We'll have to prove it wasn't you, of course. The State will do everything they can to prove it was you."

"What about fingerprints on the gun?"

"Only yours."

"So whoever fired it was wearing gloves."

"Unless it was you."

There. The comment hangs in the air between us like a black cloud. We've needed to have this particular talk.

I continue, "Could you have blanked it out?"

Mira is emphatic. "That wouldn't be like me. I don't do blackouts."

"So let's talk unconscious. Why and how did it happen? We need a story for me to give the jury."

She rubs her forehead, thinking. Then, slowly, "Tell the jury I had taken an Ambien with a small glass of wine. It knocked me out. Tell them that I hadn't slept for two nights in a row because of the campaign. Which is mostly true. We've been extremely busy since May."

I nod and think. It's enough, I decide. I can start off with that and see where it goes at trial. I decide to move on.

"All right. Next item on my list is Brianna Finlayton. She

dismissed all charges against Tory Stormont and resigned. My question to you, is, why?"

At just this moment, Harley arrives and takes a seat. She looks fresh and brings along her own coffee drink.

"I'm asking Mira why Brianna Finlayton would have dismissed the case against Tory Stormont, Harley. So let's all think about this."

Mira leans away. She is thinking. She begins slowly, saying, "I've checked around the office with some friends. Tory Stormont is a white cop who murdered a black teenager. He'll do anything to stay out of jail because with these guys if they get sent to prison their days are numbered. They die in prison. So they fight it like no one else ever did. He got to Brianna. She immediately dismissed the charges against him. I don't think it's any more complicated than that."

"He scared her off with threats against her?"

"That's my best guess. I don't think it's any more complicated than that."

"What about the District Attorney himself?"

"What about him?"

"Does he have ties to Tory Stormont? Which is probably a dumb question, am I right? I need to hear how you would answer if we called you as a witness."

She looks sharply at me. "Are you asking, is the District Attorney in bed with the Chicago police union? Of course he is. All prosecutors are. It goes with the territory. Now about Robert Shaughnessy personally, I don't know the particulars. I don't know everything that goes on inside that office."

"You weren't helping prosecute Stormont were you?"

"No."

Danny says, "What if someone wanted to wreck your run for District Attorney, Mira? Would they leave a dead body in your house to do that?"

"Someone kills Harrow in my condo so I get indicted?"

"Yes," says Danny, "why not?"

"Someone such as my opponent?"

"Lamont Johnstone?" Danny asks.

"No, I don't think he has the balls."

"What about Tory Stormont?" Danny presses. "Would he like to see you defeated in November?"

"Of course. Lamont Johnstone is known for being best friends with the police union. He would do anything to protect Stormont and Stormont knows that."

Her face goes blank for a moment and then a smile spreads over her face.

She says, "So Stormont killed Harrow, who had indicted him and was prosecuting him. And he tried to implicate me in the crime because I wasn't in bed with the union and I would be next in line to prosecute him? That sounds very complicated to sell to a jury."

Danny looks at me. "Michael, can we sell this to a jury? That Tory was plotting to control the election outcome? And that Johnstone is tied up with them?"

I look hard at her. She's done her homework and I'm grateful for it. So I take a run at her theory just to see what it sounds like. "Ladies and gentlemen of the jury, not every case is a dead body or a kilo of cocaine. The worst crime in Chicago is going on inside mahogany walls and boardrooms. Even a police officer got caught up and tried to guarantee that a prosecutor friendly to him got elected."

Harley adds to my words, "Lamont Johnstone decided who got prosecuted and who didn't. That's what first assistants do: put the District Attorney's policies into practice. But then, when Johnstone left, Darrell Harrow took over for him and Darrell went after the police officer. Darrell Harrow wouldn't play ball with the cops."

"So a cop killed him. Tory Stormont was the trigger man," Danny says. "What about it, Michael? Can you sell this?"

They all look at me.

It is coming into focus. "Maybe it was always about the election. If Mira loses the election, a cop-friendly prosecutor takes over. That means Stormont's implication in Harrow's murder case goes away."

"What implication is that?" asks Danny.

"The implication we're going to make at trial when we point the finger at Stormont and away from Mira. The world is going to know about Stormont and his motive and the gun in his back pocket. We're putting him on trial, my friends."

Mira says, "So I was indicted in order to guarantee Johnstone wins. Pure evil."

"Something stinks at the District Attorney's office," I say. "I can definitely sell it."

So that's where we leave it: Lamont Johnstone departs the District Attorney's team to run for the office himself. His job falls to Darrell Harrow. Harrow indicts Tory Stormont for killing an unarmed black teen. Then Darrell Harrow winds up murdered and stashed inside Mira's living room. Brianna is next up to bat; it's her turn to prosecute Stormont. But Stormont puts the fear of God in Brianna Finlayton and she dismisses all charges against him. Then she resigns. Now Harrow's gone, Mira's gone, and Brianna's gone. If Johnstone wins, there will be no case filed against Stormont for shooting Harrow, even with all the evidence I'm going to introduce at trial that implicates Stormont. It's the best shot we have.

Some of this is conjecture and I cannot prove it. But that doesn't matter. To the criminal attorney the only question is whether he or she can sell the conjecture to a jury. It's how criminal cases are defended. This is how it's done, pointing the finger elsewhere. You come up with a parallel fact track and you ascribe motive to someone else and you walk your client out of court.

As we continue with our trial prep, it keeps coming back to me: I'm not sure how much longer I can keep doing this. My children deserve a father who stands for something more than hiding the truth from juries.

Oh well, I shelve it for now. Duty calls.

Now to build the case against Stormont as the true killer.

That falls to me and Marcel. We've got part of it already.

But we don't have it all. At least not yet.

32

Monday morning Harley and I arrive at court early. We have a motion to present.

I am reviewing my notes as I wait for our trial judge to hear my *Motion to Expedite*. My notes pretty well set out what I think will occur at trial Monday to Monday, the week before the election:

OCT 31 Monday FIRST DAY OF TRIAL. Motion Expedite. Jury Selection

NOV 1 Tuesday: Jury Selection + Opening statements

NOV 2 Wednesday: Detective Weldon

NOV 3 Thursday: More State's Witnesses

NOV 4 Friday: Last State's Witnesses. State Rests.

NOV 5-6 (sat, sun) MG and MARCEL
Confirm Wits will appear

NOV 7: Stormont testifies, jury verdict

NOV 8: election, morning newspaper comes
out with NG verdict.

The calendar is proving accurate.

Present with me in the judge's chambers are the District
Attorney himself, Robert Shaughnessy; Miranda
Morales; Danny and Harley; the court reporter; Judge
Itaglia; and the clerk of the court.

Seating is crowded as we all jockey to get on the judge's
left-hand side where studies have shown the prevailing
party sits something like eighty percent of the time. I am
just off-center and to his left but Shaughnessy is to my
right, not a good sign. I drive such idiocy from my mind
and concentrate on why we're gathered together. Timing
is everything from here on out.

The case has moved from Judge Wang, who handled the
pre-trial matters, to Judge Itaglia for trial. She's a no-
nonsense judge in the courtroom with a great sense of
drama that just oozes out of her in chambers. Everything
is a much bigger issue than it ever actually is--in my opinion, anyway. Physically, she is a small woman, stooped
and withered with age, a woman whose face and
physique you might expect to find peddling wares on a
sidewalk in some small Italian town. But her mind is the
mind of a legal giant. She clerked for the Illinois Supreme

Court at one time and there is always talk around of elevating her to that court. I watch as her hands are always in motion even where the rest of her is not, such as right now, looking down at the litigants' attorneys as we await her signal to begin.

At last she says to me, "Counsel, it's your motion, please proceed. Please tell me why you want this trial concluded by November seven and why that should matter to me."

"It should matter to you, Your Honor," I begin, "because justice demands we give this woman, if innocent, the opportunity to present herself as a viable option to the voters when they go into the booth on November eight to select a District Attorney. If this case hasn't been resolved before the levers are pulled inside the booth, then she loses, plain and simple. Even if the jury finds her not guilty the next day, it's too late then."

"But what about the State's right to fully present its case against her? Don't I have to give the State its day in court? Why should I limit that to just three days as you're requesting?"

Beside me, Shaughnessy nods vigorously and clears his throat. He's acknowledging that he's in complete agreement with what she's just said. Three days isn't enough, his demeanor and body language cry.

I ignore him.

"The State's case is a simple one, a circumstantial one. A detective, crime scene techs, and a medical examiner and he's done. There's no way that takes more than three days as long as the court requires the State to be efficient. As long as the court doesn't allow the State to drag its feet and drag out the trial. I already expect them to do this and I will be constantly on guard against the State engaging in delaying tactics. I hope and pray the court will join me in that."

The judge looks over at Shaughnessy. He's chomping at the bit to be heard. His arguments are predictable, but he launches ahead anyway.

"Judge, the State--as you have mentioned--has a constitutional right to present its case fully. Due process of law requires no less. This is a first degree murder case. We should never forget that. This is the most important case the State ever prosecutes for the benefit of the public. This is the type of case that intimidates the killers among us, the person who would kill were it not for the fact that he learns, from cases such as this one, that he will spend the rest of his life behind bars if he follows through on his plan to murder. That's why these cases are so important in the larger view. In the smaller view, these cases-- this case--is hugely significant to the loved ones of the victim. His widow, his children, they have a right to see justice done. Justice in this case isn't about an election. It's about the meting out of punishment to their husband's and father's killer. That's the true justice waiting in the wings. It must happen, Judge. Justice cries out to be served."

Judge Itaglia's hands flutter nonstop while we are talking. She's making notes, she's thumbing through pages of white pleadings on her desk, she's moving yellow legal pads hither and yon; it makes me wonder whether she's actually hearing anything of what's being said. Then I find I needn't have worried about that at all.

"So let me see if I understand, here. The State's idea of justice is punishment and vengeance while the defendant's idea of justice is the reclamation of her professional life by the timely conclusion of the case so that her run for District Attorney can continue without the Sword of Damocles hanging over her head. Am I on the right track so far?"

It's rhetorical and the DA and I both know it. We simply nod.

She continues. "So let's see if we can whittle this thing down. First, we can hear all motions outside of court times. Before nine and after five. That way we don't waste jury hours with motions that the State might decide to file in an effort to delay things or run out the clock. This sounds like the NBA, ladies and gentlemen. So what else can we do?"

"Limit the State's witnesses," I quickly suggest. "Keep it to a certain number, two hours for direct examination and one hour for cross examination. Three hours per witness, tops."

"Impossible!" cries Shaughnessy. "My first witness, my detective, will very likely take up an entire day on his own."

The judge's eyes at that moment screw down tight on the district attorney. "I think not. I rather like the idea of three hours per witness. Now, if the State needs more time for a witness, then that extra time will be subtracted from the remaining witnesses. Until we're down to the last witness and have no other time to draw on. So the last witness is three hours, tops."

"Or you could do this, Judge," I say, "you could limit the State's case to three days. Two days to pick a jury, three days for the State's case. That gets us to Friday night. Then I get one day--Monday--to put on the defendant's case."

"Sure," says Shaughnessy, "and you're going to scream bloody murder if the jury takes longer than a few hours to reach a verdict. Would the court keep them past five o'clock Monday night to deliberate?"

Judge Itaglia is cogitating. Finally, she leaves off the train of thought and says, "I'll keep the jury here as late as midnight Monday night. We want to give the defendant every fair chance at getting a verdict before the election. To be honest, everyone, I'm not feeling that favorably toward either side in this case. The State's case is circumstantial as there's no evidence the defendant fired the gun. On the other hand, the defense case seems to consist only of a denial that the defendant did it. My guess is that the defense's case is going to be closing argument to the jury that the state failed to meet its burden of proving the charges against the defendant beyond a reasonable doubt. How am I doing so far now?"

Neither attorney speaks up. We don't wish to give away our game plans so we just don't respond.

"So here's the order. Three days for the State, one day for the Defendant. Two days for jury selection. Whoever is sitting in that jury box at the close of the day on Tuesday, that's your jury, boys and girls. Plain and simple. Am I leaving anything out?"

"How about time limits on witnesses?" I ask. "Three hours tops?"

"No, I don't think so. I think if the State wants to spend its entire three days on one witness it should be allowed to do so. But when I say three days, I'm dead serious. Come Friday night, the State will either rest its case or I shall rest it for them. Any questions?"

Shaughnessy is livid but he doesn't want to start a brawl with the judge even before we set foot in the courtroom, so he swallows it down. I would like to have seen the judge declare that the jury will have a verdict by midnight on Monday night or that she will declare a mistrial, but I haven't fully thought that through, so I don't go there.

"We're done here," says the Judge. "Let's go out and pick our jury."

With a flutter and a dive her hands finally come to rest on her bench book and notepad.

The judge is ready.

The question for me is, am I? Am I ready?

I tell myself that I am and put on my most confident face.

Beside me, Mira is elated. She had thought we wouldn't

get the judge's help in this. She is beaming ear-to-ear as we stand but I have to tell her to wipe it off.

A jury should never see a smiling defendant. At least not before they rule. After they rule, that's when we all want to see a smiling defendant.

Shaughnessy is grimacing and gives me a deadly look.

Not everyone wants to see a smiling defendant.

33

Tuesday afternoon, second day of trial in *State of Illinois vs. Miranda Morales*. We are all in our places and jury selection is just about complete. I am on my feet at the lectern, questioning the jury members about their fitness to serve on Mira's jury. Surprisingly, the State hasn't attempted to create reasons around which the judge would have no choice but to delay things--my worst fear. Shaughnessy hasn't protracted jury Q&A's and hasn't nitpicked every little issue that would require us to step up to the judge's throne and make ourselves heard in private. I'm beginning to think he has accepted the court's conditions, the ones I requested.

"It's a different kind of trial," I'm explaining to prospective juror number eight, "because the State is putting one of its own on trial. The District Attorney has indicted one of his own prosecutors. Is there anything about that kind of case that would affect your ability to serve as a fair and impartial juror?"

Juror number eight is a young woman with three children under six. Even with so many youngsters at home, she has let us know that she is determined to sit on our jury. That being the case, I know the question I have just asked her about affecting her ability to serve will draw a "no" response. Which is a good thing, because I really want her on my jury.

Without hesitation she answers, "No, that won't affect me at all. I can be a fair and impartial juror no matter who the defendant happens to be."

Excellent. Time to move along.

At which point Robert Shaughnessy himself stands at the prosecution table and asks to have a sidebar with Judge Itaglia. The judge nods so we hurry up to her station. This is only the second time this has happened in two days. I'm not pleased with the delay and will tell the judge what I think about it.

"What is it, Mr. Shaughnessy?" she demands.

"I think this juror number eight should be excused for cause," he replies.

Her eyebrows raise. "And what cause would that be?"

"She has small children at home, young ones, and clearly they are going to be uppermost in her mind throughout any trial. It's the State's position that she won't be able to give her full attention to the trial and the witnesses and their testimony. We move to excuse her for cause."

"Mr. Gresham?"

I smile. "Judge, that's about as specious as it gets. I'm no longer surprised at the lengths the prosecution in this county will go to get rid of jurors it doesn't like, but small children at home? What's next, old parents at home? Too many bills at home on the table? Too much NBA to watch on TV? The possibilities for how the State will attempt to expand on such a dangerous precedent are endless. As endless as the State's imagination, which, judging by this objection, seems boundless already. This objection is made for the pure purposes of delay. Counsel should be admonished so we're not up here again in ten minutes."

Judge Itaglia looks down at me and winces.

"That's a pretty commentary," she whispers to us, "let's try to avoid speechifying up here, shall we? At any rate, the State's request for dismissal for cause is denied. Counsel, do you wish to exercise one of your peremptories on number eight?"

"No, Your Honor," Shaughnessy says, which totally makes the case I was aiming for. If he really was worried about the juror, he would use one of his dozen peremptories. But he's not. He was just looking for a delay.

"Please take your places, gentlemen. Let's move it along now."

We sit down and I scan over my drawing of the jury box and its occupants for my next target.

That turns out to be Amelia M. Briggs, who is sitting in the number four chair loudly snapping her chewing gum. Something about her casual demeanor tells me to follow up on the judge's earlier questions to her.

"Miss Briggs," I begin, "you told Judge Itaglia that you're a graphic artist, isn't that correct?"

"Yessir," she snaps, never missing a beat with the gum.

"What kind of art?"

"Graphic."

"I'm sorry, I'm trying to ask what kinds of things do you render."

"People making love."

It is very still in the courtroom as I fire through my mind looking for ways her response might come back to hurt Miranda Morales. Thinking of none, I plunge on.

"People making love can mean a lot of things. Is what you do pornography?"

She looks askance at me. "Anime."

"Isn't anime a form of Japanese visual expression?"

Her face brightens. A point was just scored.

"Exactly! Most people are clueless about it. I'm impressed!"

"So your animations feature people making love. Would that be physical lovemaking?"

She pulls herself upright in the chair. "No, that would be people doing things that they love for a living. I work for an insurance company. One rendering was of a man mowing his grass with great care until a car came veering through his fence and ran him down. Another was of a young mother taking her child out for a walk in the stroller until a tree branch fell on them. In both cases no one was that seriously injured, but it demonstrated how unexpected life's need for good insurance can be."

"So you're doing animations for commercials?"

"Exactly."

"Is there anything about that which would affect your ability to be a juror in this case?"

"If anything," she replies through two snaps of her gum, "it qualifies me as someone with a great eye for viewing any video you might want to show us. I have a great skepticism about much of the police video I see on TV, so much of it is doctored."

"What about video taken by CCTV security cameras? Would your background in visual art make you somehow prejudiced to where you wouldn't want you on this jury if you were the one on trial?"

She smiles. "Someone like me is exactly who I *would* want on my own jury. I'm good at visuals and I'm very fair."

Those two about cover it for me. I'm finished here. This is our second full day of jury selection and it is almost five o'clock.

"Judge, the defense accepts the panel. We're very happy to have this group of twelve jurors and four alternates helping us from here forward."

Judge Itaglia nods and looks at Shaughnessy at the prosecution table. It is extremely unusual for the DA himself to try a case. But this isn't just any old murder case. This one is extremely high profile and he wants to end his term in office with a bang and a nod to the police he has protected over his entire career. Press and TV are jamming the courtroom and he wants more than anything for his office to come across as fair and unbiased.

He stands up.

"The State accepts the panel as well, Your Honor."

"Very well. The remaining contingent on this case are excused. Please report to the main jury room tomorrow for your next assignments. The other sixteen selected here today, we will begin trial at nine sharp in the morning. Please report to the courtroom no later than eight forty-five and the bailiff will show you into the court's jury room."

She then goes into the usual litany against allowing conversations or news accounts about the case and the jury is dismissed. We stand in recess.

Harley and I are on our feet while Mira remains seated between us, staring straight ahead.

Harley touches her shoulder. "Okay?"

Mira looks up at her. "Just shocked. I'm actually on trial for murder. I should be over there at counsel table trying this case for the State. Instead, I'm here in the defendant's chair. I don't know if it ever will soak in all the way."

"You're going to be fine," I tell her, and I hope the uncertainty in my heart isn't vocalized. Truth be told, the State has a very strong case against Mira. After all, it was her condo and her gun and it was she who had the fight with Darrell Harrow not an hour before he lay dead on her living room floor. Who else would be as likely to do such a thing as the dead man's lover? It is no secret, at this point, incidentally, that the two of them were lovers. The State has as much as said so in its jury list where general topics of testimony are required to be disclosed. While this doesn't surprise me, it does muddy the water. We tend to think of romance as more likely to elicit homicidal feelings between lovers than disputes between us and our dentist. It's that certain something so proliferated in song and poetry that makes men and women turn to guns, knives, and poisons, that certain something called love. Love kills. At least that's the thinking among those of us involved in criminal justice because that's what we most often encounter as the basis for violent crime. Love is, in fact, a many-splendored thing. Until it is rejected. Then all hell breaks loose.

With these thoughts in mind, I return to the office with Harley. Mira has caught a cab back to her condo, where we've asked her to lay low and remain until the trial is over. Except for coming to the court, of course. The less of an appearance criminal defendants make in the world, the less opportunity there is for the police to interfere in their lives vis-à-vis traffic stops and the like. The police like nothing more than to intimidate a defendant during a criminal trial. So we ask her to stay at home and we trust that she will heed our admonition.

"Love kills," I say to Harley as we ride the elevator upstairs to our offices.

"What the hell?" she says. Then she gets my drift.

"That's the angle they'll be using. I agree."

"So how would you handle it?"

"Simple. I would prove that it wasn't she who was enraged. It was him. He was coming there to hurt her. Put the shoe on the other foot."

I turn and watch the floor numbers click by overhead.

It's running through my mind for the umpteenth time as I begin yet another criminal trial, that the real duty of the State--the prosecution--is not to win; rather, it's to present a case without flourishes and without strategy in an attempt to help the jury get to the truth of a situation. But that notion fell by the wayside long before I became a lawyer. Today the State strategizes and tries to color situations and paint with a deceitful brush in order to win.

The truth train left the station long ago.

The door opens on our floor and we flee into our offices, where I sit at my desk and attempt to stop shaking inside.

It's an unimaginable burden on lawyers who defend murder trials. At times I kid myself into thinking it's just something I do; I try to come across *to myself* as inured to the responsibility and convince myself that I handle these cases gracefully and easily without fear.

Nothing could be further from the truth.

Like always, I am scared to death. And we haven't even really started yet.

Tomorrow will be savage as the state weaponizes its witnesses. I will resist with all my wit, experience, and creativity.

I only hope I'm up to it.

I know the State, with its unlimited resources, will be.

Days three, four, and five are stacked up against the defendant. Then a quick weekend and one day for the defense. I only hope I'm doing the right thing by telescoping it all down into one day for the defendant.

As far as I know, I'm on the right track.

But that's as far as I know. Which is never all of it.

I say a silent prayer that I won't turn up at the end, Monday night, needing to extend the trial for another day or two. It could happen.

It's my job to make sure it doesn't.

34

Wednesday morning, nine o'clock, and we begin the actual trial.

Judge Itaglia calls court to order and takes on some minor housekeeping matters with the jury. (Some want vegetarian at lunch and some want a meat eater's diet.) When she is finished, she turns to DA Shaughnessy and tells him he may now begin with his opening statement.

Ronald Shaughnessy played offensive tackle at Notre Dame. And, judging by the looks of him, he still works hard to stay in shape--the kind of guy you'd want on your team in a friendly game of touch football. He steps up to the lectern and sets before himself a small stack of note cards. That's the sign of the lawyer who isn't all that comfortable talking to juries, needing signposts in the form of notecards to guide him along the way. With myself, anymore, I take a single sheet of paper with maybe five key points I want to cover--and that's it. Each to his own. But what Shaughnessy maybe lacks in comfort addressing the jury he more than makes up for with a huge, booming voice that fills the courtroom with a pleasant, nasal sound not unlike the voice of Samuel L. Jackson. The jury is attentive as he gets underway.

"The State is going to present evidence that will prove beyond a reasonable doubt that this pleasant looking woman over here--" pausing to point out Mira, sandwiched between me and Harley--"fired a single round from her gun, killing Assistant DA Darrell Harrow. Why would she do this? A lover's quarrel. No more, no less. We will be calling a witness, Harrow's own wife, who will tell you that her husband had come apart the night before his death, confessing to her that he had been carrying on an affair with his colleague, Miranda Morales. Tearfully, he promised his wife it was over and that he would break it off with Morales immediately."

He stops and takes a sip of water. The jury is interested, leaning forward, eyes following the DA.

"So the next night, July Fourth, at the Democratic Fundraiser for the upcoming November elections, Harrow approached Morales and an argument broke out between them. A man by the name of Nathaniel McMann will testify that he heard this argument from the dais and that he thought it beyond a mere lovers' quarrel, that it was very serious. He will tell you he based this judgment on the anger levels and the threats going back and forth. That's right, Harrow said some pretty mean things to Morales, but she reciprocated in kind. Meaning, she threatened him right back.

"Detective Jamison Weldon will testify that he was the

lead detective on the investigation. He will tell you about his work out of the homicide bureau of the Chicago Police Department and he will go into what he observed and what he did at the condominium of Ms. Morales on July Fourth and early July Fifth. He has headed up the investigation ever since and will give you the twenty-thousand-foot view of things. It's very likely another one or two of the uniformed officers at the scene that night will also testify about the scene and how it was kept un-contaminated by people coming and going inside the premises."

Again with the water and a minute or so of flipping through his notes. Then we continue.

"The crime scene technicians will testify about their duties, their training, and what actions they took at the scene of this murder. They will talk about bloodstains and DNA evidence and other criminalists will talk about gunshot evidence. All of it neatly tied together by the time we're finished with them.

"The medical examiner will testify after the CSI's and will tell you about the manner and cause of death. You will be told that DA Harrow died inside Ms. Morales' condo that night from a gunshot wound. Which leaves you with the question of who fired the fatal round."

He steps away from the podium and leans across his table to whisper to Detective Weldon. They exchange words, Weldon nodding and then pursing his lips in a very serious look. They seem to be in agreement and my stomach falls. I'm not going to like what they just agreed to. Shaughnessy returns to the lectern and pushes the glasses up on his nose. Then he levels his eyes at the jury.

"One key item of evidence needs to be mentioned at this point. Let me tell you why. Darrell Harrow was found stretched out dead on Miranda Morales' living room floor. His head was nearest the wall where the entrance door is located. At his head was an upside-down cross. A Christian icon turned upside-down. This configuration is often seen in Satanic ritualism. Detective Weldon will testify about that. He will also tell you that on the wall above Harrow's head was where someone had drawn a pentagram. As many of you know, a pentagram is a five-pointed star set inside a circle that is also typically found in Satanic ritualism. What you may not know is that a pentagram with two points up inscribed in a double circle with the head of a goat inside the pentagram is the copyrighted logo of the Church of Satan. Well, this is exactly what was found drawn above Harrow's body, without the head of the goat. The drawing was primitive as it was done with a black drawing agent of some kind. Detective Weldon will tell you the drawing was made with a piece of charcoal taken from Ms. Morales' fire-place. Crime lab testimony and reports will prove this to be the case. Now why is this important?"

He gives the question pause and lets it sink in. Then he picks it up again, his pace much slower now.

"It is important because a cigarette butt has been located that involved two things. First, it had on the filter the DNA isolated from the defendant's lipstick. Second, it had smudges from the same charcoal that was used to draw the pentagram on the wall. Adding the two together, you will come to understand from all the testimony and evidence that Miranda Morales drew the pentagram, the sign of Satan, on the wall after she shot and killed Darrell Harrow with one shot from the gun she always carried inside her purse. She carried the gun because she was a homicide prosecutor in my office and was exposed by her work to some very dangerous and very upset people."

Now he crosses over to the court clerk's evidence table where all exhibits have been marked and picks up the gun used to kill Harrow. He holds it up.

"This gun was used to kill Darrell Harrow. But guess what else? This gun also has trace evidence on it of the same charcoal that was applied to the wall to draw the pentagram and the same charcoal that was found on Mira Morales' cigarette butt. Coincidence? How could it be? The evidence will connect up these three dots and you will be left with the compelling knowledge that the defendant touched all three and used two of the three to commit the murder and then tried to push the murder off on Satanists in order to disguise her involvement. How did this work? Simple. The murder appeared to be the work of Satanists as she would have us believe with the upside-down cross and the Satanic star. But in truth they were used to provide misdirection only. There was no Satanic involvement in this murder, only a lover's quarrel followed by a single gunshot. That's why we're all here today.

"And here is the final nail in the coffin. The cigarette butt found with her lipstick and her fireplace charcoal were not found at the crime scene. No, they were found in a legal file that belonged to her lawyer, sitting right behind me, Mr. Michael Gresham. The file was in his office and was discovered by Detective Weldon when he searched Michael Gresham's office pursuant to a search warrant issued by the Cook County courts. That's right, Michael Gresham removed evidence from the scene of the crime and hid it inside his file folder. All of this is conclusive proof that Morales not only committed the crime but also that her lawyer attempted to remove evidence in order to help cover it up. Why didn't he dispose of the cigarette butt? Why not just throw it away? Ladies and gentlemen, I leave it to Michael Gresham to explain that 'why' to you. I certainly don't know why."

He steps back and turns around to look at me. He then raises his right arm and points a finger at me in an accusing manner.

"Here's the last thing I have to say. Before this case is over, Michael Gresham may be charged with the crime of obstruction of justice. For tampering with evidence and attempting to hide the commission of a murder. That's who is about to stand up here and talk to you. Shall we all listen? Are you ready? So am I. Thank you."

Then he sits down and all eyes turn to me. I stand and ask the court for a five-minute recess. The court goes me one better and recesses trial for the morning, saying she has other cases that need attention in open court.

Thank God for beneficent judges. Judge Itaglia has done me the huge favor of giving me time to respond to the DA's charges that I have committed obstruction of justice.

I ask the judge if we can make a motion in chambers and she agrees. For the next five minutes, seated around the judge's desk, I and the prosecution team argue whether the case should be declared a mistrial due to the prosecutor's comments about me being prosecuted—maybe, he said—for obstruction of justice. It is extremely prejudicial, I argue, and at the very least the jury should be told to ignore it and remove it from their memory. My argument is halting and unrehearsed and I cannot tell which way Judge Itaglia is leaning as she takes my motion under advisement. Which means she's going to think about it privately before she rules one way or the other. We leave her chambers and my heart is heavy.

We walk out of the courtroom stunned. The press clamors around us, demanding a statement, but Marcel and Danny run interference for me, Harley, and Mira. Now we make the elevator and Marcel quickly punches buttons and closes the door. Only our team and our client ride the elevator down to the lobby.

"Son of a bitch," Marcel says as we grind our way on the creaky old elevator.

The rest of us are too shocked to even comment.

Finally, Mira says, "Michael, I want you off the case."

I look at her and nod.

"We'll meet in my office in thirty minutes. We'll discuss it then," I tell her.

Marcel drives my Mercedes as we silently wind our way back downtown to our office.

Finally, we park in the basement and climb on the elevator.

Not a word has been spoken since Mira said she wants me off the case.

Not one word.

35

I t is before noon and we're seated around the conference table in my office. With me are Mira, Harley, and Marcel.

"What were you even thinking?" says Mira. "Removing a piece of evidence is one thing. But hanging onto it? Seriously?"

I shake my head. She's right, it is beyond the pale. The whole thing has left me in a rage at myself for taking the cigarette butt and then keeping it around.

"I'm sorry, Mira. I've put you in a terrible position. My thinking at this point is that I agree with you. I should move to withdraw from your case. Ask the judge for a mistrial. What do you think, Harley?"

Harley pours a second cup of coffee from the carafe. She is thinking and very quiet, for Harley.

"I'm thinking you have to withdraw, Michael. Withdraw

and let me take over the defense. That is, if Mira feels okay with that."

All eyes focus on Mira.

"To tell the truth, I've never been faced with this before," she says. "I've had situations where I suddenly found that I had witnessed something inadvertently, sometime that made me a witness to the case in trial. But I've never had a case where a lawyer on either side of the street was accused of removing evidence from a crime scene. I'm just relieved that Michael has you, Harley. I don't want a mistrial. That would just allow the State to come in better-prepared the second time around. I want to go ahead without Michael at counsel table."

Then Marcel speaks up. "We do have an option here."

My head jerks up. "What might that be?"

He continues, "Let me just float this. What if we go in and say it was me who removed the cigarette butt? I could say that I removed it in order to have the smudge tested by our own crime lab. At the time I did it, the scene was under no one's control. We could argue that I put it inside the file with the intention of having it tested but then I forgot about it."

We three lawyers trade looks. Marcel is speaking beyond mere friendship. It is an act of extreme devotion that he's proposing, giving the State a shot at him.

But it can't work. It can't work because I won't let him take the fall for me.

"Can't do that, Marcel," I say, "but it means everything to me that you would offer."

"Wait a minute, Michael," says Harley, "I think you're missing the point here."

"What point is that?"

"That point he's making is that if he steps up then Mira's defense team--her lawyers--can remain on the job with clean hands. It will have become a staff error, not a lawyer error or, worse, an intentional deception. That looks terrible for Mira. This looks less terrible if a staffer did it without your knowledge or permission. Think about that, please."

"Oh my God!" I explode. "I don't want that to make sense, but it does. Someone please tell me there's another way around this."

"Not that I can think of," Mira says. "As the client, I think it's a game-saver."

"Nor I," says Harley. "It keeps the defense counsel intact and clean. It has to be done."

I shake my head violently. "I can't just let Marcel open himself up to being prosecuted for obstruction of justice. It isn't right."

"Neither is throwing your client to the wolves in order to preserve your own sense of right and wrong," says Harley. "Look, I know how you feel and I know you, Michael. Truth be told, your inner sense of right and wrong is almost too powerful for you to be doing criminal defense. Sometimes criminal defense requires that the criminal lawyer do things that violate his sense of right and wrong in order to protect the client. That's the case we have here. We can't let Mira go to prison because you have a need to feel honest in all things."

She's right. That's the quandary. It's my exaggerated sense of right and wrong that's causing the solution to the problem to go wanting. "Damn, I have so screwed us up here," I say. "Mira, I can only tell you how sorry I am for this."

Mira tosses her head. "Just tell me you'll make it right by letting Marcel take the fall. I'm not asking you, Michael. I'm demanding you do it at this point in the case. You owe me."

I can only agree, of course. "I do owe you. I'm damned if I do and I'm damned if I don't."

"But don't leave out the all-important fact that you created this problem yourself, Michael," says Harley.

Then another niggling idea floats to the surface and for just a moment I see a glimmer of hope.

"Let me posit one other solution," I say.

All eyes turn to me.

"What if we renew our motion to suppress to include the cigarette butt?"

"Keep it out of evidence altogether?" says Harley. "How's that work when Ronald Shaughnessy has already mentioned it to the jury?"

"It works by the judge giving the jury an instruction that

the District Attorney's representation to them was improper and that the court has found it was also untrue."

"Wow," says Mira. "That is an alternative, Michael."

"It does save Marcel from prison bars," says Harley. "But I can't see the judge telling the jury the District Attorney lied to them. That's not going to happen."

"I agree," says Mira.

"What about this?" I say, as the truth of the case settles over me. "What if I admit taking the cigarette but tell the jury I was going to turn it over to the police but they beat me senseless and then I forgot about it."

"Bingo!" cries Harley. "Then we get it in front of the jury that the cops beat you up and we explain why you had the evidence in your file. It works! This is what we'll do."

"Agreed!" exclaims Mira. "They did beat you up, Michael. And something tells me this scenario is probably closer to the truth than anything else on the table."

"I'm liking it, Boss," Marcel agrees. "A closed-head injury with serious neurological repercussions--that's enough to win the jury's sympathy right there. They need to hear about it and Mira needs for them to hear about it. So do you, now that the State's Attorney stuck his knife in your back."

"Then that's what we'll do," I state. "So what's our scenario? Harley?"

"We file a motion to allow you to testify even though

you're trial counsel, for openers," Harley says. "Second, we move to call you out of order in the case. We move to have you testify regarding the District Attorney's claim that you hid evidence. We do it bundled together with a motion to strike what's been said."

"But that would be held outside the jury's hearing, that kind of motion," says Mira.

"She's right," I say. "But we want the jury to hear it. So how does that happen?"

"I've got it," says Harley. "We don't call Michael at all. We cross-examine Detective Weldon on the issue. Ask him about the beating as a possible explanation. I get to do it. Leave Michael out of it."

"And here's the nail in the coffin," I say. "As our first witness, we call the District Attorney himself, Ronald Shaughnessy. We call him as an adverse witness and cross-examine him regarding the beating."

"Do we all agree?" Harley asks. "Let's see some hands. All in favor of a motion to strike?"

Four hands are raised.

"All in favor of calling Shaughnessy as our first witness?"

Four hands again.

"Cross-examination of Weldon on the beating?"

"No-brainer," says Marcel. We all nod our agreement.

"I'll whip up the motion to strike," says Harley. "It will be my motion to argue. I'm going to love this."

"Sounds good," I say.

It beats hell out of me going to prison for hiding evidence. We have come a long way in a half hour. But now it's time to move along to court.

Detective Weldon will be first up. I will be ready with my cross-examination of him. This will actually be fun, I realize for the first time all day.

"Weldon is my witness on cross," I say.

No argument, only nods.

"Good," I say. "Then let's go to court and watch the heads roll."

36

Wednesday afternoon. It's one o'clock when court resumes.

Detective Weldon looks every bit the part of the professional detective when he comes into court this afternoon. His hair is perfectly combed and neatly parted; his starched white shirt is obviously brand new and sparkling; his pinstripe suit fits perfectly in the shoulders and back without a wrinkle. He is here with us in the courtroom ready to do some serious damage to me and to Mira.

Now we will find out just how far he can get.

After the jury is settled and court called to order, Shaughnessy calls Weldon as the State's first witness.

"Your name?"

"Jamison Weldon."

"Please tell us about your current job and your work history."

"Detective with the Chicago Police Department, homicide bureau. I've been a law enforcement officer for nearly twenty years, beginning in 1996 when I graduated from Loyola with a degree in criminal justice and then went to the CPD police academy. Upon my successful graduation, third in my class of eighty-eight cadets, I was assigned to patrol in South Chicago. That assignment lasted about eighteen months. Then I was assigned to a gang task force, also in South Chicago. I was still wearing a uniform but walking a beat every day, keeping my ear to the ground, gathering information on gang crimes and gang members. Our team would arrest and prosecute anyone found wearing gang colors for even the most minor infractions like loitering outside a candy store. Our job was to keep the pressure on the gangs."

"Any promotions during this time?"

"Well, two years in, I made sergeant. One of the youngest ever."

"Why do you suppose that happened?"

Weldon grins modestly. "I received two commendations for meritorious service. Our group had put over a hundred gang bangers behind bars in our time on the street. The mayor liked that, which meant the chief liked it, which meant I got promoted."

"So your service was highly commendable. Well, what happened once you made sergeant?"

"That went on about a year and then I made detective. Working vice then robbery-homicide. Been there ever since."

"You've been working robbery-homicide how long, Detective Weldon?"

"About fourteen years, give or take."

"And over the past six months, have your duties been more on the robbery side or on the murder side?"

"Murder, definitely."

"Were you working robbery-homicide on July Fourth of this year?"

"Yes, I was."

"Describe your involvement, if any, with the Miranda Morales case that day."

Weldon leans back in the chair and crosses an ankle over a knee. His jacket falls open but he buttons it and uncrosses his legs, remembering the posture rules when testifying. Those rules go way back to the police academy and all cops know them.

"I came on duty at noon on July Fourth. A stack of paper-work maybe three inches deep took up most of my after-noon. This was interrupted with calls from witnesses and informants and vics--victims. I would have come off duty at nine o'clock except my partner called in sick and I had to work up his paperwork too. Paperwork doesn't have sick days, we always say. Someone has to do it, so partners cover for partners."

"Please continue."

"About eleven I got called out to the defendant's condo. Someone had called in a dead body. Later I found out it had been called in by defense counsel, Mr. Gresham."

"So Mr. Gresham was at the crime scene before you?"

Weldon's forehead wrinkles. "He was on the crime scene before any law enforcement official or officer."

"Did that present any problems?"

Weldon smiles wryly. "It certainly doesn't help. Defense lawyers have been known to clean up a crime scene before the cops arrive."

"Objection," I cry, "move to strike. Relevance. Foundation."

"Objection sustained. The jury will ignore the comment regarding defense lawyers. Please continue, Mr. Shaughnessy."

Shaughnessy turns away from the judge and back to his witness. His huge shoulders hulk over the lectern as he finds his place in his list of written questions.

"So you proceeded to the crime scene?"

"I did. My partner was off sick so I went alone. That's not that unusual. I arrived downstairs and waited for the uniformed officers to arrive and secure the scene. When that finally happened I went upstairs. By now, CSI had arrived and they joined me."

"What happened upstairs?"

"We buzzed and knocked and entered the condo. Michael

Gresham let us in. We found the defendant and Mr. Gresham's investigator around the dining table. The shooting scene was fresh--the blood wasn't completely dry. I talked to the three people and got some basic info. Then I investigated the scene itself. I told CSI what I wanted, including camera shots and angles, bullet trajectory particulars, hair and fiber, trace and transfer, and possible sources of DNA evidence of the crime."

"How long did that take?"

"Not long. Five minutes, maybe."

"Then what did you do?"

"I returned to the defendant and her lawyer and his assistant and asked some follow-up questions."

"What did you learn?"

"Not all that much. The defendant is a heavily experienced homicide prosecutor in the District Attorney's office. She wasn't going to give me a statement, if that's what you're driving at."

"Did she tell you anything about what happened?"

"Her lawyer wouldn't let her talk to me. All we obtained from her was gunshot residue swabs and a blood draw. We also searched the premises."

"Now, without going into any prior proceedings in court, was the gun that killed Darrell Harrow ever recovered?"

We have worked this out beforehand. Rather than tell the jury they "found" the gun in the trunk of my car, the jury is going to be told that the gun was recovered not in the defendant's possession. That's as far as it can go.

"Yes. The gun was recovered."

"Where from?"

Weldon looks hard at the jury. "Not in the defendant's possession."

"Very well. Now, for the record, please describe the victim."

"The victim was lying on his back, his head facing the north wall, the entrance wall. He was dead, I checked. So did the medical examiner, later. A Christian cross was upside down on the floor just at the top of his head. On the wall was the drawing of a pentagram. It was done in charcoal. Lab reports have identified the drawing charcoal as the same as what was in the defendant's fireplace."

"You said the victim was Darrell Harrow?"

"Yes. I did the ID based on his wallet's contents. This was later confirmed at the morgue by you, Mr. Shaughnessy, the District Attorney himself."

"What time did your team finish up at the crime scene?"

"The scene was turned back over to the defendant at twelve-oh-two the next day. Right about noon. That's when we left. I went straight home and went straight to bed. I was exhausted."

"I want to back up a minute and ask you about a cigarette butt. Did you recover one in this case?"

"Yes. One at the scene. And then there was a second one."

"Please tell us about that."

"Yes, my team searched Michael Gresham's law office and his file and found a cigarette butt inside the file."

"Describe the condition of the butt."

"It had lipstick on the end of the filter. It also had black smudge marks on the filter."

"Did you have the butt tested?"

"Yes, the Illinois Crime Lab tested the butt at my direction."

"What did they do?"

"DNA testing and spectrography."

"What, if anything, did that testing reveal?"

"That the defendant's DNA was on the cigarette butt. I think it was found in the lipstick marks. That's one thing. The second thing it revealed was that the black smudges on the cigarette butt were from the same charcoal that was used to draw the pentagram on the wall. It was the same charcoal as was in her fireplace."

"Whose fireplace?"

"The defendant's fireplace."

"So you're saying there were three tests done on three different charcoal samples?"

"Yes, the fireplace, the drawing, and the cigarette butt."

"And it was all the same charcoal?"

"Yes. The Crime Lab report came back conclusive."

The direct examination then re-tracks all the previous testimony, this time through adding in all the details. Exhibits are introduced. The murder weapon--Mira's gun--is introduced into evidence and discussed. One-hundred-and-ten photographs--previously marked and stipulated--are passed to the jury. It all takes hours.

37

I t is late afternoon. The State's case has been presented through Detective Weldon. Now the cleanup witnesses will be called and the case will be made. I won't be able to have it dismissed through the motion for directed verdict that is presented by defense attorneys at the end of the State's presentation. There is just enough time for me to cross-examine Weldon--to try to unring some bells--before we finish up for the day. I need to score some points so the jury doesn't go home and have all night to brood on the State's proof. Without cross-examination the prosecution's case is extremely persuasive. Miranda Morales is definitely guilty if we stop right here.

But we don't.

Shaughnessy steps away from the lectern and goes to his table. He flips through two legal pads, obviously looking for questions he may have forgotten to ask. His assistant whispers in Shaughnessy's ear and then both men nod. They are done.

"That's all the direct I have, Your Honor," Shaughnessy tells the judge.

The judge looks across at me. "Counsel? We have forty-five minutes remaining in our day. You may cross-examine."

My chance to change this trial forever comes around at last.

"Mr. Weldon, please tell the jury about the police beating I suffered as a result of my defending Mira Morales in this case, and please don't leave out the part where you come to my ICU room and try to talk to me and try to take my statement after I've been beaten so badly by four police officers that I suffer brain damage."

"Objection!" cries Shaughnessy and he is on his feet, requesting a sidebar. The judge waves us forward and we move to the side of the judge's throne farthest from the jury. Judge Itaglia isn't smiling; she's clearly unhappy.

"Counsel?" she says to Shaughnessy. "What's the basis for your objection?"

"Obviously counsel poisoned the jury. His injuries at the hands of police officers not involved in this case are totally irrelevant and totally prejudicial. We move to strike and ask the court to instruct counsel not to go there again."

"Mr. Gresham?" she whispers to me. "What say you?"

"Judge," I begin with all feigned innocence, "Mr. Shaughnessy told the jury I was guilty of removing evidence from the scene of this homicide. My question now will be followed up by additional questions that dispute those statements. To prevent me from doing that after the State has poisoned the jury would be prejudicial and grounds for reversal on appeal."

"I tend to agree with that, Mr. Gresham. The objection is overruled. You may continue. But only as far as you're trying to contradict his opening statement and not just trying to prejudice my jury."

"Judge," Shaughnessy continues, "this is outrageous! Not one of the police officers who were attacked by Mr. Gresham has or had anything to do with this case. It is totally irrelevant, the fight he had with them."

"Counsel," says the judge, "I would have agreed with you had you not opened the door by telling the jury Mr. Gresham removed evidence from the scene of the crime. Now I believe he has the right to explain his actions. Please retake your seats, gentlemen."

Shaughnessy sits at counsel table while I return to the lectern. I can hardly wait. I will open the wound slowly and let it bleed out.

"Mr. Weldon," I begin again, "please answer my question."

Detective Weldon slowly shows us the beginning of a smile. "I don't remember the question."

The court reporter reads it back at my request: "'Mr. Weldon, please tell the jury about the police beating I suffered as a result of my defending Mira Morales in this case, and please don't leave out the part where you come to my ICU room and try to talk to me and try to take my statement after I've been beaten so badly by four police officers that I suffered brain damage.'"

The witness turns red on his face and neck. It is quite pronounced above his starched white shirt.

"I don't know. I wasn't there."

"Tell us what you've read about it in departmental reports, then."

"According to the arresting officers, Mr. Gresham was being transported to the Cook County Jail and, in the parking lot, he suddenly turned and attacked the officers accompanying him. According to Officer James Miller he was struck and kicked by Mr. Gresham. In order to protect himself he used his nightstick to subdue Mr. Gresham. Mr. Gresham was injured in the melee and taken to the infirmary. He was later transferred to UC neuro."

"That's all?"

"That's all I've read."

"You didn't read anything about me being down on the ground and being kicked by the police officers?"

"No, sir."

"You didn't read anything about me being down on the ground and being kicked in the head repeatedly by the police officers?"

"No, sir."

"All right, then. Tell the jury about coming with your partner to my area in the ICU and attempting to take my statement."

"We didn't know how badly you were or weren't injured. Our hospital call was just routine."

"Do you recall being told by my lawyer that I had suffered a serious head injury and remembered nothing about the attack?"

"Something like that. We learned you were much worse off than we first thought."

"Would it surprise you to know, Detective Weldon, that I suffered brain damage at the hands of the police?"

"I don't know if I would call it surprised. If you were struck in the head, I guess that's always a brain injury to some degree."

"Would it surprise you to know that the beating and kicking I received caused such significant injury that I couldn't practice law for a long period of time?"

"It wouldn't surprise me, no."

"Would it surprise you to know that with regards to the item I retrieved from the crime scene that I simply forgot to notify the State that I wanted to turn it over for examination?"

"You're saying you were going to turn it in?"

"I'm asking you whether it would surprise you to know

that the beating I suffered at the hands and boots of the police simply removed all memory of the cigarette butt from my mind. Would that surprise you?"

"I don't know. Nothing much surprises me anymore."

"So when DA Shaughnessy told the jury that I removed evidence from the crime scene, he didn't actually know the whole story about why it was done and what I intended to do with it, did he?"

"I guess not."

"So would you like to rephrase what the jury has been told about my removing evidence?"

"I guess I would tell them that you meant to have it tested and turned over. At least that's your story now."

"Do you have any evidence to contradict my story?"

"No."

I pause and allow this Q and A to sink in with the jury, most of whom are furiously making notes. I take a drink of water from the glass on my table and I catch a look passing between the DA and the detective. It is an aggrieved look. It tells me they've caught their foot in a deep hole they should have anticipated, something they would have been wise to have left alone and not brought into this courtroom. Harley's eyes catch my own and I see a twinkle. She nods ever so slightly. Mira is sitting beside her writing. Her head is bowed and she is making notes on a legal pad opened many pages deep below the first one.

We resume.

"Now, Detective Weldon, I'd like to ask you to look over at the jury and tell them all the different ways I interfered with the crime scene before the police arrived on July Fourth."

Weldon lifts his hands but then drops them onto the ledge at the jury box.

"I can't" he says. His mouth is grim and his voice very quiet.

"What do you mean you can't?"

"I don't know how you interfered."

"Well, you told the jury I'd been alone at the crime scene and that defense attorneys alone with crime scenes are very suspicious. Do you remember saying that?"

"Something like that, yes."

"So look over and tell the jury what it was you meant. How was I suspicious?"

"I don't know."

"You don't know of any ways, do you?"

"No."

"So you were attempting to mislead the jury, weren't you?"

"Not mislead. Not exactly."

"Then you were lying to the jury, weren't you?"

"No, I wasn't lying."

"Then tell the jury how your words about me were truthful."

"I can't. I don't know how."

"That's because you were lying to the jury, isn't it?"

"Objection! Asked and answered."

"Sustained. Counsel, please move along."

I nod and skim over my notes, looking like I'm shifting gears. But I am not.

"Tell the jury how I disturbed the dead body of Darrell Harrow to take the blame away from Miranda Morales."

"I can't."

"You can't because there's no evidence I did that; am I correct?"

"Yes."

"Tell the jury how I prepared the defendant herself for your appearance on the scene."

"Well, you told her not to talk to me."

"No, I'm asking for how I changed her testimony, her physical attributes, anything that proves I somehow interfered before you arrived on the scene to take the blame away from Miranda Morales."

"I don't know."

"You don't know because you had no evidence I had done anything when you told the jury that defense attorneys can't be trusted at the scene of a crime, correct?"

"Correct."

I pause to go over my notes and take a drink of water. Breathing space: that's what I'm giving the witness. I don't want the jury to get the impression that I'm badgering him.

Then I continue.

"So you tried to mislead the jury about Ms. Morales and what I might have done, correct?"

"I guess."

"You guess or am I correct that you tried to mislead the jury."

"I didn't intend to. If I did mislead them, I was wrong."

"You lied to the jury."

"I wouldn't call it a lie."

"What would you call it?"

The court interrupts.

"Ladies and gentlemen, we're going to stop here for the day."

Judge Itaglia then gives the jury the usual admonitions about speaking to anyone about the case and about avoiding all news accounts of the case and the rest of it.

When the jury is taken out and returned to the jury room, the court declares us in recess. The press scrambles to the aisle leading out of the courtroom, prepared to get comments from counsel.

Bobbie Carroll from Channel Five catches me and Harley outside the courtroom. Her cameraman has us in his viewfinder and she's ready with her microphone.

"Mr. Gresham," she says, "Is your defense of Miranda Morales going to be that the police lied to the jury after they beat you up?"

For once, I stop and respond.

"Our defense is that Miranda Morales didn't shoot anyone. And the State knows it can't prove she did, so they're attempting to come after me and what I might have done to hurt their case."

"What have you done to hurt their case?" the reporter asks.

I smile and look into the camera lens.

"What have I done? I showed up here. That's what I've done to hurt their case."

Harley and I then turn away and make our way to the elevators.

It has been a good first day.

"You know," Harley whispers on the ride downstairs, "they really can't prove Mira did this. At first I was skeptical, but you're making me into a convert."

I smile at her. "They can't prove it because they arrested the wrong person."

The doors open onto the lobby. Now we can speak freely.

"So what are we going to do to prove they arrested the wrong person?"

"I think we have to put the killer on the witness stand and expose him."

"How do we do that?"

"The cop with the gun in his back pocket. Tory Stormont."

"Yes."

Harley smiles and pats me on the back as we wait at the curb for Marcel to arrive with my car.

"We don't prove it," she says. "We intimate it."

"We suggest it."

"We offer it as a possibility."

"So the jury has a way out, a way to find Mira not guilty."

"Exactly."

"This is going to get very interesting."

Marcel pulls up to the curb and we clamber inside, Harley up front, me in back.

"Very interesting," I say.

"And the motion to strike won't be necessary," she says. "No need to strike what the DA told the jury about your involvement in the crime. You killed them on that today."

"It did go rather well, I thought."

She sighs and looks out of her window.

"Thank God for sympathetic judges," she says.

"Thank God for fair judges," I reply. "She was only doing her job. Do we still call Shaughnessy as our first witness?"

I've been thinking about this. A part of me thinks that maybe calling him would be overkill. All he can really say is that he was wrong in his comments about me.

But I quickly discard any worry about overkill. He can't be killed in front of our jury enough. I'm ready to take him on when it's my turn. My guess is that he will toss and turn in his bed tonight because he knows what's coming.

For me, it can't come fast enough.

38

Thursday, trial is spent with the District Attorney trying to rehabilitate Detective Weldon after the beating he took yesterday at my hands. But it is difficult because I get to re-cross-examine and I simply hammer home my points a second time.

Then the District Attorney spends several hours presenting his scene witnesses: two CSI's testify about the scene and evidence retrieved; then he presents his medical testimony by the medical examiner who did the autopsy for the Medical Examiner's Office.

After trial I head back to the office, where I meet with Marcel. He has been trying all week to serve a subpoena on Tory Stormont, who I want to put on the witness stand and implicate in the murder. It was Stormont whose arrival at the scene of the crime through the lobby of the condo building isn't found on CCTV security video except in civvies—but that's only a maybe, not a sure thing. We do see him a second time, in his police uniform at the upstairs elevator but that footage isn't preceded by him coming through the lobby.

And it is Stormont who, at the elevator and inside the elevator and coming off the elevator in the basement is seen carrying a gun in his hip pocket. Finally, Marcel has spoken with Brianna Finlayton and she's going to appear by subpoena and describe Stormont as the man who came to her apartment and threatened her and had the case against himself dismissed. Do these things add up to a murder conviction against Stormont for the killing of Darrell Harrow? Certainly not. But they totally implicate him in that murder by virtue of his departing the scene with a gun in his back pocket and by his demonstrating his willingness to commit a crime by going to Brianna Finlayton and threatening her as well as her family.

"I don't know, Boss," says Marcel, "I've staked out his home and haven't seen him coming or going. I've staked him out at work and he never appears during his shift."

"You're getting his work hours from someone on the inside?"

Marcel nods, saying, "Straight from the horse's mouth. His sergeant is feeding me the inside story on the guy's shifts. It seems like he's calling in sick every day."

"Where's he calling from?"

"He says he's at home, but I can't locate him there. Or maybe he's just not answering his door all week. I don't know. He's a will-o'-the-wisp, I guess."

This isn't good. Our case dies on the vine without Stormont. My plan is to put him on the witness stand and ask him all the questions I can about his possible involvement in Harrow's death. It's not that his answers will matter as much as the implications I can make by simply asking him the questions, much as I did with Detective Weldon. Without Stormont with us in court I don't even get to ask the questions. It's not looking good, not at all.

So I send Marcel back out to his house. I've asked him to get the manager of Stormont's apartment complex to let him inside on the pretense that Marcel is a family member to Stormont, who isn't answering his door and who the family fears is ill. It might work; it might not. If not, we might need to pick his lock and let ourselves inside: a very dangerous proposition given that Stormont is a police officer and that means he will be armed and very dangerous. He will understand that he has the right to shoot anyone who breaks in; this is enough to put the quietus on any notions of a break-in.

IN TRIAL on Friday morning Shaughnessy shifts over to a police officer who was at the scene. He testifies about keeping the scene from becoming contaminated. He follows it with a diary of all who came and went during the time the shooting scene was under the control of the Chicago Police Department. His name is Tomas Algernon and he is a Latino from Guatemala who has been naturalized since coming here fifteen years ago as a young boy. I tell the judge that I do have questions for the witness and step up to the lectern.

"Officer Algernon, one name that appears on your diary is the name of Tory Stormont. Do you see that on your list?"

"Yes, I do."

"And who is Tory Stormont?"

"He's a Chicago police officer."

"Do you know him personally?"

"Not really. I had to get his badge number and ask him his name. Just seen him around the station. That's about it."

"Now, it says on here that he arrived on-scene after you arrived, is that correct?"

"Correct."

"And you arrived sometime after eleven o'clock--I think you have it down as eleven-oh-four, correct?"

"That would be correct."

"Were any other police officials there when you arrived?"

"I arrived in the lobby and waited, as instructed by the dispatcher. There were no other police officers there."

"Or detectives?"

"Or detectives. Detective Weldon arrived about five minutes later. Close behind him was CSI and close behind them was a member of the medical examiner's staff. No, I'm wrong. The M.E. came much later, about three in the morning if you look at my diary."

"Describe what happened after you all had assembled in

the lobby of the building."

"We all went upstairs to twenty-five in one elevator. We got off and proceeded to the defendant's door."

"And then?"

"Detective Weldon rang the bell. Then he pounded on the door. Finally you came and let us in."

"What time did you actually enter the condo?"

"That would have been at eleven-sixteen."

"What did you do?"

"I was posted at the front door. I had the diary to run."

"What can you tell us about Tory Stormont?"

"He helped with the search of the premises, far as I know."

"What time did he leave?"

"He came and went. When the last time was, I don't know. I've got it down as two-seventeen in the morning but he actually might have come back after that."

"He might have returned?"

"Yes, he might have returned. With the uniforms we don't make entries for every time they come and go because we'd run out of paper. I mean some guys are getting police tape, sometimes they're getting traffic cones, or first aid supplies, or video equipment--you never know. So you just kind of ignore them."

"Do you show him returning after he left at two-seventeen?"

"Officer Stormont? No, I don't show him returning. And I don't have an independent recollection, either. It was a kind of boring scene compared to some we get. Sometimes we got family members trying to get in, or kids crying, or neighbors trying to give us statements, or other police jurisdictions showing up, or FBI snooping around. You just never know. But this was just CPD and the M.E.'s office."

"When Officer Stormont left the crime scene at two-seventeen, did he take anything with him?"

"Well, you'd have to look on the inventory sheets for who took what. I don't have that information."

"Let me put it this way. Do you recall him carrying anything out when he left?"

"I have no recollection of him leaving, period. So I'm guessing he probably wasn't taking anything or I probably would remember. We're pretty tight on what leaves an active crime scene."

I then end my examination of Officer Algernon. He has been able to provide very little except that he did place Tory Stormont at the scene after the main police force arrived. Which leaves me asking, how did he get inside the building? There's no video of his arrival. I make a note to review the video with Marcel again.

Next up is Natty McMann, who was present at the Democratic fundraiser and heard Mira arguing with the victim. Natty testifies about what he saw and heard. I don't bother to cross-examine him except for a few questions to prove that Mira was not the instigator of the upset; he is an eyewitness to an event that is very damning but if I belabor any of it he just gets to tell his story again. So I ask very few questions.

The victim's widow, Denise Harrow, testifies about the loss of her husband and what it's meant to her and their children. She is a good woman, a respiratory technician who labors at twelve hour shifts in a local hospital; the jury likes her. It is prudent to leave her alone in her grief and anger, and I do.

Next comes a records custodian who enters Harrow's human resources file into evidence. It turns out he was an exemplary employee with no black marks in his file. We should be so lucky as to find a suitable replacement for him. Everyone can see that.

The state then calls a crime lab firearms technician who testifies about the gun, the caliber, the firearms and bullet testing that was done and she finally concludes with the proof necessary to establish that it was, in fact, Mira's gun that murdered Darrell Harrow.

A shooting reconstructionist then testifies about the direction and angle the death shot traveled. It is his testimony that the bullet came from someone who was probably lying on the sofa in Mira's living room, someone with her arm raised just enough to point the pistol at Harrow's head as he came in through the door. It is an upwards angle the bullet travels, indicating that the shooter was lower than the target, indicating, again, that the shooter was very likely reclining. They have no way of knowing for sure that they have anticipated Mira's story to the effect that she was asleep on the sofa when the shooting occurred--at least that part of her story that places her on the couch. I am struck with just how accurate shooting reconstruction can be and I am hopeful we don't need to call Mira to testify, which would only lead to her admission that it was she, in fact, who was lying on the couch when the door opened and Harrow came inside her condo.

By late Friday afternoon, many witnesses have been called out of order, which is common in criminal cases, given the fact many of these professional witnesses are testifying in other courtrooms on the same trial days as our own.

The state finally rests its case and the usual motion for directed verdict is offered by me and it is of course denied. The State has made a prima facie case and now it's the defense's turn.

Then we are dismissed for the weekend.

Very little cross-examination was required as the witnesses basically did not hurt us that much. Yes, there was a crime scene and yes, evidence was collected. Yes, there was an autopsy and yes, the victim died by a gunshot wound at the crime scene. Yes, the victim left behind a beautiful family and yes, they will miss him greatly and forevermore. But there is no eyewitness, and that hurts the state's case more than anything else.

Returning to our office, Harley and I discuss our feelings about the case where it stands right now. The jury has learned that there was a relationship between Darrell Harrow and Miranda Morales. They learned through Natty McMann that a fight ensued between the lovers on the night of July Fourth and that two hours later--give or take--Darrell Harrow lay dead on Miranda Morales' living room floor, shot to death by Miranda Morales' gun. The circumstantial case is very strong at this point and, if we present no evidence, offer no explanations, and fail to prove an alternative theory, Mira will be found guilty of first degree murder and spend the rest of her days in prison.

From the front seat of my Mercedes, driving us back to the office, Marcel listens to all of this. He is quiet--a good sign, because when Marcel is quiet that means the wheels are spinning in his head. And very often that means he's close to offering up a solution for whatever problem we're facing.

"So, Boss," Marcel slowly begins, "I'm thinking we need to confront this Tory Stormont over the weekend. Bust into his place if we have to in order to serve the subpoena. I'm thinking he took out Harrow because Harrow was prose-cuting him. Plus, we can play the video with him leaving the premises with a gun in his back pocket. Am I right?"

"We do need him," Harley offers. "But so far he's refused me every time I've asked to meet with him. In fact, he doesn't even answer my phone messages I've been leaving at the police department."

"I'll double down on that," Marcel adds. "I spent all after-noon bird-dogging his apartment. Still nothing. The manager also refused to let me inside Stormont's apartment. He wasn't buying that maybe the guy was ill. He said the guy's a cop and someone might get shot if he uses his passkey. So he wouldn't cooperate in my little scam. Imagine that."

"Do we have any other way of contacting him? Where does the guy live? Where have you been hanging out?"

"Arlington; his place is guarded day and night by other cops. They're protecting him from those folks in South Chicago. Jesse Jackson and his Rainbow people have condemned him often enough that his life's in peril every minute."

"Any family living with him?"

"No. Divorced, lives alone, mostly keeps to himself from what I can gather. You think I should drive over with you and see if he'll talk to you? See where we get together? Maybe the manager will take you more seriously than just me?"

"I'm thinking," I say. "If he won't even respond to Harley, he sure as hell won't talk to me. So I'm nix on that. I think we need to step it up."

"How about we bust in, kidnap the guy and force a confession out of him?" Marcel is only half-kidding. But we both know the guy's armed. There's zero opportunity to break-in. Way, way too dangerous.

"What if we sued him for some civil tort and took his deposition," Harley says. "You still don't want to do that?"

"We talked about it before," I say, "but he's not going to admit anything to us in a deposition. Not if he's the shooter. Look, let's get back to the office, have a cup of coffee and let's really think about this. This has to happen. We have to get him served."

"Good idea, Boss," says Marcel. "Have you back to the office in twenty minutes, tops."

Back at the office, Marcel and I loop though the CCTV footage, trying to spot Tory Stormont's arrival in the building wearing a police uniform. We've done this before but this time we flip through frame-by-frame. No luck; there simply is no video of Stormont arriving at the building and coming through the lobby wearing a police uniform.

We spot several men who match his build more or less, but out of them we cannot really get good facial shots and both are dressed in civvies. Two are wearing porkpie hats, one made of what appears to be a summer straw and one made of blue sailcloth. The first guy has sunglasses perched on top of his hat; the second guy does not. We then loop ahead and we see second guy get off the elevator on twenty-five. We see him walk out of view from the elevator. He's also carrying a shoulder bag that is large enough to hold a police uniform. Very clever if he did it, arriving in civvies then changing into his police threads. My guess? He probably let himself into Mira's unit and changed out his clothes there. Then when she arrived home he subdued her in order to shoot Harrow, who he knew was close behind her.

But can I prove all this?

Not yet. But I'm sure moving in that direction.

39

F riday, after trial is recessed, we can't come up with a plan, Marcel and I, for getting a subpoena served on Tory Stormont. More than ever, I need him at trial. He's my secret weapon.

When we get back to the office we sit down and wrack our brains. There's just no way to get to someone if they're armed and holed up and don't want to talk to you. In the end we head out for Arlington. I want to take a look at the setup for myself.

We take Marcel's truck. He's driving and I'm riding shotgun without a clue as to what we'll do once we get to Stormont's complex. At the last minute, Harley demands to come along. She's persistent and refuses to be denied, so we finally relent and here she is with us. She's in the backseat of the crew-cab. Before we leave, Marcel has me slip on my shoulder holster and gun. He's already armed, as usual. Harley is told about my gun. We offer to put a pistol in her purse or inside her jacket pocket. But she refuses, saying she won't be getting into the line of fire so she has no need of a gun. She also tells us she knows nothing about combat shooting and asks me whether I do. I have to admit I know very little and that what I do know is what Marcel has taught me out at the range. In true Marcel fashion he began my lesson with the admonition, "First rule of combat shooting is don't get shot."

Right.

Westbound traffic out of the city is heavy. It's Friday night and people who work downtown are racing home to get the weekend started. Plus, many city dwellers are headed west to homes they keep in the suburbs with small horse acreages.

Twenty-five minutes later, we take the Arlington Road off-ramp and head south into the city.

At Essex Road we head west for five minutes and finally arrive at an apartment sprawl that extends along both sides of the street. It's a neighborhood area that is quite old, with huge ancient oak trees and maples, houses set far back from the sidewalks, while the apartments themselves are relatively new--having been built in the last twenty years. The neighborhood houses are probably from the 1940's and earlier.

Friday night is quiet along here. We park on the far end of the street and climb out of the truck without slamming the doors--an unnecessary precaution but we've all seen enough TV that we think that's how it should be done. For just a minute I am astonished at how ridiculous it is for the lawyer in a case to be out chasing down an armed witness. But I let go of that thought. As long as Marcel's willing then I want to be with him to offer my moral support if nothing else. Firing my gun is the last thing on my mind. Nevertheless, its weight below my armpit and thumping against my ribs as I walk is reassuring on the one hand and a reminder on the other hand that I'm way outside my league. This suspect is a cop, someone trained in firefights with guns, someone I have no plans of shooting it out with. I almost wish I hadn't brought the gun along, as if that would somehow exempt me from participating in any fireworks.

"Cross here," Marcel says softly, and we follow him across Essex Road.

We step up on the curb and cut across the grass strip, cross the sidewalk, and then catch the concrete walkway leading up to two buildings in the complex. The place is French Provincial, brick exterior, steep roofs, tall second-story windows with arched tops and porches with full balustrades. All of this detail is registering in my mind as the fear uncoils inside my chest. It is as if my mind is taking full inventory of every item before my eyes. Marcel points to a window three down from the front wall and we begin creeping along the walk toward it.

The window is dark; no light is emitted from the rear or other rooms, either. The unit has the appearance of being uninhabited but we know just how deceiving that can be. Again with the TV shows. Marcel ducks below the window and creeps up to the door. With the flat of his hand he pounds the door. Of course there is no response from inside. He pounds harder. Within ten seconds the next door down opens, startling all three of us. I find myself reaching for my gun and then stop my motion with a stupid half-smile on my face. I have no business having the gun with me; that was pure reflex and it was totally out-of-sync with reality, for the head that pops out of the next door belongs to a neighbor lady. She eyes us querulously, as if we have interrupted her TV viewing with our racket.

"He's not home," she says through the screen of her front door.

"Any idea where he's gone?" Marcel asks.

"My husband said he left and asked him to keep an eye on his place. That's why I opened my door. He said some unsavory characters had been trying to roust him out and he was leaving for a few days, that it was connected to police business and we shouldn't be alarmed. But we are alarmed. Do I need to call the police or will you be leaving?"

"What?" says Harley, stepping nearer to the woman. "It's illegal in Arlington for someone to knock on someone's door? I don't think so, lady. Now why don't you get back to *The Voice* or whatever you're watching and let us do our job."

But she doesn't leave. "What job might that be?"

"Actually, we're with the Cook County Court system. This police officer is needed in court and we're trying to track him down."

"You got ID?" she asks, surprisingly persistent. We should

all have neighbors like this one when we're away, I'm thinking.

Without missing a beat, Harley produces her wallet from an inside jacket pocket and displays her bar card to the woman.

"That only means you're a damn lawyer," the woman says distastefully. "Show me something that says you're from the court or I *am* calling the cops."

"How about this," says Marcel. "How about you get back inside your own place and mind your own damn business! We have as much right to be on this goddam sidewalk as you do, lady!"

The woman steps back and the door slowly closes behind her.

Marcel turns to us and winks. "Gets them every time, a little sinful cursing."

"Well done," says Harley. "Couldn't have put it better myself."

"Okay, so where are we?" I ask. I'm very uncomfortable being out here at night when there's a chance we have an armed suspect behind the door we're standing around. It's probably not our best thinking that's got us here.

"We have two choices," says Marcel. "We can either go home and forget about it, or we can wait around until we get eyes on the little bastard. Me, I'm for sticking around. But then I'm paid by the hour," he smiles.

"I'm for waiting around too," says Harley.

I start to reply, "I'm--"

When suddenly there's a gunshot from inside the cop's apartment. I turn in time to see Harley's hands fly up to her chest. She teeters on her feet and then, in one motion, crumples to the ground. Marcel and I stand over her, and in the dim light of the courtyard we see a red flower spreading across her chest.

"My God," she says in a small voice, "I'm shot and I'm dying."

"Quick," shouts Marcel, "give me your handkerchief to plug the hole."

He knows I always carry one. I rip it from my back pocket and watch aghast as he slowly threads it into the hole, then he stands straddling Harley and takes her by her wrists. He steps backwards, drawing her prone body up against the wall just down from Stormont's window. A bullet hole the diameter of a cigar can be seen in the window glass, I realize, and I run to the end of the walk nearest where we entered the courtyard.

"Come back!" hisses Marcel. "Help me get her out of here."

With a sudden boldness I push myself from out of the shadows back into the dim light of the sidewalk and approach Marcel and Harley.

"Take her legs up under your arms and start walking backward. She's light."

I do as ordered and soon find myself doing what I never in a million years thought I would ever be doing: carrying one of my employees out of a firefight. It honestly hadn't crossed my mind that there might actually be someone in the cop's apartment after we knocked and there was no answer. It just hadn't registered with me that we three presented an easy target.

As we steal along the shadowy wall I realize Marcel is talking into his phone, which he is carrying in his breast pocket. Evidently he has called 911 and he's giving directions to us. At that exact second, the cop's apartment door suddenly flies open and I see a shadowy figure emerge and begin running directly away from us. Of course there will be a parking lot out beyond the quadrangle wall he's headed for. There always is. But we cannot abandon Harley and run after him.

Reaching the front of the building, we ease Harley down onto the sidewalk, on her back, and Marcel kneels and listens to her chest. Then he puts his ear to her mouth. Now he pulls her lower jaw open and pushes his index finger around the inside of her mouth. Then he is breathing into her mouth and intermittently pumping her chest with the heels of his hands. Coming out of my stupor I realize he's breathing for her and that he could use my help. So I take over with the hands on the chest while he continues breathing air into her lungs. It's a very primitive CPR when it's done without instruments or cannulas or bags of any kind, but it is reputed to save lives so we continue.

"Harley!" I hear him saying. "Open your eyes!"

The eyes remain closed. I look down at her in shock and disbelief. This beautiful, gifted woman is, I'm realizing, probably already dead and there's absolutely nothing we can do about it.

We keep applying CPR anyway. Then the EMT's are there and taking over and Marcel and I are ordered to stand back. We surrender our positions and watch as the pros take over. There are stethoscopes and moments of listening for pulses and breath sounds, but the EMT's faces remain grim, stony, as if a battle has already been lost. A portable EKG is in place and its leads are attached. The monitor lights up and all eyes fall to its small window and its LEDs. They remain glued there for a good fifteen seconds then, one by one, they look up and resume their CPR and ministrations but this time without much enthusiasm. I only sense this, as the efforts are mechanically the same. But there's a dead woman on the sidewalk before us and their faces show it.

At last the nurse among them calls it.

"She's gone," she says. "No pulse, no breath sounds, flat-line EKG. I'm calling it. Time of death is seven forty-eight p.m. Somebody make a note and let's stand aside and let the M.E. in here."

The nurse turns to Marcel.

"The bullet pierced her heart. She was gone before you called us."

Marcel shakes his head and it's clear he's losing control. "I should've known! I should've known he was inside."

"Wait here. Lots of police officers are waiting to talk to you."

A sudden rush of tears fills my eyes as the reality comes screaming into my brain. Harley is dead. The words bounce around inside my head and I hear them with diminishing disbelief each time they come around. She really is gone. Her body is small and looks almost child-like there on the cement at our feet. Then I feel a strong hand encircle my upper arm and I realize I'm being steered away from her body. I am moved across the grass strip up over the curb and placed into the backseat of a police cruiser.

I have been detained.

40

T en minutes tick by. I am still detained.

    Finally, I look up and try to figure out where they've taken Marcel. And why isn't he right here with me?

Then I think I see him in the next car over, an unmarked black Ford with fat tires. He sits there in the backseat, his chin on his chest, his upper body moving slowly back and forth. I want to rap on my window and call out to him but I don't. Something tells me not to draw attention to myself at this moment.

So I sit and stare straight ahead. It occurs to me--the lawyer kicking in--that they have no right to have me detained. I reach up and try the door handle. It is locked. I really am being detained. So what's that make me, a suspect of some sort?

Looking straight ahead I see the tight knot of cops and medical personnel surrounding Harley's body. A wheeled cart has been pushed into their midst and, even as I watch, her limp body is lifted up to the cart and she is gently placed upon it. Many hands have helped move her from the dirty sidewalk up onto the sterile-looking cart. But it's too late for sterility, I realize as I watch the little drama unfold. It's too late because there will be no more medical effort on her behalf. There is, simply put, no reason to keep her body sterile any longer. At this point it's done out of respect for the dead.

Harley is dead.

My mind cannot even conceive of the ramifications of this news. A small cry works its way up through my chest and escapes my mouth. I realize I am angry and that I am calling out for attention.

"Someone come talk to me!" I cry against the thick glass of the backseat prisoner enclosure.

But no one gives a damn. I'm unsure anyone can even hear me anyway.

So I call out again. This time I see a slightly familiar face turn from the tight clutch of cops overseeing things, and it begins moving toward me. Then I realize. Detective Jamison Weldon.

What the hell?

He's supposed to be home, escaped from the courtroom where we've all been pent up all week. So what in the world is he doing out here at this homicide scene?

Which is the moment I realize. Detective Weldon and Officer Stormont are connected. I don't know how--I haven't made it that far yet--I only know that it's true. There is a link between them of some kind. And I suddenly know that if I can understand that link then I will be very close to solving the mystery of the murder that occurred in my client's living room. No, Weldon isn't here in an official capacity as the detective on call. Hell, this is Arlington. He's not a member of their police force; he's Chicago PD. But who called him?

Then it comes into focus for me. Stormont called him. Probably before the shooting incident. He was probably on his way over to lend a hand to Stormont, to run us off from his front porch. But where were the other cops, the ones we were told were watching out for Stormont 24/7? That in itself is a mystery. But Weldon *is* here. That picture is becoming clearer by the minute.

My mind keeps going over it: Stormont and Detective Weldon. The murder happened on Weldon's watch because that's when it was supposed to happen so that Weldon would be the one to answer the call. That's why Weldon's partner was off sick that day. He was supposed to be off sick. There it was, neat and tidy. They were in it together. That's how Stormont got away with the murder weapon in his back pocket. Otherwise he would have been questioned about Mira's purse and gun after he searched her bedroom. Weldon knew Stormont would find the gun. And he knew Stormont would remove the gun in order to place it inside the trunk of my car.

But why me? They sure as hell didn't know I would be on the scene to help Mira.

Of course it didn't matter who came to help her. Whoever

it was, they would be framed with the planted gun. Only I had gone a step further and even given them a second shot at me with the cigarette butt. They must absolutely love me, I'm thinking, as Weldon approaches the car where I'm being held.

Then a funny thing happens. He comes up to where he's standing just outside my window when he looks down on me and I can see his face up close and in focus. He gives me a fierce smile from ear to ear. Then he shakes his head and walks on by. No one saw him do it and there are no witnesses standing around watching.

But the message is clear.

They knew we were coming and they had been ready. Now one of our trial team is dead and the other is being held on a Friday night in the back of a cop car in connection with--God knows what. A murder? In the next second I realize the holster beneath my armpit is empty. They have seized my gun. And why wouldn't they? It is evidence. Evidence of my plot to come here and shoot Tory Stormont. Terrified for his life, he had shot one us first. Then he had fled, running for his life. I can hear the story already. We are about to be prosecuted under the felony-murder rule which says that one who is participating in a felony crime at the moment someone dies is guilty of the murder as if he pulled the trigger himself. It doesn't matter that I was only standing outside the door, waiting for someone to answer. There was a shooting and I was there, engaged in the crime of--what? They will figure out what. Obstruction of Justice, maybe, a Class Four felony in Illinois. There is a whole book full of felonies to lay on me and Marcel. They only have to choose. Then we can be charged with murder and Mira's trial will go to a mistrial.

And there's more coming into focus. She will lose the election and Lamont Johnstone will step in. Lamont, friend of the police union, friend of Tory Stormont, the poor cop who was threatened and had to shoot his way out of his home to avoid being attacked.

Suddenly my head drops to my knees and I throw up.

Then I repeat.

I lay my face on my knees and the pain starts surging up through my chest, into my eyes, sweeping across my face as I am wracked with the horror of what I have stumbled into. Not only is the trial lost, not only am I lost, but Harley is dead.

And, according to the law they're going to pull out and use against Marcel and me, we killed her.

We are guilty of murdering one of our own.

It's a short jump from there to visions of a long prison term.

At that very moment, I feel like I deserve no less. My own stupidity, my own need to win Mira's trial at any cost, brought me to this place. Brought me here with a gun hidden on my person.

And in the next breath it all comes rushing out in a long, pained cry.

The gun, my gun, hidden on my body.

I have no license to carry a concealed weapon. The application to do so is still in my office, beneath a stack of papers that had priority, waiting to be filed.

Weldon's face appears again outside the window. Only this time it is all in my mind.

I am losing control and then, in a rush, I am gone, unable to think another thought that would require that I consider the reality that has grown up all around me.

I am finished.

41

I t is six-forty-five on Saturday morning and we've just marched into Pod 3 eating hall. I was brought here to the Cook County Jail last night by the Arlington PD, and I've had the hell scared out of me all night. Imagine me with thirty-six men, each having committed a really evil deed, spending the night together on concrete slabs, the great majority drunk or stoned, and waking up feeling refreshed. Honestly, I have never felt worse. Marcel has disappeared out of my life. I have no idea where he's been taken. He would handle this much better. I'm a nervous, twitchy, train wreck who stayed awake all night in enormous fear for his life.

A jailer guides us into the tables and I find myself sitting between two gigantic black men with the shaved heads and the black panthers whose legs curl around the upper arms. They both only stare straight ahead when I twist my legs and body into the small space separating them. Each tightens the body side that touches me so that I don't feel flesh touching my shoulders but instead feel case-hardened steel. Nothing is said as we eat, of course, and after five minutes the guards have us on our feet and filing out the other end of the place so our replacements can get to the tables and cheese slice with apple.

They march us directly back down the hall to an area new to me: the dayroom. It is octagonal, as wide as a normal pool, with back-facing TV's in the center, each tuned to a different channel and adding a different soundtrack to our day. I make my way around the exterior walls until I am met by a wood chair. Making myself as small as possible, I let myself down on it. No one pays any attention to me and for that I'm hugely relieved. These are not the kind of people I'm around even as an extremely experienced criminal lawyer because in here no one is putting on his court manners in an attempt to endear. What you see is what it is, I would tell one of them if asked how I see the place. What you see is what it is.

I do not relax.

Nearly two hours later, I hear my name being called. I find that I have fallen asleep upright on the wood chair because it's daylight and there are lots of eyes about, making it safe to snooze off. My head jerks up from my chest and I wipe a thread of drool off my chain and look around. It is a blue-uniformed jailer and he's calling me over. So, I go.

"You're Michael Gresham?"

"Yes. How did you know?"

"It's a Caucasian name and not a Washington or Jefferson."

"Oh." Racist, but I think no one gives a damn in here.

"Your lawyer wants to see you. She has a right to come in twenty-four-seven. And you also have the right to refuse to see her. Do you want to accept her visit or reject it?"

"Accept."

"Come through the two doors and I'll be waiting to take you to her."

"I'm coming."

The doors buzz sequentially, fifteen seconds apart, and we meet. He tells me to walk ahead of him down the hall and through two doors to where the attorney conference room is located and where my lawyer is waiting. So I lead the way and am buzzed through two more doors.

He steps up behind me and says, "Turn left, second door."

I obey. At a small table someone is waiting for me.

Then here she is. Danny Gresham, the most beautiful wife in the world.

The jailer leaves the small room, closing the door behind him.

Danny and I run at each other and collapse in a bear hug. I am kissing her hair, the top of her head, her face, snuggling against her shoulders with my own, and we are just crying how glad we are to see each other. Tears roll down her face but mine remain in my eyes, making the scene a blurry one for me.

"Thank God," I say.

We sit down beside each other, hands clutched and squeezing.

"What am I charged with?"

"So far? Illegal concealed carry. Who knows what's close behind, but you can bet something is. I'm thinking felony-murder from what I'm seeing in the papers and hearing on TV. Seriously, Michael? You? In a shootout? With a *gun*? What in God's name were you thinking!"

"You're not sounding like my lawyer. You're sounding like my wife. Maybe even my mother; forgive me, but it's true. Let's try talking about how the hell we're going to get me out of this before all the rest of the stuff that's going to make some counselor a million bucks. I did everything you mentioned and no one regrets it more than me. But I could regret it even more if I weren't locked up in here."

"Bail hasn't been set. You can't get out."

"Oh, my God!" I moan. This can't really be happening. It's Saturday morning and I won't see a judge until Monday. "Can't you call a judge this morning? How about Judge Itaglia. She's going to want me in her court Monday morning. Not in some criminal court down the hall."

She's way ahead of me. "Listen to me. I've got an idea. We go to Judge Itaglia and notify her you're being held in jail because Tory Stormont shot one of Mira's defense team. We tell her that Stormont is your witness and we make the case to her that you have been arrested in order to deprive Mira Morales of due process in not getting to call Stormont to testify and in arresting you and depriving her of her counsel of choice. What do you think?"

"I think it's pure genius. Let's make it in the form of a petition for habeas corpus where I'm delivered into her court today and where she issues an order releasing me on my own recognizance. If you can get that order, I'm out of here today."

"I'm on my way, Michael."

"I love you just for trying. Thank you. Oh, and one other thing."

"Yes?"

"Do this for Marcel too."

"Done."

BACK IN THE DAYROOM, I go so far as to sit down with a dozen other inmates and watch cartoons featuring the talking crows. I try to remember whether I ever watched these things; I do this to make myself recall my reality as I feel it slipping away in Pod 3.

Five hours later, the same jailer as before comes for me. I'm starting to recognize a jailer face or two. This one has the job of moving solo inmates around the halls. Which explains why he's enormous and heavily muscled. No one's trying to get the jump on this guy. He guides me back toward the attorney conference room except this time we pass it by, turn right, and buzz through a final door. Now I'm in the front office of the jail and Danny is waiting there, the bail order spread before the assignments officer.

"Welcome out," Danny says, and I am handed a bag containing my clothes and told to step into a side room and shed the jail garb. I comply and five minutes later I emerge ready to walk outside, get in a car, and get the hell away.

Then we are under the overcast skies of November Fifth.

The election is three days away.

42

W hen I walk into Judge Itaglia's chambers at eight o'clock Monday morning, as I've been told to do, I am immediately greeted with the news, from the judge's secretary, that officer Tory Stormont has been subpoenaed by Judge Itaglia to appear in her court at eight o'clock. The clerk then looks up from his screen and tells me he's been told the officer is in the building, that he's waiting in the courtroom. Evidently he was picked up at his house by CPD and brought straight to court up here on California Avenue.

Judge Itaglia gathers us around her desk in chambers-- Shaughnessy, Danny, Mira, and me--and she calls court to order.

She begins. "We're going to take a look at what facts the court was asked to rely on in releasing Mr. Gresham from Cook County Jail. There were many verbal representations made to me by Danny Gresham and the court needs to determine if those are confirmed or misstated. If confirmed, the release on recognizance will continue. If misstated, Mr. Gresham goes straight back to jail and, I kid you not, Danny Gresham with him for misrepresenting facts to me. That said, let's move out into the courtroom. Officer Stormont awaits us there. And just so you know, Marcel Rainford, Mr. Gresham's investigator, is still in jail while we make our inquiry. All else being equal, he will be released OR too if Michael Gresham prevails out there."

So that answers my question about Marcel's whereabouts.

We all step into the greater room as directed and take our seats. Once again I have Mira beside me at counsel table, but we're unbalanced at the other end. Harley is missing and this no longer feels right. DA Shaughnessy is set to go at his table, with Detective Weldon beside him. Just in front of the bar sit two huge deputy sheriffs and between them sits Officer Stormont. He looks calm and unruffled and I hate him for it. I know who he is and what is he, but what I don't know is whether I can prove it.

"Mr. Gresham," the judge says to me, "please proceed with the presentation of your motion to release OR."

I lean forward and nod at the bench. "Thank you, Judge Itaglia, and thank you for your help in this case thus far. Your Honor, I am prepared to prove to the court that Officer Tory Stormont removed Mira Morales' gun from her home the night of the Harrow shooting; that Officer Stormont had the opportunity and reason to shoot Darrell Harrow; and that Officer Stormont and our very own Detective Jamison Weldon are acting together to prevent a defense verdict in this case for political and criminal reasons."

"Very well; please proceed, counsel."

"The movant calls District Attorney Ronald Shaughnessy to the witness stand."

There are complaints and emotional pleas to the court, but in the end the judge orders Shaughnessy to the stand. An Assistant DA steps up and takes his place at the State's table.

Shaughnessy pauses before he sits down in the witness chair and the clerk swears him in. Then he stands alone, looking around, blinking hard, perhaps deciding whether he will even sit. The judge clears her throat and Shaughnessy takes a seat.

The judge then has the bailiff bring the jury in and they are seated. She simply advises the jury that we're proceeding with the trial, that the defense is calling its first witness, and that the witness just happens to be the District Attorney himself. Then she looks at me and nods to proceed.

"State your name for the record," I tell Shaughnessy.

He looks at me long and hard. Again, as if mulling.

Then he says, "Ronald Shaughnessy."

"You are the Cook County District Attorney?"

"Yes."

"And you have served in that capacity up to this point in the trial, correct?"

"Yes."

"You are a Democrat?"

"Yes."

"And you are acquainted with CPD officer Tory Stormont?"

"Vaguely. I might know him if I met him in the hall."

"Did you? Did you meet him in the hall?"

"What? No!"

"How do you know him?"

"My office investigates all police shooting cases in Cook County. We don't have jurisdiction to do that, so we do it as a public service. We investigated Officer Tory Stormont who was eventually indicted by my office for second degree murder in the shooting death of a young citizen of Chicago, a Mr. Johnny Washington."

"So you're prosecuting Officer Stormont?"

"Not me personally, no. My office is doing that."

"What's the name of the attorney in your office who got that indictment?'

"Darrell Harrow."

"Would that be the same Darrell Harrow who is the victim in our case in which you are claiming Miranda Morales was the shooter?"

"The same."

"What do you think of this proposition, Mr. District Attorney: Darrell Harrow indicts Officer Stormont. Officer Stormont shoots and kills Darrell Harrow. Does that make sense to you?"

"Not at all."

"You see no connection between a man who is charged with a crime and how he might feel about the people who are claiming he committed a crime?"

"No connection."

"Then tell me if this is more of a connection: Darrell Harrow indicts Tory Stormont. Tory Stormont was present at the scene of the crime where Darrell Harrow was murdered. Except the District Attorney, instead of suspecting Tory Stormont, picks out another prosecutor in his office, the same prosecutor who was on tap to take over the prosecution of Tory Stormont and, as if that's not enough, the same prosecutor who, if she's elected tomorrow, will bow her neck and make that case against Tory Stormont stick. Do you get the connection?"

"No."

"Well, let's try this. What if Stormont figures out how to kill the prosecutor who indicted him and make it look like it was done by the new prosecutor who, if elected, will come after him next. Does your mind grasp a connection on these facts?"

"No."

He is weakening in his resolve to keep playing the "no" card. You can sense it in the courtroom air. The jury is no longer on his side as it might have been since juries always are always siding with the witness at least up to when the first answer is given. He has lost that advantage now. Surely someone on that jury is thinking, *This guy must be absolute bonkers if he doesn't see the connections between these people!*

Which is the point of this whole exercise: to alienate the jury and the judge from Shaughnessy by making them see him for the manipulator and liar he really is. If A equals B and B equals C then you just can't deny for very long that A is also equal to C. Before long you're going to find a whole roomful of people who are going to call you out for that. It is my job to make that happen. I can't get a confession out of Shaughnessy--nobody can--but I can get denials of truth out of him and expose him. That *is* my job.

"Mr. Shaughnessy, isn't it true that your office is tight with the police union?"

"Define 'tight,' please."

"You're in bed together?"

"You mean like literally in bed? Not hardly. I'm much choosier than that."

A light ripple of laughter crosses the jury but I come right back.

"I mean like conspiring to allow crimes by the police to go un-prosecuted. That's what I mean by tight and in bed together. Please answer, have you been conspiring with the police union?"

"No."

"With its police membership?"

"No. Look at my prosecution of Stormont to see this."

"Not *your* prosecution. You told us it was *Harrow's* prosecution. And that it happened without your approval, correct?"

"No. It had my approval."

"Good. Then perhaps you can bring us the email or office memo where you order Harrow to prosecute Stormont. The jury would like to see that if it's not too much trouble, sir."

"It's not too much trouble."

"Good. Then will you have it here at one o'clock when we begin the afternoon session?"

"Of course I will."

"Thank you. That is all. For now."

"Counsel," says the judge, "may the witness be excused?"

"No, Your Honor." I reply. "I will need to call him once again after another witness or two."

"Thank you. Please call your next witness."

43

"**M**ovant calls Tory Stormont," I proclaim.

The bailiff steps into the hallway and returns with Stormont in tow. Stormont, on my earlier motion, has been barred from the courtroom while other witnesses have testified throughout this trial. This is his first visit here with the jury present.

Stormont takes the witness stand.

He is a burly man, rough around the edges like Shaughnessy. I am struck by the resemblance between the two men: both large and raw-boned, rough-hewn, with solid jaws and that kind of charisma that makes you eager to vote in their favor. For his part, Stormont radiates it. The man will be hard to hate. But it must happen. Now.

"Tell us your name."

"Officer Tory Stormont."

"Your first name. It's 'officer?'"

"No. It's Torrance. The 'officer' designates that I'm a sworn police officer with the Chicago Police Department."

"Well, thanks for straightening that out."

His answer hasn't been angry, not even heavy-handed, as I had hoped it would be. He has been friendly and not at all insulted or belittled.

"Are you acquainted with District Attorney Ronald Shaughnessy?"

"Distantly, I suppose. He was prosecuting me."

"For what?"

There is a long sigh. "Murder in the shooting of Johnny Washington, a young black man in South Chicago. Mr. Shaughnessy must have thought I was guilty because he turned Mr. Harrow loose on me."

"Really? Has he told you he thinks you are guilty?"

"No."

"Has he sent you a letter or an email saying he thinks you're guilty?"

"Well, he was prosecuting me."

"He was or his office was?"

"Well...his office, I guess. But his name's on all the papers, including the indictment."

"Because it's all being done in his name as the elected official, correct?"

"Yes."

"Not because he's personally on your case?"

"No, I guess not."

"That was Darrell Harrow, correct?"

"Correct."

"Until you shot him to death, correct?"

"Shot him to death? Are you serious?"

"It's true, you shot him and tried to make it look like Miranda Morales was the shooter, didn't you?"

"No. I mean *no*!"

"Not only that, Friday night you shot and killed a lawyer on my defense team, didn't you?"

"Yes, but only after I was threatened by her."

"How did she threaten you? Look over at the jury and tell them that."

"She--she was with you and your bodyguard outside my door. I know you had guns!"

"Did Harley Sturgis have a gun?"

"I don't know."

"Did you know when you shot her to death Friday night?"

At this point a juror stands up and begins waving her arms. "Wait a minute, Judge, are we talking about that nice lady at the lawyers' table? She's been *shot*?"

"Ladies and gentlemen, the court has just learned over the weekend that Attorney Harley Sturgis of Mr.

Gresham's firm was shot and killed Friday night by Tory Stormont. I have seen the initial police reports and know this to be true. Tory Stormont has claimed the shooting was justified. Your job is not to decide that. This is neither the time nor forum for that. Your job is to decide whether he's giving truthful answers to the questions put here today and that is all. Please proceed."

The jurors sit back uncomfortably. The scenery has been changed. There are no raised hands, no questions. But they are clearly upset. Several are crying openly, two women and one man.

I lean down to Mira. "We are making progress," I whisper.

She says nothing.

"I'm waiting to hear your answer, Officer Stormont. Did you know Friday night when you shot Harley Sturgis whether she was armed?"

"No. I didn't know."

"Did you later find out whether she was armed?"

"I did."

"And what did you find out?"

"Detective Pamlico of Arlington PD told me she was not armed."

"What?"

"She was unarmed."

"What?"

The witness looks at the judge.

"Let me rephrase," I tell the court. "Are you telling us that you just shot and killed your second unarmed civilian in Cook County last Friday night because you felt threatened by her?"

Dead still, deathly quiet.

It is a good point. The jury has picked it up and embraced it.

The man is a killer.

"When speaking to you, we also need to keep in mind you shot and killed Johnny Washington this past year because you felt threatened by him too. So let me ask, do you feel threatened right now? Should we feel threatened by you?"

At that point, the prosecution against Mira is all but over and I know it. It is just a matter of finishing out the trial at this point. Finish the trial and wait for a defense verdict of not guilty.

But there is one more thing. I'm going to break this wide open with the video that Marcel so carefully put together for me. Danny comes forward and keys it up for me on my laptop.

"Permission to play the defendant's video for the witness, Your Honor."

"You may proceed."

I nod to Danny. She presses PLAY and we all watch the video where Officer Stormont enters the video view surrounding the elevator vestibule. The camera mounted on the far wall recorded a gun clearly bulging in Stormont's hip pocket. When we are finished we turn up the lights and I again approach Stormont.

"Now, let me ask, since we're all wondering. As you're leaving the Morales floor the night of the murder of Darrell Harrow, whose gun is it we see bulging in your back pocket?"

His eyes dart around the courtroom. "You know, I want to talk to my lawyer. I'm taking the Fifth Amendment. I'm done here."

So I look up at the judge.

As simply as I can, I say, "Your Honor, the defense rests its case."

The defense case would never be stronger than at that very moment. Something about quitting while you're ahead.

So I quit. I have bagged my man.

He is my first kill of the new week.

And it's only Monday.

44

While the jury is out deliberating, Danny and I walk back outside and down to the jail. We ask to see our client, Marcel Rainford.

Ten minutes later, we are alone with Marcel in a conference room. He looks very tired but he is keeping his spirits up, he tells us, by reviewing court papers with other prisoners who are coming to him for advice. "I'm not a lawyer, I told them. But that doesn't matter. I work for a lawyer and that's enough for them. It keeps me from thinking every second about Harley. I got that girl killed, you know."

"No, Stormont did that. We were just doing our job, trying to serve him with process. Please don't beat yourself up, Marcel. We're all in this together."

He looks to Danny and back to me. We both nod that we're in agreement on this. It was a horrible thing, but, in the end, it was part of our job.

"So how close am I to getting out? Any movement on that?"

"Yes, the judge signed an order releasing you OR. You'll be out in the next hour. We just didn't want to leave you hanging."

"The jury's out?"

"The jury's out."

"How did it go?"

"Well, you know I didn't have a confession or even a statement from anyone because the police never did investigate this case beyond immediately pointing the finger at Mira. And of course Stormont made himself totally unavailable, so I went with what I had."

"Which was?"

I sit back and lace my fingers together on the table.

"I went with logic. That good old standby, logic."

"Also known as common sense," adds Danny. "He was terrific. He called Shaughnessy and Stormont and drew the lines that connected them. The jury definitely bought it."

"They didn't have much choice, once Stormont shot poor Harley. He as much as admitted he had also killed Harrow when he did that. *Sayonara*, fool."

"It sounds like a defense verdict is on the horizon for some time today, then," Marcel says.

"Yes, then it's off to the news media. We've got a hell of a story that we have to get out there before voting starts tomorrow."

"How's Mira feeling?"

"You know, when we left she said she was going to go for a long walk. I asked her why. She said she needed some space to start thinking about her staff as the new District Attorney. She's come back around."

"That's good to hear," says Marcel. "She's been through hell over this."

"Yes," says Danny, "she was a pawn in their little game. Pure and simple."

"That's all over," says Marcel. "Thanks to our boy, Michael Gresham."

"Thanks to all of us," I add. "We're all responsible for whatever happens next."

Speaking of which, the jailer comes for me one last time.

"The court called," he says. "You have a verdict."

The three of us look at each other.

"How long they been out, Boss?"

"Less than two hours."

"Oh, my God. I'll be over as soon as they spring me out. Please stick around."

"You know we will, Marcel. We'll be waiting right there."

Danny and I leave the room and walk outside. Early November snow is spitting. The air is flaked with sideways-blowing particles of the white stuff. A vulnerable part of me deep inside suddenly wants to get home away from all this. Away from the court, the black robes, the detective shields, the police uniforms, the jail and jailers. Get home and never leave again. That just might happen, too.

Mira is already at counsel table when we walk into the courtroom. Judge Itaglia is on the bench, the courtroom is packed with media and court watchers, and the State is settled in at their table.

"Mr. Gresham," says the judge, "the court has received notice from the bailiff that the jury has a verdict. Are you ready, sir?"

"We're ready, Your Honor, thank you."

"Very well, the bailiff will bring in the jury."

Minutes later they are led in single file, all twelve of them--the alternates have been excused--and they take their places in the box. The verdict is passed from the jury forewoman and handed to Judge Itaglia, who studies it. She then hands it back to the clerk.

"The clerk will read the verdict."

The clerk stands and studies the paper, then he reads. "We the jury duly impaneled in the case titled *State of Illinois v. Miranda Morales* do find the defendant not guilty on all counts."

"Ladies and gentlemen of the jury, is this your verdict?" asks the judge.

"Yes, Your Honor," says the forewoman. The others nod their assent.

"Very well. Then the jury is excused. The defendant's bail is exonerated and she is free to leave the court. We are adjourned."

Judge Itaglia leaves the bench and pandemonium erupts. Microphones appear out of nowhere and the print press is shoving recorders at us. Unlike some other trials, this time we remain at counsel table and answer each and every question the press asks. This goes on for pretty much the next hour. Why? Because we want the story out there. Mira's success with the voters demands it. So we go on and on, all of us, including Mira, answering everything that's asked.

Sometime during that hour Marcel makes his return to the courtroom, his first time back since last Friday night. He makes his way to us and shakes my hand, shakes Danny's hand, and gives Mira a hug. "I can't thank you enough," she tells him through damp eyes. She has already told me and Danny the same thing.

Finally, the bailiff tells us the judge has a two o'clock hearing and that we need to leave the courtroom. She needs her courtroom back. It's an unscheduled proceeding, we are told. But then the bailiff pulls me aside. "You might want to stay and watch," he whispers. "You won't be disappointed."

Sure enough, we're not disappointed.

The Attorney General's minions have arrived in court and they are full of hustle and bustle. They are presenting affidavits and search warrants that will allow them to search the office of the Cook County District Attorney and the Chicago Police Department. As it develops over the next several minutes, the etiology of the Attorney General's involvement becomes clear: Judge Itaglia has called them in. It is she who is requesting the investigation.

I wouldn't have missed the show for anything. The search warrants are signed and delivered back to the Attorney General and her investigators and they rush out of the courtroom to begin the business of investigating the District Attorney and the police.

Now we are free to leave. The press is satisfied, the news accounts are spreading across the city, the voters are being informed, and voting begins in a little less than sixteen hours .

Yes, there's a certain comfort that comes from knowing one has friends in high places. As evidence of this, just think about my relationship with Miranda Morales, the new District Attorney of Cook County. We are law partners, in the very truest sense of the words although we don't share an office and we don't share clients and we don't share net profits. But what we do share is mutual respect.

I don't demand special favors from her when I'm defending the next bad guy.

And she doesn't prosecute me.

All in all, a very fair trade.

Six months have gone by. News accounts of the prosecutions of Tory Stormont, Jamison Weldon, and Ronald Shaughnessy fill the papers and TV screens every day. The entanglement between the Shaughnessy DA's office and the police union and its membership is much more involved than any of us might have first guessed. A trial is on the horizon and word on the street is that the defendants are jockeying to see who gets to sell out the others and testify for the State in return for some degree of leniency. Your typical dogfight.

Harley Sturgis was remembered and her life was celebrated in a ceremony at the United Methodist Church the Wednesday after the election. It was well-attended, defense attorneys and prosecutors alike. Danny and I sat on the front row and wept openly as endearments were offered and memories stirred. For me, I will never forget the woman who stepped up when I had lost my freedom and had been beaten down by the same cops who were now under indictment. Harley stood in the gap for me and fought back with everything she had. In the end, she saved my life and gave me my freedom back. Danny remembers her likewise.

As for me personally, I no longer like to leave the house that much. Our little family of four is enough for me. There's no longer a drive to defend the scourge of society, the forgotten among us who, without me and others like me, would be lambs led to the slaughter by the criminal justice system. So I stay home as much as possible. Danny is running the office now; she still has the fire in her belly where I do not.

Dania, our oldest, is learning to read and constantly has me beside her on the couch as she reads book after book to me and explains story plots that I might otherwise miss. She's also drawing pictures of mommies and daddies and new baby brothers and yellow suns and houses with smiling windows. She loves her baby brother and wants to do everything with him. Especially feed him, which she'll do for thirty minutes at a time, situated on the sofa with a bottle and a smile. She's at peace and that is helping to put my heart back together. Our new baby is named Michael. We're calling him Mikey. He is beautiful and looks just like his mother but clearly has his grandfather's peace and calm as he's already sleeping through the night. We never knew we could love these children as much as we do and we'd both die before we'd let anything happen to them.

But I cannot stop thinking about Harley. I am stuck there.

Perhaps I will give up the practice of law. It has been extremely harsh these past few years and I have been very lucky to come through it all somewhat intact. Not totally, but somewhat. I don't know what I'd do without law but I'm sure the next pathway in my life will sooner or later become clear. I've thought about writing some of the stories down. I have a world of them. Maybe, I am thinking, just maybe it's time to share some of them with the world. I don't know.

It's June now and the sun is hot and the humidity outrageous. We'd all pass out without air conditioning. And I'm still hanging around home as much as I can. I'm beginning to realize that I'm done with it all--the practice of law is a diminishing dot in my rearview mirror. I have gotten over it.

But one thing remains. And that is my memory of Harley.

So in early July I buy a motorcycle. That's right, a big black Harley-Davidson from just up the road in Milwaukee where they make the things. It's a beast and way more bike than I should probably be starting out with, but it's mine and after a week or two I want nothing more than to ride it whenever and wherever I can.

August 8. That's the date of the Sturgis Rally in South Dakota. Harley riders from all over the world will attend.

Including me.

It's my way of honoring her, the friend who saved my life.

Harley. Sturgis.

Works for me.

The day before I'm to leave, Marcel comes to my house. With him he brings a dossier I have had him prepare. We retreat into my office, shut the door, and he explains his findings. Tory Stormont, despite having murdered three innocent people, remains free on bail. My mind swirls. I cannot begin to believe what I'm hearing.

Stormont, says Marcel, follows a daily routine. He has moved back into Chicago and now lives with two other single police officers. They share a three bedroom home on the near north side. Every day he drives alone to his postoffice box and retrieves his mail. Marcel has photographs and videos of this routine as he has seen it for the weakness it is.

We talk about Harley and what she would want. Marcel argues with me. But I refuse to budge. I am finished with the part of my life where I always color inside the lines.

Danny knows only that I'm riding the bike to Sturgis when I kiss her goodbye early the next morning. My saddlebags are stuffed with fair- and foul-weather gear. I dress in my leather riding pants and leather Harley jacket and pull on my black helmet. The clothing provides the anonymity I require. My last preparation consists of removing the license plates from my bike. They slip into my saddlebag along with the screwdriver I will need to replace them later this morning.

Then I ride to Stormont's postoffice. It is a block off the main drag. I pull into a fifteen minute parking slot and kill my engine. I enter the postoffice with a long white envelope and take up my position at the courtesy table, where I appear, to all the customers coming and going, to be addressing my letter. They don't even notice that I am wearing gloves. In America, I have learned, we are all so busy with our lives that we make poor witnesses to what is about to happen. That's how people like me get away unobserved.

He arrives within minutes, like clockwork, like the clockwork that Marcel has promised.

He bends to his postoffice box and inserts his key. He doesn't notice me, at the table, still wearing my helmet, when I abandon my letter—it contains nothing, no handwriting, no address, no names—and I slip up behind him.

In one smooth motion I withdraw the Glock from the shoulder holster inside my HD jacket and place the muzzle of the gun against the back of Stormont's head.

I HAVE BEEN RETURNED from Sturgis less than a week when, out of the blue, Mira Morales, our brand new District Attorney, calls me on my cell.

"How was the trip to South Dakota?" she asks.

"How did you know I went to South Dakota, Mira?"

"Easy. I asked Marcel. I've been looking for you."

My heart misses a beat. My hand tightens around my smartphone.

"Well, you've found me."

"I guess you heard the news about Stormont."

"I did. Good riddance."

"Agree," she says. "My office isn't going out of its way to find the person who blew his head off."

"I can't blame you for that."

"But that's neither here nor there. Why I'm calling, Michael, I want to offer you a job."

"Doing what?"

"Using all your skills as a criminal lawyer to put bad guys away. I understand you might have some interest in doing that."

"I don't understand. When have I ever told you I have any interest in putting bad guys away."

"Let's just call it my intuition. Want the job?"

"As an assistant district attorney? I'd have to think about that. I'd need to talk to Danny."

"I just did. She said to call you, that it would be your decision. So when can you start, Michael?"

"Is Monday soon enough?"

"We have our daily meeting at eight. Please be in attendance."

I promise that I will arrive on time.

When I hang up, I notice how calm I'm feeling. Dania

hunts me down and wants to read to me. I swoop Mikey up out of his playpen and the two of us sit down on the sofa next to Dania where she begins reading out loud.

These are the best of times.

THE END

UP NEXT: CARLOS THE ANT

"I gave it a 5 because I couldn't give it a 10!"

"We were grabbed in immediately and had so much trouble stopping!"

"Carlos the Ant is the first I've read of the series and loved it!"

"Carlos the Ant is one that kept me spellbound from the start."

"This story about Carlos leaves nothing out. It hits high speed from the start."

"If you like legal thrillers with a surprising ending, this is your book!"

Read Carlos the Ant: CLICK HERE

ALSO BY JOHN ELLSWORTH

THADDEUS MURFEE PREQUEL

A Young Lawyer's Story

THADDEUS MURFEE SERIES

The Defendants

Beyond a Reasonable Death

Attorney at Large

Chase, the Bad Baby

Defending Turquoise

The Mental Case

The Girl Who Wrote The New York Times Bestseller

The Trial Lawyer

The Near Death Experience

Flagstaff Station

The Crime

La Jolla Law

The Post office

SISTERS IN LAW SERIES

Frat Party: Sisters In Law

Hellfire: Sisters In Law

MICHAEL GRESHAM PREQUEL

LIES SHE NEVER TOLD ME

MICHAEL GRESHAM SERIES

THE LAWYER

SECRETS GIRLS KEEP

THE LAW PARTNERS

CARLOS THE ANT

SAKHAROV THE BEAR

ANNIE'S VERDICT

DEAD LAWYER ON AISLE 11

30 DAYS OF JUSTIS

THE FIFTH JUSTICE

PSYCHOLOGICAL THRILLERS

THE EMPTY PLACE AT THE TABLE

HISTORICAL THRILLERS

THE POINT OF LIGHT

LIES SHE NEVER TOLD ME

UNSPEAKABLE PRAYERS

HARLEY STURGIS

NO TRIVIAL PURSUIT

LETTIE PORTMAN SERIES

THE DISTRICT ATTORNEY

JUSTICE IN TIME

ABOUT THE AUTHOR

For thirty years John defended criminal clients across the United States. He defended cases ranging from shoplifting to First Degree Murder to RICO to Tax Evasion, and has gone to jury trial on hundreds. His first book, *The Defendants*, was published in January, 2014. John is presently at work on his 31st thriller.

Reception to John's books have been phenomenal; more than 4,000,000 have been downloaded in 6 years! Every one of them are Amazon best-sellers. He is an Amazon All-Star every month and is a *U.S.A Today* bestseller.

John Ellsworth lives in the Arizona region with three dogs that ignore him but worship his wife, and bark day and night until another home must be abandoned in yet another move.

johnellsworthbooks.com

johnellsworthbooks@gmail.com

EMAIL SIGNUP

Click here to subscribe to my newsletter: https://www.
subscribepage.com/b5c8a0

AMAZON REVIEWS

If you can take a few minutes and leave your review of this book I would be very honored. Plus, with your support you will be helping me write more books!

Made in United States
Orlando, FL
18 August 2024

50496644R00221